HURON COUNTY LIBRARY

D

TELL ME WHO YOU ARE

3420

FIC   Dixon, R. G. Des.
Dixon   Tell me who you are / R.G. Des Dixon. --Toronto :
         ECW Press, c1995.
            233 p. : ill.

         722925   ISBN:1550222317 (pbk.)

         I. Title   DISCARDED

4872   95SEP28   3559/he   1-399489

TELL ME WHO YOU ARE

R.G. Des Dixon

ECW PRESS

OCT 0 3 1995

Copyright © R.G. Des Dixon, 1995

CANADIAN CATALOGUING IN PUBLICATION DATA

Dixon, R.G. Des

Tell me who you are.

ISBN 1-55022-231-7

I. Title.

PS8577.I86T4 1995   C813'.54   C95-930413-4

PR9199.3.D58T4 1995

This book has been published with the assistance of
The Canada Council and the Ontario Arts Council.

Design and imaging by ECW Type & Art, Oakville, Ontario.
Printed by Métropole Litho, Sherbrooke, Québec.

Distributed by General Distribution Services,
30 Lesmill Road, Toronto, Ontario M3B 2T6.
(416) 445-3333, FAX (416) 445-5967,
(800) 387-0141 (Ontario and Quebec),
(800) 387-0172 (other provinces).

Distributed to the trade in the United States exclusively
by InBook, 140 Commerce Street, P.O. Box 120261,
East Haven, Connecticut, U.S.A. 06512.
(800) 243-0138 FAX (800) 334-3892.

Distributed in the United Kingdom by Bailey Distribution,
Learoyd Road, Mountfield Road Ind Est,
New Romney, Kent, Great Britain TW28 8XO.
0679 66905 FAX 0679 66638.

Published by ECW PRESS,
2120 Queen Street East, Suite 200,
Toronto, Ontario M4E 1E2.

*for my namesake John Robert Tomas Barron
who arrived in the world at the same moment
as this book with as much chance as the kids in the
story that his schools will know who he is*

CHAPTER ONE

At 7:15 p.m. on his fourth day as a high school teacher ex-lawyer David Halper stands in the doorway of his den looking down the black-and-white marble hall.

He calls, "I'm sorry, Liz. At least I'm . . ."

The front door slams. Above it, leaded glass shakes. Rainbow reflections tremble on bevelled edges and flashes shiver across polished marble. Halper winces as though stabbed by shards of light. His wife of nineteen years departs for the theatre alone. Her BMW pulls away, tires screeching on driveway curves, while he stares at the heavy door in gathering gloom.

David Halper's previous three evenings and weekend have been devoted to lesson preparation and tidal waves of term-opening trivia lugged home in nineteen folders: forms, agendas, memos, letters, announcements, requisitions, questionnaires, course outlines, deletions, additions, timetables, reports . . .

"At least," he trails off to the empty hall, "I'm working late at home."

He means at home instead of in the high-rise offices and executive-class plane seats that were his plush prisons for twenty years.

"Sorry? Why should I be sorry?" he thinks. "She should be sorry."

As night approaches and rain clouds close in, black marble darkens and white marble, infused with the last glow of daylight, brightens in contrast. Halper stands staring, thinking how well they understood each other — thought they did — when they met as undergraduates. She ignored his diffidence, took him in hand. He ignored her assumptions, followed. Her circle became his.

They chose the same literature courses, read Marlowe and Congreve to each other under the trees in Queen's Park, went to plays at Hart House, attended Victoria College teas with little sandwiches and Northrop Frye, borrowed her mother's station wagon and drove to Expo in Montreal, fell in love. The whole country was in love in 1967. That was before law school, before babies, before mortgages, before success, before grief.

Theatre? How could he put his mind to another two-hour benefit ritual with a cast of six familiar players on a puny proscenium stage when every day at school is a ten-hour spectacular in the round with a cast of hundreds, so many that he will never know their names let alone their characters. He is a featured performer but he hasn't had enough rehearsal. The lines they taught him don't work. He has to improvise. He has stage fright, a perpetual nervous edge piqued by the fear that he is an amateur, not a real teacher, not good enough. But on cue, some visceral rheostat turns on. He feels the surge and senses himself lighting up classrooms.

At 7:18 David Halper sits down to mark his first English assignments: two grade nine classes, sixty-eight students, 'Write at least four paragraphs that TELL ME WHO YOU ARE.' Next week he will have thirty-two more papers from his senior English class, 'Write at least four pages double spaced that TELL ME WHO YOU ARE.' Even his fifty-six law students will tell him who they are.

The first paper he reads is from his home room, 9c. It is untitled and unsigned and written at various angles in pencil on the back of a sheet torn from a calendar:

I an Frank an 15 with red hair an turkeys but not to job for 2 monts my birtday October be 16.

My dad think to me compuputer in cheneer give up to tel my tatoo frum he think for me but who care.

No for pen than pencil but not frum Becky neether. Ha. Ha.

I gess no mor who are.

That would be Frank Stringer using Becky Kowalski's pencil — Becky who has been late for class every day so far, Frank Stringer who announced his presence the first moment of school by arriving with his red hair in spikes dyed turquoise (turkeys) and by standing in answer to his name (instead of just saying 'here') and by rubbing his sandpapered crotch while pointing to his rattlesnake tatoo, thus displaying all at once his three claims to fame.

Frank Stringer will be sixteen next month. TELL ME WHO YOU ARE. Involuntarily, Halper pictures for the ten-thousandth time that Friday night over two years ago, his son Simon's sixteenth birthday.

Halper, still dictating into his tiny recorder, automatically pulls through the wrought iron gate and feels for the automatic door opener as his headlights sweep left to right, right to left, around curves in the driveway, reaping the flowers of June. Late lilacs fly past his windows like white and mauve balloons, but he barely notices. He has flown in from Los Angeles on the last flight, gone straight to his downtown office at Tory Tory DesLauriers and Binnington for three undisturbed hours, and is home at 3:06 a.m. anticipating his nightcap.

As the garage door rises, Halper sees the new red Jeep and remembers Simon's birthday. He and Liz have given Simon the Jeep keys embedded in birthday cake. He must back up to jockey his own car into the third space.

Simon is sitting behind the wheel of the Jeep. The motor is running. The note on the windshield says: 'Dear Dad, I missed you. I saved you some birthday cake. Thanks for the Jeep. It's really nice. But I didn't come first, not even second, just seventh. I'm sorry about everything. Love, Simon.'

Simon's report from Trinity College School is attached to the note. The stench of car exhaust gives way slowly to the scent of lilacs.

Halper forces himself to concentrate and leafs through all the 9c papers looking for Becky Kowalski's. He knows her by name and face so early in the year because she is glued to the colourful Frank Stringer whenever both are present. She seems bright enough but dreamy, always preoccupied. The first day, he had thought she might be on drugs but now he thinks not. TELL ME WHO YOU ARE. As he leafs through the papers a second time, he has a vision of Becky being born late, taking ten months to gestate, and then happening upon the birth canal by mere chance. That picture changes to his older daughter Jillian being born suddenly, purposefully, impatiently, two weeks ahead of schedule. There is no paper from Becky Kowalski.

The second 9c paper Halper marks is eight pages of laser printing with a cover sheet in various sizes of print:

WHO I AM (I THINK)
(in 26 paragraphs instead of 4)
by
CLAUDIUS J. ITO
class 9C
Midhill High School
the first assignment given by
MR. DAVID HALPER, English teacher

I Claudius thank you, kind sir, for caring who I am. I thought nobody in this school would ever ask. Not that I have an answer ready, but I'm almost over being twelve (thank God I'll be thirteen in October) and I'm beginning to have some suspicions that I don't mind sharing.

I've pretty much decided that I'm not a budding manic-depressive, a diagnosis once suggested by my mother to Dr. Bell, my psychologist. My mother says such things in front of me so I can have my say. My mother is the interior designer Keiko Ito and between you and me, sir, I suspect she's just assuming genetic predisposition to manic depression since her father and two ancestors (one a concert violinist who jumped into Mt. Fuji) have all displayed certain symptoms of that condition, but I'm half something other than Japanese — maybe French since my mother was in Paris at Parsons School of Design the year before I was born — so maybe I haven't got the jumper gene.

I asked my mother about my father and she said only God knows who he is. (Her exact words were God only knows.) She said bus loads of students from art schools went sketching country mansions for a week and converged the seventh day near Chambord for wine tasting and a special son et lumiere at the chateau with nobody around on a Saturday except hundreds of art students because it was off-season for tourists and chilly, so wine overflowed from the afternoon into the night, lights flashed, cannons boomed, symphonies played from the sky and I joined the party (so to speak) when my mother passed out among the bushes opposite the chateau where a bunch of people were sharing blankets and wine and other things. She called me Claudius because the book she took along to read on the bus was *I Claudius*.

Maybe being created with all that son et lumiere is why I seem to be in a permanent manic phase, semi-manic anyway, except for occasional temper tantrums (which Dr. Bell says I have found to be an effective strategy since I'm too small and too poor — my allowance is a measly ten dollars a week — to control people any other way). I keep telling my mother that anger and depression are two different things so I must be in training for a manic-aggressive, not depressive.

But I assure you, sir, I'm not aggressive unless crossed and mostly I just keep quiet and groove away on sci fi in my head even when things are bad, and I smile a lot even when life is not that great, just okay, which is most of the time, when people leave me alone because they don't notice me. I'm the kind that nobody notices unless I wear socks that don't match. Once in a while I horse around and dance and stuff like that when I'm on a real high which is mostly when I'm with somebody nice who notices me and in a place where you can feel safe.

And all of this is, I assure you sir, without benefit of my mother's uppers, not even a snort of her vodka, not so much as a whiff of the grass which is readily available in the pockets of her boyfriends, not to mention the locker corridors at school. So far I'm clean.

Halper wonders if Claudius Ito goes through the pockets of his mother's boyfriends for the same reasons Simon went through his father's pockets. Looking for what? Nothing was ever missing. Looking for a father? Halper knows that Claudius Ito is one of half a dozen oriental-looking boys — three or four in each grade nine class — who so far have not volunteered any information during lessons. He thinks he knows which one, the little one with the baseball cap. He reads on:

The reason I have a psychologist is partly that my mother hired her when I was three to test my IQ because I started reading to my daytime baby-sitter (who was Polish and was so bad in English that she couldn't read me the same stuff the night sitter had read to me so I read it to her), and partly because I started dressing up in my mother's clothes when I was four (because that's the only kind of grown-up clothes there were in our closets and besides my mother was a flashy dresser in her younger days and had some outfits that I used to think were like clown costumes), and partly because I had bad nightmares when I was four, and partly because I stole the odd thing at school when I was five and six, but mostly because I set fire to several things including my toy box and the garden shed when I was seven and eight.

The reason I started the odd fire in my younger days was not because I was playing with matches — I knew how to use matches — I was just trying to make things go boom, which Dr. Bell thinks is a hobby that may have something to do with the fact that my great grandparents were incinerated at Hiroshima and my grandmother got so much radiation that she died later of cancer, which is why my mother told me all about Hiroshima lots of times when she was teaching me Japanese — because she says it's my heritage as much as the language is and because she still cries about her mother dying of cancer and her father falling silent after that and dying slowly of despair. My mother also told me about Japanese soldiers raping Korean girls but that didn't make me a rapist, but then I don't have the equipment yet to do rape (though I sure wish I did — have the equipment I mean, not that I've got the slightest interest in using it for rape) but I've got the equipment to do blasts.

I used to have my lab in the rec room but my mother made me move it to the attic because she says, 'If there's a blast in the basement the whole house goes up but if there's a blast in the attic only the roof and Claudius go up.' Ha. Ha. Actually, I've moved on from little bangs to the big bang theory and I've got my computer and telescope set up under the skylight so I can get into astrophysics and —

The phone rings. It is Halper's youngest daughter, Alison, fourteen, calling from boarding school. Halper expects she will bubble with stories as usual and wonders what it will be this time: her new roommate? riding? sports? something horsy she has just read?

"Daddy, I need a formal. Margo's got three. She's my roommate. Mummy says to ask you. And a full-length coat. You know, dressy. And —"

"Honey, you just had a thousand dollars for clothes."

"That's nothing. Uniforms and stuff. Mummy says I need about two thousand more. I need some decent dresses and heels. Everything's too small and childish."

"I'm sorry sweetheart. That thousand, plus your allowance, is all till Christmas."

"Honestly Daddy." She hangs up.

Alison is like her mother. Halper bites the end of his red marking pen and pictures Alison stomping down a hall, tossing her blond ponytail, slamming a door . . . TELL ME WHO YOU ARE. Even if she had chattered on as usual about horse stories or dressage or field hockey he would have found out less of substance than Claudius Ito tells in a paragraph.

At 11:55, when his wife returns from the theatre and goes directly upstairs without a word, David Halper has marked two thirds of his grade nine papers. Midnight, and he feels as he does in the crush of school corridors: sardined with a teeming catch of kids in the ooze of youth, at once stimulated and numbed by the juices and the press. He flips open his journal to record the image, but the hall clock chimes twelve and he closes the book without writing and turns back to his marking. He must speed up, cut corners.

He writes only one comment on Claudius Ito's paper: 'I feel privileged that you have told me so much about who you are, Claudius. Thanks. I look forward to getting to know you in person. Let's have some meetings to talk about everything in your paper. Meanwhile, would you consider breaking some of your longer sentences into shorter ones and running both of us a copy of the new version? I'm not sure shortening will improve clarity or impact but I think it might, and we can compare the two versions at our first meeting. Please consider also whether you want to read all or none or just parts of your paper to the class.'

On every other paper, at least once, usually several times, Halper draws an arrow to a problem too complicated or too subtle to explain with a marginal note and writes at the top or bottom, 'See me about this.' Often he circles passages and draws arrows to places they should be moved to improve organization.

He circles hundreds of grammar, punctuation and spelling errors and, more often than not, inserts the corrections even though he knows it would be preferable, if there were time, to have every student try again and again for the correct form. He hates this compromise, resents the model of schooling that makes it necessary. Keeping up with the syllabus. Covering courses instead of uncovering them.

He makes non-sentences into sentences. He adds connecting

sentences where they are missing. He fills margins with questions and comments: 'What does this mean? This doesn't follow logically from the previous sentence. Is this how you really feel?'

It is necessary to staple a blank sheet to most assignments to make enough room for all the comments he has to write to clarify shortcomings. On many papers he writes, 'You have told enough about sports, music videos, clothes, parties and dates but not enough about your thoughts, feelings, fears, hopes, emotions, beliefs, opinions . . .' In giving the assignment, he had written all of those words and more on the blackboard, and the sample paper he wrote about himself and read to his classes covered all those bases.

Most of his grade nine students are fourteen. At that age, Halper reflects, he was in grade ten, awash with feelings, fears, hopes. But he recalls that he told nobody at home or school. He remembers that Simon at fourteen told nobody. He at forty-five is able to tell. Claudius Ito at twelve is able to tell. He and Claudius have been through intensive counselling where they learned not only the willingness to open up but also the concepts, the vocabulary, the content of self-revelation.

Halper thinks his students have no idea how to discover and declare themselves because the school has never taught them, and he knows from experience that homes do an even worse job of it. Home talk is babble. Alison is too close. Simon was too close. Schools could do it Halper thinks — teach self-literacy — but they don't even teach reading/writing literacy.

On all but four papers he prints in big red letters, 'Rewrite and hand in by next Friday.' He reckons he and his classes could spend the whole term, the whole year, on this one assignment, forever conferring and rewriting. TELL ME WHO YOU ARE. He considers making it a continuing composition activity, not the only one but the basic one, and it could be a running theme in all his English literature classes: TELL ME WHO YOU ARE Macbeth and Oliver Twist. TELL ME WHO YOU ARE Claudius Ito, Frank Stringer, Becky Kowalski, David Halper . . .

While he records marks and sips coffee and craves a drink or even a cigarette, Halper decides he was wrong to tell his students they would read their TELL ME papers aloud in class as he had read his. Too personal. Too soon. An invitation to posture, be superficial. For now, his grade nines with nothing to say should read aloud their residual up-the-Amazon or at-the-horse-ranch stories while working with him one-to-one on TELL ME WHO YOU ARE. His seniors should read their earnest paeans on save-the-environment and feed-the-starving-Somalis when what they really care about is sex, money and popularity.

By 2:20 he has marked all the papers, tabulated the results and sorted them into piles: two illegible, five so garbled as to be almost unintelligible, seven inept, eight failures by any reasonable standard, fifteen barely passable, three adequate but dull, seven good, three excellent, one outstanding, six indicative of psychological or behavioural problems (not including Claudius Ito's), the rest — eleven — not handed in, Becky Kowalski's among them.

He decides to take *Macbeth* to bed in case he can't sleep. Copies of the play are still not available for his senior students so he has been showing them the Orson Welles film version as an introduction. He will pick some passages and follow up today's video screening with class discussions based on oral readings that suggest shades of character in Macbeth and Lady Macbeth.

When he slips in beside Liz he kisses her sleeping eyes. She used to love that, flutter awake, smile, reach out for him. But that was before Simon's death. After Simon she would keep her eyes closed and clutch his hand. Tonight she turns away and mumbles, "Turn off the light."

"I was thinking about Simon tonight."

"Let him rest in peace, David. You rest in peace."

"We should have taught him to express his thoughts and feelings. Should have told him ours."

"It's late, David. Turn off the light."

"We taught him impeccable manners, sent him to the best schools, bought him the best clothes, taught him to reach for the top, instilled the work ethic."

"For God's sake stop blaming yourself. Stop blaming me. All we did was encourage Simon to get in the race and win. Without that he would have withdrawn into his own little world — books, gymnastics, and computer games. I thought teaching was supposed to help you get on with your life." She reaches over and turns off the light.

Halper lies there in the dark wondering how Simon saw him. Colourless of course, because David Halper has always been colourless. Banker's gray, a colour indelibly dyed in him by his own father. Simon must have seen him as a big gray rock. Not cold though. Warmish. A gray rock warmed by the son. Maybe also from within. Yes, warmed from within too by some pent-up magma. A rock chiselled into something traditional by Simon's mother and grandfather. A pillar, chiselled into a pillar, like the ones in front of the house. But still gray, still colourless.

At 8:47 a.m. David Halper says to James Fenton, the principal of Midhill, "They can't write at elementary school level so what are they doing in high school?"

Halper already knows about Fenton's public appearances. The two are standing in the new-wing foyer, in front of the office, where Fenton exposes himself most mornings as zero hour approaches, when hall traffic is heaviest. Four such strategic exposures per day (morning arrival, two at noon, and afternoon dismissal — a total of sixty minutes), along with two sweeps of the corridors (another twenty minutes), establish his universal presence. Most students should see him most days, should carry home with them to dinner table conversations an impression of the school ship that includes the captain solidly at the helm, missing nothing as he scans the potentially treacherous sea of faces.

"Ah, well," Fenton says with a smile for passing teachers. "That's just our little cross to bear, Daniel, we who labour in the vineyard of education. For compensation there's the other extreme. Like Billy Parr over there speaking to Mr. Duchok — always a top scholar, Billy, and captain of the Midhillers hockey team, and student council president. Or my son Lincoln in your senior English class — brilliant boy, Lincoln. Loves to read and write. You'll see."

"But how do we carry our little cross through the vineyard of education without slipping on fallen grapes?"

James Fenton — most of the longtime teachers call him Jimmy — is slightly older than David Halper, slightly taller, slightly heavier, slightly grayer, with a bristly gunmetal moustache. He moves in a permanent aura of boiled spices from some heavy cologne which Halper assumes is intended to cover the odour of cigarettes. The combined smell causes Halper to step back a pace and wonder if it has the same effect on students.

Fenton stands erect with an air of authority, his arms folded, his fists clenched so that his huge birthstone ring with its flashing facets and his massive matching cufflinks look like three police beacons. While he considers Halper's question, Fenton straightens his yellow-and-black tie and fastens the top button of his Tuesday suit, a single-breasted grey pinstripe with an unusually long jacket. Halper assumes that Fenton found the suit at a bargain price on the extra tall rack and had the sleeves shortened.

Halper takes momentary comfort that his own suit fits and he will not have to worry about clothes for years since his closet is full of tailored suits left from his Bay Street days.

"That's where you come in," Fenton says, jovially. "You teach them to write. Among other things, we're a repair shop, Daniel."

"David. David Halper."

"David. We repair problems at Midhill, David. Now if you'll excuse me. Could we discuss this another time? My door is always open. Just see if my secretary can squeeze you in next week."

Fenton is alternately smiling and frowning, mostly smiling, at passing students. Halper knows it is the principal's way of communicating pleasure or displeasure with dress and decorum and that he takes pride in the power and clarity of the messages he feels sure he is sending with the raising of his eyebrow, the twisting of his mouth, the running of one finger along his moustache. Once or twice each morning he points and the river of youth parts, allowing Fenton to cross safely to some student illegally wearing a bun-exposing mini or jeans so shredded as to make total disintegration, or at least organ exposure before noon, a probability.

"Repair work? Are you saying I should stop using the grade nine English course and go back to the level they're really at to repair them?"

"Well of course you have to teach the course. But individualize. We meet individual needs here."

"With sixty-eight kids in these two classes? Not to mention all my other classes, interruptions, announcements, attendance checking, people missing, classes cancelled, books lost, bells ringing, hyperactive kids, lethargic kids, hungry kids, malnourished kids, kids on drugs, behaviour problems, gang vendettas, kids who fall asleep every class . . . Everybody knows school is set up to deal with job lots, not individuals. Why not say so? These two job lots are supposed to be grade nine, but half of them write at grade two, three, four, five — I don't know what level. I just know it's not related to the course I'm teaching."

Fenton is smiling at the passage of two other new teachers who are young and nervously excited, not forty-five and outspokenly critical. He answers Halper briskly without looking at him. "Just do the best you can Halman."

"Halper. David Halper."

"Halper. David. Call me Jimmy. Look David, don't let all that stuff go to your head. What they told you at teachers college. Just be practical. Why don't you see the English head. See the special education head. A few of your students must have been identified for special education."

"Which means about three from each class will be withdrawn from my room now and then and get further behind by missing my lessons — in order to learn some fragment they should have learned years ago — and then come back into my room and pretend they know what's going on. And what about the other fifteen or so in both of my classes that can't write worth a damn? How come nobody ever put them through an identification process?"

"Identification is to identify special education students — multiple problems, dyslexia — not people with ordinary language deficits."

"By ordinary language deficits you mean functional illiteracy."

"I mean everybody with language deficits."

"Can't read. Can't write."

"What difference would it make anyway if we did identify them? We have mainstreaming. Everybody ends up in the same classroom whether they read and write well or not. Just make sure you run a tight ship. Otherwise they'll walk all over you."

Halper thinks the ship analogy is consistent with the jargon word mainstreaming. But he notices ethnic eddies in the river rushing by. Six black boys in faddishly baggy clothes, shaved heads and multiple earrings banter loudly and bounce a basketball back and forth. Fenton frowns at the ball and wags his finger. Several Chinese girls in designer outfits pass books among themselves. Half a dozen whites of both sexes in tight t-shirts, studded jeans, and black boots exchange flirty jibes. Five East Indian girls in plain Western clothes and a lot of gold jewelry interrupt their closed conversation to smile respectfully at Halper and Fenton.

The torrent tosses up a shrivelled man in a shapeless gray suit who shuffles up to Halper smiling slightly, smelling stale. He looks older, Halper thinks, but must be under sixty-five or he would be retired. The half smile seems to be permanent. Halper has seen the same man at faculty meetings sitting, gnome-like, smiling wanly, nodding off, almost falling from his chair. Halper recalls being told in a whisper by the teacher beside him that the old man is the head of mathematics and has solved the problem of how to survive staff meetings: sleep through them.

"David Halper," the old man says. "It took me a while to place you. But you haven't changed as much as I have. And I had the benefit of seeing your picture now and then in the business pages."

Fenton takes advantage of the interruption to duck away. Halper tries to remember.

The old man says, "Oak Park Junior High. 1960. You were in the gifted program."

"And you taught math. But not to my class. And you ran the stage crew for school shows, and you coached after-school swimming. Mr. Wilkinson. Right?"

"Wilkins. Art Wilkins. Now what on earth possessed you to become a teacher?"

"People like you. You taught me how to organize backstage

for the skits I wrote and how to run water-ball games to raise money for children's services at East General."

Wilkins is gray all over but not a gray rock. He is gray powder. His hair, the bit that remains, his exposed scalp, his wizened face, even his limp clothes seem to be sprinkled with fine ash. Halper marvels at the corrosive power of chalk dust. A third of a century ago this ruin was a wiry man with thick brown hair. Halper remembers Wilkins's hair slicked back and glistening when he shot up from under water like a sea lion after demonstrating dives.

Arthur Wilkins moves his books from one arm to the other and shifts his wispy weight from one leg to the other as though dodging danger. He blinks his watery eyes and says, "Ah, well, a mistake then. My mistake. I should have told you teaching is for mediocre men. Teachers are just stage crew in this show, David, makeup, lighting — at best walk-ons, extras, chorus. Administrators get a few lines, but Mother School is the star, director and producer. Even in her decrepit condition, half paralyzed. Why throw your life away tending the old bitch? She's incontinent you know. Mother School shits herself and teachers have to clean up the mess. They don't tell you that at teachers college."

"You're not mediocre. Those trophies over there say this school wins math contests and swimming meets."

"Not this school. Not me. A few kids win. An insignificant number out of all these masses. The same kids would do it if they went to most other schools. That's the way the system works. It serves a few who fit the mould. And even them it doesn't allow any power. The very best are bored but knuckle under and get out of here as fast as possible. Jake Zimmerman — over there, that framed certificate — math olympics gold medal, kept his mouth shut and won every math prize going. Others do what they have to but seethe with discontent, or mouth off, or both.

Gordon Wing. You've got him for English and law, he tells me. Dazzling mind. You'll see. Along with everything else Gordon Wing is a fine swimmer. Championship material. But he's too sapped fighting mediocrity and obsolescence to swim his heart out. The rest, the masses, drop out physically or mentally. The system also serves teachers who fit the mould. The rest get out or burn out. I burnt out. What you see is a cinder barely warm at the centre."

Halper recalls that Wilkins was never very warm. Not somebody to talk to. But with an infectious energy. Good at challenging kids. He knew how to hand responsibility over to kids even though he could never make himself available emotionally. Halper thinks of the ashen look before him as the residue of Wilkins's own cremated ambitions. The three-minute warning bell rings.

"Bells ring. That's what it's all about," Wilkins says. "Routines. There's no place for a keen teacher to go but up and down corridors. No place for ambition, creativity, new concepts. Midhill and every other high school in the world are living proof that the universal model of schooling lacks a regeneration factor. You suck Mother School's withered tit or else she rolls over and crushes you. I've heard your questions and comments at faculty meetings, David. Perceptive. Intelligent. Not welcome. And nobody welcomes your references to education literature either. Ninety-nine percent of teachers and principals don't read the literature of education and they're suspicious of anyone who does. We should talk about all that some time." Wilkins shuffles off in obedience to the bell but turns, smiling slightly, to say, "You should shut up or get out, David."

Halper assumes that if they can't write, his grade nine students can't read either, so he skips lunch to ask the head of English for a test to give them.

Mrs. Lemon, Diane, is in her cubbyhole office of ceiling-to-floor shelves, standing on top of her time-worn desk, counting out used copies of *Macbeth*. The room is a former storage cupboard in the old wing and is jam-packed with one desk, two four-drawer filing cabinets and two folding chairs. The bits of plaster wall not obscured by books and shelves are painted parchment brown that may have been ivory eons ago. The walls remind Halper of tombs he and his family toured in Egypt. He glances up at Mrs. Lemon and thinks of saying, "I see the mummy but where are the hieroglyphics that tell me who she is?" He decides against it and just says, "Hi Diane," as he steps in.

A half eaten ham-on-rye sandwich sits on a big ink stain at one side of the desk. With its green pickle skewered by a toothpick it looks to Halper like an obsolete sailing ship drifting aimlessly on an ink-stain ocean. He recalls his well-appointed office at Tory Tory. At Midhill he has no office except the trunk of his car, and this is the office of a department head who spends her time counting books.

Diane Lemon smiles and says from up near the ceiling, "Close the door, would you David?"

Looking up at her carefully painted face and artfully burnished hair Halper is reminded more of a puppet than a mummy. He rather likes the puppet but he knows someone else is pulling her strings. He thinks of his mother performing devotedly for him but manipulated by his father.

But who is pulling Diane's strings? Not Fenton, Halper decides, not some superintendent. They just service strings. An image clarifies as he looks into the blue smoke above him. Old Arthur Wilkins is right: the string puller is the institutional monster. Teachers are talking dolls. The model of schooling is the Gorgon he has to fight to cut the strings Fenton is trying to tie on him.

The one tiny, high-up window is wide open and every few moments Diane leans toward it to exhale smoke. It is a hot day in late summer. The school, like most, is not air conditioned. Nonetheless, the door is closed to keep smoke from the corridor. The tomb of texts is sweltering.

Diane sips coffee from a mug which sits on a high shelf along with her ashtray. She wears a calf-length white smock swinging open over stylish beige slacks that match her high-heeled sandals and the small flowers in her gold blouse. Her red fingernails match the larger red flowers in her blouse. The narrow sash around her trim waist is gold and red. The easy stylishness reminds Halper of his wife but he can't imagine Liz in a closet counting out books for a living.

An old electric fan sitting on a biscuit tin on top of a battered file cabinet whines and growls and oscillates jerkily beside a coffee pot and kettle. The only decoration is thumb-tacked to the door: an old Christmas card with a colour photo of two cats wearing red and green ribbons.

"You don't need a test," Diane Lemon says. "Their reading scores are on file. That's sixty-six *Romeo and Juliet* and thirty-four *Macbeth* with a minimum of offensive graffiti if you don't count such everyday expletives as 'Romeo is a necrophiliac' and 'Lady Macbeth is a ball buster.'"

"On file where?"

"Student Services, the guidance department. I'm short three *Moby Dick*."

"Why not in the English department?"

"Why would we duplicate what's readily available? Where would I keep that many files?"

"On your computer. Along with all these relics. You could put all these books on one CD-ROM and have lots of room left for current literature."

"Ha. Maybe in the next century. This isn't Bay Street, David. We still have one hundred percent paper books and tons of paper files. Guidance people use reading scores, that kind of information, more than we do. Can you see any *Moby Dick* in those odds and ends behind you? What's that one with no cover?"

"*Heart of Darkness.* You mean guidance people teach reading to the ones with low scores?"

"No, of course not. But they need to know all about the ones in trouble. It stands to reason. Low reading scores usually correlate with behaviour problems. Would you mind? Take these *Merchant of Venice* and start a pile on that chair. Six. Twelve . . ."

"But who takes the kids with low reading scores and gets them up to standard?"

"Eighteen. Some time this week or next, resource withdrawal teachers from special ed will start coming to your room and taking the identified kids out for tutoring now and then. Twenty-four. Thirty. Thirty-one."

"I know, but that's three or four kids in each class. Who takes the other fifteen or so who I assume can't read since they can't write?"

"We don't have people to do that, teach reading. They do that in public school."

"Obviously they don't."

"Tell *them* that."

"*Someone* should tell them and you, Diane, and Fenton and the school board, that it's grounds for a lawsuit. Malpractice."

"Where am I? How many did I say? Look David. You're a new teacher. Trust me."

"My senior English class is almost as bad."

"Listen David, I juggled kids in the senior classes, I bent over backwards, to make sure you got two or three of the best. That loudmouth Gordon Wing who calls himself the yellow peril —

obnoxious, but the highest mark in English and nearly everything else last year, editor of *The Midhiller*, which he's made the best school paper anywhere. Billy Parr, president of the student council and saviour of the world — unctuous, but smart and the best writer in the short story club last year. And you've got Lincoln Fenton, Jimmy's kid, an unknown quantity since he didn't go here last year, but according to Jimmy, Lincoln's the biggest brain this side of Harvard, writes like a Nobel laureate, and he's read the entire national library."

"A few stars, a lot of mediocrity and too many dregs. Doesn't it bother you that more than half the kids in this school can't read the stuff on these shelves and never will? They just sit through it. And where's the modern literature?"

"Over there. *The Old Man and the Sea*, *Grapes of Wrath*, *The Wars*, *The Diviners* . . . I'm coming down. Give me a hand will you?"

"Fifteen to fifty years old, or more. That's the history of literature. Why aren't there shelves full of this year's novels, plays, poetry, short stories. Why not all the current literary magazines? That's what's relevant. Hemingway and Shakespeare don't have a monopoly on universal truths. And why not current films? That's the literature of our time."

Diane Lemon steps from her chair to the floor and keeps hold of Halper's hand. Her helpless smile reminds him of his mother's when he used to complain to her, over milk and cookies, about his father. His mother, a teacher before marriage, used to reach across the kitchen table and take his hand and press another cookie into his palm.

Diane says, "Have a cookie, David."

"Not for me, thanks."

She lets go of Halper's hand with a sigh. "The board office has a reading consultant if she hasn't been cut for budget reasons. Nice woman. You can call and sooner or later, a month or two, she'll respond and waste a lot of your time and then disappear and leave you with a pile of vague stuff you haven't got time for. Or worse, she might try to involve all of us in some hopeless game plan that will make the other English teachers mad as hell at me and you for starting the whole thing. You're going to find it hard enough to cover the English course without worrying about what somebody else didn't teach, David. You'll be lucky to get 150 teaching days a year after all the days cancelled because of exams, football, field trips, assemblies, professional development days, snowstorms, God knows what else. It's not a year. More like a third of a year. Not to mention that ten to twenty percent of your kids will be absent every day. Coffee?"

"Some other time."

"Damn," Diane says. "I've left my cigarette and coffee up there. Give me a hand will you? Listen David, if you want to be conscientious, figure some way to cover the course and still teach everything two or three times without boring the few who got it the first time. That way you accommodate the ones who didn't get it the first time because it's over their heads and the ones who missed it because they were away getting their hair done or keeping house for single parents or working part-time jobs. Keep your sanity, David. Survive. Half of new teachers don't last past the fifth year. Just teach your courses and keep things running smoothly."

She hands Halper her ashtray and climbs down again clutching a mug crazed with age and bearing the remainder of some eroded inscription. Halper deciphers the words Secondary School Teachers' Federation.

"Don't forget the department meeting at 4:00," Diane says. "Here's the agenda — extracurricular assignments and committees."

"I've already got student council and short story club."

29

"Student council is category A, front office assignment, not my business. Besides, you share council with another teacher and all you have to do is approve agendas and make sure nobody makes off with the take from chocolate bar sales. Short story club is category B: yearbook, newspaper and all that. Short story is considered the plum, except maybe for the poetry club. Small group. No deadlines. I hoped you'd also take theme issues of the newspaper. Just two or three specials a year. Somebody else gets the regular issues. Each of us also gets a C category: half-time shows for football, drama club, spring revue, graduation show, special assembly programs, all that. I rather hoped you'd take the spring revue. We do that and the musical in cooperation with music."

Halper is leafing through the six-page agenda looking for the items she is rhyming off. She continues, "Would you mind dropping that little box — the *Macbeth*s — off at 211? Think about department committees too David. Page five, column D. Each of us gets three or four. I think you might like examinations, curriculum revision — that's board level — and media literacy. We all get a turn on race relations, gangs, violence, destreaming, all that stuff in the last column. And the other box is your *Macbeth*s, thirty-two, right?" The puppet is smiling and puffing just like a real person. "And close the door behind you, would you please? Thanks David."

While his 9c students are silently reading *The Highwayman* for the first time, Halper looks at the seating plan and finds Claudius Ito second last in the middle row, behind a large girl with big hair. To see Claudius, it is necessary to walk down the aisle and look around the friz. There he is, slipping a paperback under the baseball cap on his desk. Halper lifts the hat: *Robot Dreams*, by Isaac Asimov.

"I always carry a little something to read, sir. Helps pass the day. I did *The Highwayman* as a recitation in grade four."

"Good. I'm glad you mentioned that, Claudius. Maybe you could recite it for us."

"Now?"

"Well, you'll need time to refresh your memory. Tomorrow?"

"Okay sir."

"Good. And maybe you could tell the class about the poet, ask them some questions, make sure they understand the poem, lead a discussion. I'll be right here to help out if you need any help, so it's nothing to worry about. Would that be alright?"

"Yes sir."

"These are the notes and questions I intended to use. Maybe you and I could get together after school today and go over them, do a little practising, not the recitation unless you want to, just how to lead the discussion. Okay?"

"Okay sir."

"Good. And later this period I'll be handing back your TELL ME paper so we can discuss that after school too. And right now you could start practising for *The Highwayman* by going over there in the corner and helping Frank and Becky with the dictionaries."

Frank Stringer, with his hand on Becky's thigh and the turquoise spikes of his red hair perilously close to Claudius Ito's eyes says, "I don't get it man, you know like I mean 'across the purple moor.' So like you know man, we look up moor but I mean basically it says you know like some funny stuff I mean about here look man — 'a tract of peaty heath' — so I mean like basically I'm looking for all that stuff. I don't get it man. What's he riding, a Harley or what?"

Between bells Halper dodges body traffic with the carton of *Macbeth* for his senior English class. He is rushing to write his thought for the day on the blackboard before students arrive. The principal's son, Lincoln Fenton, is the only one already in the room and he sits reading, without looking up, stroking his thick black moustache. Lincoln always comes and goes alone. Halper is reminded of Simon, home between school and camp, sitting beside the pool reading, always alone.

Halper is about to ask Lincoln to distribute books as a way of engaging him and having a first chat. But Gordon Wing bursts into the room. He wears a t-shirt which says SCHOOL DAZE. Halper looks at it and smiles.

Gordon says, "Colorfast. One hundred percent cotton. Pre-shrunk. Fifty messages to choose from. Mild ones like this are for the dweeb market. Note the cut. Design by me and my brother Arlix. I import them from Hong Kong and Arlix prints them. Twenty bucks. For you, fifteen."

"Why do I get a bargain?"

"Because of that stuff you read us about yourself. TELL ME WHO YOU ARE. First time I ever heard a teacher blow his cover. Mostly they tell you nothing or bullshit about how great they are."

"I think I see why you call yourself the yellow peril."

"Mainly when dealing with the white blight. Not that I'm racist. Smart people aren't because it's irrational to be ethnocentric. The stupider people are, the more they congeal into ethnoblobs. The stupidest ones, like my father, act like packs of jackals because they've got the brainpower and instincts of animals. Multiculturalism feeds them so it's just another obnoxious ism like racism, ageism and sexism. That's from my editorial for the school paper which Fenton censored out of print. He's the white blight and that's why I'm the yellow peril."

"I take it you're Chinese."

"Ethnically. More or less. Converted rice. I'm Canadian."

"Did you want to see me, Gordon?"

"About TELL ME WHO YOU ARE. What you read us about yourself sounded like a short story, almost. Not bad. A bit sanitized. Kind of shapeless. Inconclusive. Not as good as my stories but not bad. How about this — instead of a four-page bio, how about if I hand in a real story about me? Longer. Something that happened six months ago. Tells you who I am. But I've got the first issue of *The Midhiller* to get out next week so I need more time."

"Take it. Rewrite half a dozen times at least. Good writing is mostly rewriting. Great idea, Gordon. Maybe some others would like to do a story. Why don't you suggest it? Make an announcement."

"Preacherman Parr is the only one I know that writes a lot. Mr. President. Billy Parr. Mostly bowel-moving tracts for the Christian student club, and one-page-wonder stories that win the yearbook prize for sweetness and light. I'll give him one thing though — his hockey reports for the paper never need editing. And last year he wrote a pretty good defence of hockey in reply to my editorial panning it."

"And I hear his presidential campaign speeches were so good the school board printed all three in their newsletter."

"Sermons. Cute, but sermons. Preacherman Parr writes sermons exclusively. He didn't like my t-shirts saying DIED AGAIN CHRISTIAN and DOG SPELLED BACKWARDS IS GOD so he wrote a sweet piece in supplication for my soul, and I printed it. But right beside it I ran my piece for careers day which said theology is just a branch of mythology, of marginal relevance, and the required training for every clergyman should be a Ph.D. in astro physics. The only reason Fenton didn't censor that was because he didn't check final copy on a safe-looking topic like careers. I doubt if Preacherman Parr would spill his guts in a real story, if he's got any to spill. I'm not that sure about doing it myself if it gets read by anyone but you."

"How about if we make the full-length personal story an option for my eyes only unless the writer wants to read all or part of it in class or maybe in the short story club?"

Lincoln Fenton, twisting one end of his moustache, reads on without looking up.

Halper gets to Student Services the following day at noon by skipping lunch. There are a dozen students and a man in a silk suit lined up at the door. Halper is told student files are not available. They are being sorted, regrouped, reviewed and updated by guidance teachers who are tied up all day interviewing students about switching courses. Halper has exasperated words with a fat woman in baggy jeans who is clutching a stack of files to her damp bosom with one hand and holding a box of cookies with the other. Halper is reminded of his fat mother clutching folded laundry in one arm, pulling cookies from the oven with the other, perspiring, telling him he can't always have what he wants, rushing off upstairs, leaving a trail of scents: lavender, laundry, cookies, fresh sweat.

The smell lingers when the fat woman kicks open the door to her cubicle, passes through, and kicks the door closed behind her. She is Brenda Sprung, head of guidance.

Halper wonders if he should persist, knock on Ms. Sprung's door. All he knows about her is a remark of Diane Lemon's that Brenda wanted two daughters to call Melody and Frolic, but being unmarried and unable to bring herself to artificial insemination, has settled for the two cats whose photos are on all her Christmas cards and, as Halper can see through the window, are also framed in gold on her desk. The cats are Melody and Frolic. Frolic is a neutered male.

Behind the counter, a teacher with short sandy hair and an amiable freckled face, his shirt sleeves half rolled up, is sorting files. He wipes moisture from his face with one sleeve and says, "I'm sorry. We're understaffed and Brenda's overworked. We've had cops in here all morning about two sex abuse reports and half of yesterday about a knife fight in the parking lot. A social worker is due in ten minutes about students he's found working all night in some gigantic bowling alley. And that dressy private eye in the hall is waiting to see us because he says some parents hired him to watch their own astronaut kids — that's what we call well-off Chinese kids left here alone in huge houses while both parents are back living in Hong Kong."

Halper wonders if it makes much difference whether missing parents are in the high-rise offices and posh clubs of Hong Kong or Toronto. Missing is missing, unless you see a lot of therapeutic value in chance encounters at the front door.

"I'm assistant guidance head, Russel Haynes. I'll put together the grade nine files you need and call you. I was wondering. Halper's not a common name. When I saw it on the faculty list I wondered if you're related to Simon Halper who went to Trinity College School."

"My son."

"Nice boy. I taught at TCS when Simon was there. What's he doing now?"

"Simon died. Took his own life."

"Oh, I'm so sorry. Forgive me."

Haynes comes to the counter in front of Halper and says again quietly, "I'm sorry. He was such a nice boy. Trying to cope. It's so hard for gay boys."

A trap door gives way. Halper feels himself hurtle down through the hole. He is yanked up short, but the rope has give to it. He bungees up and down, slows, comes to a halt facing the patient eyes of Russel Haynes.

"Simon? Simon was gay?"

"Yes. I'm sorry. I thought you knew. He said he was going to tell you at the end of term. But I left there to come here."

"He told you?"

"Yes. Well, I asked him. Then we talked about it three or four times. I knew him quite well from coaching gymnastics, and I was his counsellor."

"What made you suspect?"

"I'm gay, and he reminded me of my own up-tight cover-up at his age. Look, I'm sorry I blurted this out."

"No. No, I'm glad you told me. I only wish Simon had told me." TELL ME WHO YOU ARE.

Halper decides there is nothing to be gained by telling Liz. She would feel guilty, bear it silently, suffer some more. Or she might make something of it, make him feel guilty, more guilty, for spending too little time with Simon. So he won't tell Jillian and Alison either. But he will tell his classes because he told them about Simon's suicide in his TELL ME paper. Now he can tell them more about the reason why, information which might help someone in distress.

Hours later, driving home at dusk, that decision darts about dark corridors of his brain till it hits a light switch: *he can't tell his family about Simon but he can tell his students*. He misses his freeway exit and drives on distractedly watching familiar territory fade into twilight in the rear-view mirror.

When he finally gets all the files, Halper finds that his grade nine reading scores range from grade three through twelve, one feeder school used a different test, many transfer students from other school boards have scores from still different tests, and several students have no scores at all or scores three years old.

He also finds he doesn't know what much of the filed test information means. He is relieved to find an anecdotal note from a grade six teacher reporting that Claudius Ito 'went to Stratford for a week with his mother and is now rereading works of Shakespeare which he first read at seven.' At least, Halper thinks, he knows what that means.

David Halper's degrees are in English literature and law. He has twenty years experience as a corporation lawyer followed by eight months of teacher training, much of which was spent listening to lectures about lesson preparation and then teaching practice lessons in various schools — lessons carefully prepared and applied like pre-packaged splints to identically afflicted patients. He, and nearly all other teacher trainees, learned almost nothing about reading tests.

Nonetheless, he devises a simple, written, sight-reading test which consists of thirty questions based on four pages from *Oliver Twist*, a book which Claudius Ito describes on his answer sheet as 'another Victorian tear jerker about childhood, only slightly less maudlin than David Copperfield.' Claudius aside, Halper is able to sort his grade nine students into ten reading levels which he thinks might approximate grades two or three through college entry.

It is almost midnight. He stands in his den, leaning with one arm on his desk, looking at the ten piles and fanning himself with Claudius Ito's paper. He realizes by studying just the top sheet on each pile that he is untrained to diagnose the exact causes of each problem much less design remedial work specific to each cause. He also realizes his wife has returned from bridge and is drumming her fingers on the frame of his den door.

"I don't have two grade nine classes Liz, I've got ten levels in each class, not to mention Claudius Ito. Not to mention my senior English class. Not to mention my law classes. Half of them can't read or write well enough either. Most of them can't speak, can't carry on a decent conversation, make a point. Many of them don't even know how to listen. All of us teach literature — or law or history or something. None of us knows how to teach reading, writing, speaking and listening. And even if we knew, it wouldn't be on the timetable so there wouldn't be time."

"You know this isn't working."

"Don't start, Liz."

"I'm not starting. I'm continuing. *You're* continuing. At first I thought all this was grief reaction that would go away. Then I thought it was middle-age identity crisis that would go away. I thought instead of getting yourself a Porsche or a bimbo half your age you got a teaching certificate. But it's not going away and you're right back buried in work again. You won't stop till you have a stroke like your father, will you? Or start drinking again."

"You know I haven't had a drink in two years, not even a smoke, and I've been jogging every day — except the last couple of weeks with the rush."

"Why can't you just teach school? Why couldn't you just have been a successful lawyer eight hours a day instead of sixteen?"

"You know I entered law to please my father. And you. And I kept doing it to please you. I racked up 2,500 billable hours every year on your behalf."

"That's a lie, David. You buried yourself in law for reasons that have far more to do with you than me."

"Because law wasn't me. I had to conquer it, do it better than anyone else, to make it worthwhile spending my life at it. I always knew I should be a teacher or a writer. You're the one that wanted this kind of life — like your parents' life, this kind of house."

"And now your so-called salary will be a sixth of what it takes to run it. Less. You know we'll lose this place and you don't care. Two years and three months since Simon died. That's how long it's been since you earned anything. Two years and three months of hiding, scribbling in that journal and reading books — psychology, sociology, education theory, history of childhood . . . You've brought home hundreds of books and no dollars. Our investments are almost gone. What's next? My inheritance? If you think the bit my father left me is going to disappear on groceries while you hide out in some school you've got another think coming."

"We could manage a smaller house. You could get a job."

"As what? Receptionist at my hair dresser's? I can't get a decent job with an arts degree. In a recession. No training. No experience. Age forty-five. You're the one that wanted me home chauffeuring the children to hockey, figure skating, gymnastics, riding, dancing, acting, piano . . . The girls can't do any of that anymore. No more dressage. No more camp. We won't be able to afford their Branksome fees by next year. Or two cars. Or the Granite Club. And for what? Where's the peace of mind you were going to find in teaching?"

"I didn't know education was such a mess."

"And you're going to fix it. Prove yourself all over again. Do it better than anyone else to make it worthwhile spending your life at it. Or to prove to yourself your father was wrong and you're finally free of him. Which, David? Why can't you just do a job? Why do you have to take on the world?"

"Why do you have to nag?"

Halper decides to work early every morning in the classroom where he meets 9c to mark attendance. When he pulls into the parking lot at 7:10 a.m. he is surprised to see some of his students among the dozen or so already hanging out beside an all-night donut shop in the ageing strip mall across Midhill Avenue. Frank Stringer, pounding his feet like pneumatic jack hammers, clutches to his breast a big blaster which sprays the morning air with hard rock. Some boys, mostly black, and three or four girls, all soaked in sound, jump and gyrate in a circle that almost surrounds Frank and his partner, a copper-skinned girl in beads and bangles. She is doing a whirling dance which Halper thinks of as a powerful drill to complement Frank's relentless hammer.

Halper recognizes the girl as Zina the Mexicali Tamale, the name she gave him yesterday after someone in the cafeteria lineup called her a hooker and Halper broke up an incipient scuffle. Zina, Halper learned from Russel Haynes in the guidance office, is one of a hundred or more Midhill students living alone on welfare. She insists she no longer has a family and consequently no family name. Zina incorporates a prolonged good-morning wave to Halper into her spinning dance.

Frank grooves on but three other boys, two black and one white, amble over to the chain-link fence while Halper is at the trunk of his car unloading several boxes of books his own children enjoyed over the years. All three clutch the chain link like visitors at a zoo and make friendly banter. Halper feels like a primitive primate who has appeared at an unexpected hour to amuse the alien crowd with primordial antics. He asks if anyone would help him carry the books. All three volunteer.

Inside, Halper asks if they will shelve the books and list them for borrowing. The boys argue about how to do it but Halper mediates and they set to work. One looks at a fly leaf and reads aloud, "Simon Halper, September 1990." The book is *A Separate Peace*, by John Knowles. Halper looks at the small, tight, left-handed writing. Simon would have been fifteen then. Halper flips through the pages and is surprised to see that Simon has written comments beside many passages: silly, weak, unconvincing, unmotivated, nonsense, give me a break, get serious . . . On page

1 2 3 where a boy wonders about 'moving his bowels,' Simon has written in, 'real boys say shit.' Halper agrees with Simon but suddenly realizes that Simon would never have said shit in his presence.

On an impulse, Halper says, "This is about some boys at a private school fifty years ago. My son thought they were phoney. See what you think of them." He begins to read aloud, the first chapter, twelve pages. He stops. There is silence for a moment. Then one boy says, "Read more."

Halper says, "Not till you tell me what you think of the boys. How about Finney?"

A tall black boy with three rings in each ear and hands the size of baseball gloves makes huge circles with his thumbs and forefingers and says, "Finney got balls this big, man."

"Like shit, man. I mean Finney trip that other guy. Like jump that guy."

They sit around threshing over Finney's character for twenty minutes and then the boys ask to have the same chapter read again.

Halper says, "It's too late today. Tomorrow morning, if you like."

The principal is at the door beckoning Halper, his flashy ring signalling urgency. In the corridor, as arriving students mill past, James Fenton glares at Halper.

"What's this my son Lincoln says about you telling the class your son killed himself and you had to have therapy?"

"I did. Grief therapy for six months, my wife and I. And I saw a psychiatrist the rest of that year. That's what decided me to leave law and enter teaching. That and a lot of writing and reading I was doing at the same time."

"So now every dinner table conversation will be about this teacher of mine who had a nervous breakdown. A psycho. You've got a lot to learn, David. You keep your distance from students. Be friendly but remember your place. Keep your mouth shut about your personal life. Maybe a little something about your accomplishments. I played for the Argos so I talk about that."

Gossip is the other stimulant that flows with caffeine in the faculty lounge as teachers dash in and out to get fixes. Halper has heard whispers that Fenton's first wife attacked him and Lincoln, that Lincoln was enrolled at Midhill last year but showed up just once to register and only began attending classes a full year later; and Fenton has never explained any of that to teachers let alone students. He barely even mentions his daughter Nita who attends a private school.

"I disagree. I'm not having any of the discipline problems lots of new teachers have and I think it's partly because I levelled with the kids about who I am. I told them the truth about my father, my kids, me as a kid, why I quit a job that paid over six times as much as this one, why I gave up drinking."

Fenton stiffens. His voice lowers. "You're an alcoholic?"

Halper has heard murmurs about Fenton's first wife being an alcoholic, showing up drunk at school functions.

"A workaholic. I fueled my work machine with scotch and nicotine. I gather from the yellow on your moustache and fingers that you still puff. I recommend you give it up."

"And I recommend you learn your place, Halper. And learn something about kids. Have lunch with Jerry Duchok. Make sure you do that. Vice-principals know kids."

The next day, there are five students waiting by the chain-link fence, four boys and Zina. By the end of the week, word of mouth has increased the number to eleven. Two students are reading science fiction under the direction of Claudius Ito; and the sci-fi group is also writing a newsletter explaining the early-morning activities to parents. They are using computers in a back corner of the room.

In front corners, students are reading aloud to the other two groups. Zina is in grade ten and is a fairly good reader and a very good actor, so her group is animated and loud, but the other groups seem not to notice. Halper is moving from group to group when Billy Parr looks in to get approval of his first agenda as president of the student council.

Billy's courteous smile, his preppy look, the Ralph Lauren clothes, remind Halper of Simon. He wonders, as he glances at the agenda, about the many dimensions of self that make a gentle boy like Billy also a breakneck hockey player and a kind-hearted boy like Simon also a daredevil gymnast.

Halper recalls his own recklessness when, in spite of his shyness, he played intramural football and tried out for the Goliaths at East York Collegiate, the times he drove much too fast, the time he rolled his father's Buick at sixty miles an hour on Dawes Road and ended up in Dentonia Creek then in East General Hospital. He thinks all brash teens are venting pent-up rage over powerlessness. He knows teen boys are programmed genetically to begin being men, to fend and defend on behalf of the tribe. But their natural job has been taken from them and their lives trivialized by a model of childhood which infantilizes them, gives them no useful role. TELL ME WHO YOU ARE.

It is a long agenda, sixteen items. Halper scans it and says, "Mascot drive $3,000. What's that?"

"Chocolate bar sales, sir. To buy a mascot costume for half-time shows. For school spirit. Custom made. By a company called Sugars. Mr. Duchok says they're the best. They made the Pillsbury dough boy. We need a mascot to symbolize Midhill."

"Three thousand dollars worth of junk food buys a plastic caricature inside which a real student hides. That's what symbolizes Midhill? And look at these other items: pep rallies, parking, party decorations, folk dancing . . . Looks trivial to me, Bill. But it's your baby."

Halper initials the paper and hands it back to Billy Parr who looks surprised, even dismayed.

"Race relations isn't trivial, sir. Interfaith sharing and dress code aren't trivial."

"Agreed. Depending how deeply you deal with them. But why aren't there items here about curriculum, teachers, punishment, homework, exams, part-time jobs, money, sex, housing, missing parents, loneliness, all the things that really concern students. Isn't that what governments are supposed to do, deal with the real concerns of their constituencies?"

"Yes sir, in Ottawa and Washington, but we can't do anything about that stuff."

"I read a book this summer called *Future Schools*. The chapter on student government says, 'The test of student government is this: is anything being managed by school or school district officials that could be managed by student government? If so, student government is not functioning properly.' "

The usually articulate Billy Parr is without words but his face is back-lit by epiphany. Halper can see revelation unfolding in the bright eyes fastened on him. He knows why he is a teacher. No multi-million-dollar boardroom coup while he was a lawyer ever gave him such a rush. Billy poises his pen on a pad. "Would you say that again, sir?"

"I'll lend you the book. The author lives in Toronto. You can call him up."

Claudius Ito bounces up to meet Billy Parr and announces that he has just been elected to student council as class representative for 9C.

Frank Stringer shows up at 7:15 on a rainy morning with three friends, two of them not in any of Halper's classes. The next day, Becky Kowalski drifts in at 7:25 with a bag of muffins from her father's donut shop across the street. Mr. Kowalski also sends a message that he will supply any specified number of day-old muffins free of charge every morning and that he is grateful not to have the kids hanging around his place. While they are eating and Halper is explaining why bran muffins are superior to chocolate chip, a janitor comes to say Halper is wanted on the phone. As they walk down the corridor the janitor complains about food in classrooms, about kids in the school so early, about the office staff not being on duty yet, about not being a messenger boy . . .

Halper's oldest daughter Jillian is on the phone. She is breathless, almost shouting, over music. Someone in the background is yelling hurry up. Three or four others are arguing, something about rent.

"Daddy, will you call Mummy before the school does? I wasn't there last night. I'm going with Rick. Remember I told you. The one from the film workshop. I'm going on a shoot. I have lines, Daddy! Will you call the school and pick up my stuff?"

"Honey, where are you? We have to talk about this. You're only sixteen. How about Saturday? We could have lunch, spend the afternoon, all day if you like."

"There's nothing to talk about, Daddy. I'm quitting school. I love Rick. I want to be an actress. He says I'm good. I know I'm good. I have to go, Daddy. Will you send me some money?"

"You just got your allowance."

"A hundred dollars!"

"Every month. And you just got a thousand for fall clothes and before that a thousand for summer clothes and activities. And last March two thousand for your birthday."

"You gave Simon a YJ Laredo when he was sixteen. Rick says that's twenty thousand at least."

"That was then. This is now. Jillian, sweetheart —."

She hangs up.

The police are polite but unimpressed. No foul play. Over sixteen. Voluntary departure. There are twelve thousand street kids in Toronto, most of them younger than Jillian. They phone around from the police station and find the film is shooting in Vancouver. Halper tries to dissuade her but Liz flies there that night. Halper marks papers, TELL ME WHO YOU ARE.

CHAPTER TWO

The cafeteria air smells of french fries, boiling oil, peanut butter, body odour, gym shoes, hair gel . . . Whoops and hollers punctuate the constant roar of giggle and chat. Exhaust fans so loud they have to be turned off when the room is used as an auditorium are defeated utterly but drone on gamely as background noise. The young and eternally hungry devour stockpiles of donuts, chocolate bars, hamburgers, daily specials, whatever they can afford and can cram in quickly. The ambience reminds Halper of his one visit to a federal prison on behalf of a corporate client, except that the prison food was better.

Halper is on tiptoe, craning, looking over cafeteria fare trying to find something not full of fat, something he can bolt in twenty minutes without getting heartburn. He intends, as usual, to look around the crowd and find one or two of his students or someone on student council so he can make use of the time conversing. That may require eating while crouched beside a crowded table, or leaning against a wall, or sitting on the floor. He spots Alexandra Bagaras looking for a place to park.

Another familiar smell announces Fenton who emerges from his privileged path behind the steam table, headed for the teachers' lunch room, bearing a heaped cold plate the caterer has prepared for him. He beckons Halper aside and says, "Jerry Duchok tells me you haven't had lunch with him yet."

"No time. I have kids to see, dozens, hundreds. Over there in the wheelchair, Alexandra Bagaras. She shakes every time a teacher speaks to her, trembles. But less each time I talk to her. She smiles all the time and she's pretty so it's easy to miss the nervousness. Even easier to miss the low self-esteem that separates her more than paralysed legs."

"Leave those matters to guidance. The union fights to get rid of chores like cafeteria duty and you hang around purposely. Get your priorities straight, David. Good vice-principals like Jerry can tell you more about kids in fifteen minutes than you'll learn in fifteen hours table hopping."

Halper knows from faculty meetings that, like Fenton, Jerry Duchok is an ex-football player, ex-physical education teacher, ex-coach who at forty or so feels he brings the wisdom of all his previous incarnations to his present high office. Everybody at Midhill knows that Duchok is fearless, that he has a collection of knives confiscated from students. The entire community knows that last semester he waded into a schoolyard fight and disarmed a gun toter. Press clippings about the gun victory, along with many about his athletic prowess, are in an album with black pages and a white plastic cover which Duchok keeps in his briefcase. Halper has already had one showing — in the parking lot, on the lid of his car trunk, when he happened to park beside Duchok. TELL ME WHO YOU ARE.

"I hear from Jerry at staff meetings. I don't need another fifteen minutes on football or ten on detention procedures. I'd like to talk shop but only about education issues and only after I've got to know the kids. I can sit with one or two every day at lunch."

"How much of that do you need? My son Lincoln tells me you spend a lot of time in class sitting with the kids."

"Yes but there the purpose is different. I'm teaching them how to operate in groups — chair, present, analyze, criticize, synthesize, recap, evaluate content and process . . ."

"You're teaching English and law not group discussion."

"The content is English and law. The method is often discussion."

"Lincoln says they spend class time discussing smart remarks you write on the blackboard that have nothing to do with the course."

"Everything has to do with my courses. The subject matter of literature is life. Same with law. I leave thoughts written on side boards so the kids find them the minute they arrive and have something to discuss till starting time. Today in grade nine English the message is, 'Adults try to eliminate the symptoms of youth problems when they should look for causes and remove them.' Today's message in senior English happens to be 'A social critic's job is to tell you when beliefs you think are self-evident cease to be true.' For my law classes it's 'Truth emerges from the interplay of competing ideas.' But sometimes the message is subject centred. Yesterday, the day after I gave every senior student a literary magazine to read, the message was, 'Too many modern writers are sucked into the whirlpool left when James Joyce struck a literary deviceburg and went down in a sea of symbols.' "

"And who writes these gems."

"I do. But soon I'll have kids doing it too. Part of becoming cultured is creating hypotheses for discussion."

"You've fallen for that child-centred malarkey. The fact is discussion is just one tool, just something good teachers lead now and then. With good teachers to ask the right questions kids do it naturally."

"Not so. Even my senior students don't know how to do it because they've never been taught. Most teachers don't know how to do it, including those who break big classes into groups once in a while. Teachers keep on controlling things, even keep on peddling data instead of teaching kids how to deal with data: find, sort, organize, present, question, discuss, interpolate, evaluate, especially evaluate. So bright kids like Lincoln are not challenged to think, to take the initiative, to accept responsibility, to organize and manage classroom activities. Instead, they just mouth off or else sit there sponging up facts they can squeeze out again on examinations."

"That's reality, Halper. Reality. Lincoln and all the others need the highest possible mark so they can get into the best possible universities. Your job is to meet that need. You do that by preparing your lessons to make the best use of every minute. I'd like to see your lesson plans for this afternoon."

"I'm prepared to the teeth but it doesn't translate into a neat lesson plan for each period. That's a concept useful only on occasional days when teachers are the presenters. Even then I don't always need a written plan. Once a week or so I teach grammar for a whole period because so many kids know none. But a few know a lot. I start from some mistake a student just made and let it roll. Kids get involved at blackboards — the ones that know helping those that don't. I supervise from the back. They like it. What do I write as a lesson plan for that? Freewheel grammar?"

"Take my advice, Halper. Your department head, me, the superintendent — everyone who evaluates teachers — believes in teachers teaching lessons. Stand and deliver the curriculum. That mush about kids doing their own thing is dead if it ever lived. We want rigour at Midhill."

"My kids don't do their own thing. They do what's expected of them, which is master the process as well as the skills and the content. They and I check the curriculum guideline every day to make sure we're on target. You want rigour? My kids work their asses off in English and law. And on top of all that they're actually learning to read, write, speak and listen."

Two days and no news of Jillian. One call from Liz to say she has found the film crew but not Jillian who is off scouting locations with Rick. Halper stands at his den window looking out at the lamp-lit terrace where Jillian did aerobic exercises to loud music. She started that right after Simon's funeral and kept it up whenever she was home from boarding school. Most evenings. Every morning. Even when they jogged together she wore earphones and played tapes. Noise filled the void between father and child as much as it did between the dead and living.

The terrace is empty now. Its flagstones still wet with rain are shiny as tombstone granite. Fallen petals from white mums stick there like snow that won't melt.

The hall clock strikes midnight. Halper lets go the window drape, turns off the terrace lights, and returns to his marking. The first short story handed in is from Lincoln Fenton, who always ducks out right after class and has never even mentioned that he will submit a TELL ME WHO YOU ARE story instead of a four-page bio. Halper begins reading with his mind more on Jillian than Lincoln:

Four weeks and three days into computer camp my mother finally calls and I'm all set to tell her about my new moustache when she opens with, "Lincoln, sweetheart, I'm in Paris. Sorry I couldn't call from Istanbul. Lincoln, sweetheart, I met a very nice man on the cruise. We decided to ride the Orient Express."

Two relics riding a relic. I'm fifteen and I'm willing to believe there's sex after forty, but in a train berth? My mother's nearly six feet. With some old guy puffing and grunting more than the train? With the train car swaying through the Alps? That's grotesque. I'm nearly six feet and I've tried it in the back seat of Gramma's Mercedes, parked. That's grotesque enough.

"Lincoln, sweetheart, the greatest news — I'm married! His name is James Fenton and he's got a daughter about your age. Nita. Very cute."

Halper sits up straight and re-reads the first three paragraphs. Can this be Lincoln who broods through classes with his elbows welded to the desk, fingers of both hands knit like chain mail shielding his face, speaking only when spoken to. Can this be the son, even the stepson, of that clinker in the front office? He checks the cover sheet again and reads on:

I decide not to tell her about my moustache. I picture Nita waddling into my life. Her double chins are covered with pimples and a few whiskers. She has tree-trunk legs and hammer toes. Already I'm planning how to handle monthly meetings with my mother in Manhattan. At the Guggenheim I'll walk beside my mother and ten feet behind Nita and her father.

"I hope the three of you will be very happy. So what else is new?"

"Mr. Fenton, James, your new father — he wants you to live with us."

"No way. Gramma's seventy-four. She needs me after all that chemo."

I'm lying. Nobody needs me since my father died. Least of all Gram. It's been over three years since her chemotherapy and she's been back on the seminar circuit for two years, and during that time we've toured Central America and Eastern Europe. Her sidekick, Iris, could do everything I do for her and lots more. I doubt if Gram ever needed anybody. I mean, she loves me and all, and she loved my dad, but everything about Gram's life is like the four sailboats she inherited and still sails in the Sound: other people are welcome aboard but only if they crew for her.

This guy Fenton doesn't need me. He just wants my mother in his bed, so he's handing her a line about wanting her kid and she's dumb enough to fall for it. My mother is not noted for rational thinking anytime, but especially when she has the hots, which is most of the time. I inherited my horny genes from my mother, not Gram. Gram doesn't like horny people. I can tell by the way her eyelids drop half way and she glares from under them while she puffs out breath, especially at guys showing off on the beach.

That's why I haven't told Gram I'm so horny that right after I say goodnight to her I imagine I'm whatever guy I'm reading about, doing it with whatever woman he's doing it with in the book. When I'm home with Gram I have to make sure to clean up the mess and throw the Kleenex in the toilet and not get any on my pajamas or sheets. Some nights I have to make two or three trips to the bathroom.

Halper wonders if Simon masturbated. Of course he must have. Jillian's and Alison's first periods were greeted with much mother-daughter communication, support, affirmation. The norm, Halper thinks. But a boy's first ejaculation is always a guilty secret, never validated. Imagine any twelve-year-old saying, 'Dad, I got a hard on last night and when I rubbed it it felt good and it shot this white stuff all over my belly.'

It's safe to tell my mother about anything like that because she only hears what she wants to hear, so she never gets upset. I told her a bit about my bedtime reading habit while we walked around the zoo and she said, "That's nice, Lincoln. You'll know what to do when you grow up and have a lady friend of your own. Look sweetheart, the lion is pawing the ground." My mother sketches zoo scenes like that for her idea file which is a six-foot pile of five thousand unsorted drawings in the corner of her studio.

This camp's not great, but okay. Massachusetts coast. Computers all day. No dumb organized sports or 'activities' except a few optional ones which I skip — except for sailing and swimming and guest lecturers and one bus trip to Boston to check out computer applications at M.I.T. People are mostly friendly but there's nobody to hang out with unless you're in a clique, which I'm not.

There's one big guy who really shouldn't be here because he isn't smart enough. He started something — calling me Einstein and suck. The first week he jumped me from behind at swimming and took me down before I knew what was happening, but I heaved him off and dove on him and broke his nose and loosened his front teeth. That surprised me as much as him. In our family, nobody is supposed to lose their temper or fight or even yell. So before the camp director got hold of my grandmother, I got her on the phone and told her, and she said it was okay under the circumstances. Anyway, they let me stay, and now the big dummy leaves me alone. So does everyone else.

WYSIWYG. What You See Is What You Get. Three postcards from my mother. I keep them taped to the mirror above my computer and read them whenever I check my moustache: 'Having a glorious time on Capri sweetheart.' 'Glorious colors around the Parthenon sweetheart.' 'Topkapi is glorious sweetheart.'

For an artist, my mother's not very creative — with words. Her illustrations for kids' books are something else. Also her clothes. Also her love life: one failed copy-writer writing — make that not writing — the great American novel for kids while living on Mom and booze, one social worker of the street type saving homeless kids from drugs while stashing his own under my mother's bed, one preacher writing a children's Bible in rhyme while cheating on his wife. Eight that I remember, maybe nine. About one a year. Whenever I mention one of them, my grandmother says, 'echoes of 67,' which was the year Mom was a flower child in Greenwich Village, right after high school.

Every night when I phone my grandmother at bedtime I remind her how many days it's been since my mother called from Paris. Gram says not to worry, Mom probably met somebody new between Paris and London and is busy getting a divorce from Fenton. Gram is my father's mother and I don't know why I bother mentioning my mother to her because there are some things Gram doesn't have anything good to say about so she says hardly anything except the odd jibe. One of them is my mother. Another is all women who aren't feminists. Another is right-wing Republicans. Another is men, except for a few, mostly professors or lawyers or writers like Gore Vidal — except when he goes on too long about sex.

Every night at camp I lift weights same as at home. My dad did weights when I was a little kid, and he gave me tiny weights so I could lift along with him, so now it comes naturally to lift the heavy weights he left behind. And I play my violin and write stories or write in my computer journal and read another novel and wait. I don't know why I wait for my mother to call but I do it all the time, even at home. I know by now she hardly ever calls and I really don't care all that much, and I like to write and read anyway.

The last full day of camp I get a call from Iris, who lives across the hall from us in Manhattan. My grandmother is dead. Drowned. Sailing the dinghy alone on Long Island Sound. Overboard. Rain. High wind. . . . Iris is whining like the wind. Capsized. Coast guard. Exhaustion. Washed up. . . . When the wind subsides I can hear myself answering questions. 'Yes, I understand, Iris. Yes, I have a ticket back to New York. Yes, I can manage. Yes, I know where to reach my mother. Yes, I'm okay, Iris. Thanks for calling.' Click.

I sit staring at the dead phone in my hand and hear myself saying out loud to nobody, "Dead? Gramma?" It's hot and humid and still and two o'clock in the afternoon, but I feel cold and my throat is so tight and dry it's hard to breathe. My stomach burns and I keep swallowing the sour taste of lunch.

At the funeral I get my first glimpse of Fenton right off the plane: chain-store navy pinstripe off the rack; tacky birthstone ring the size of Rhode Island with cuff links to match — a steal, he explains, from some street bazaar in Istanbul. We're sitting in Riverside Church right in front of my gramma's casket waiting for the service to start and he leans across my mother to tell me this in a hot whisper that smells of beer and cigarettes and a blast of cologne as strong as room deodorizer. Turkey for turkeys, I think to myself as I check out the dime-store cut glass Fenton is flashing, and wonder if my mother is brain damaged. But I keep my mouth shut. WYSIWYG.

Outside the church, when people are milling around deciding who goes to the cemetery in which car, Fenton steps in and organizes everybody just like a teacher in a schoolyard. With his hand on my shoulder ushering me into a limo he wants to know which I prefer — American or Canadian football. Never mind brain damaged, I wonder if my mother is brain dead. But I keep my mouth shut. I say 'thank you, sir' for the birthstone ring Fenton has brought me and gives me while we ride to the cemetery. Fortunately, it's too small for any of my fingers because my mother thinks I'm still six years old.

Fenton says he'll give the ring to Nita and buy me something nice. I'll bet. All I can see is the hearse in front of us glittering in the sun like Fenton's cuff links. Fenton tells me Nita has been with her grandmother all summer at some lake in Canada. At least she had the decency not to show up in New York for my grandmother's funeral. Why didn't Fenton stay away too? It's none of his business. He never even met my gramma.

My mother could also stay away for all she cares about Gramma. They only ever saw each other on Christmas day. Not that they fought. Just that they had different tastes about everything, except maybe a few kinds of art, and my dad, and one recipe for apple pie they both used because it was my dad's favourite and mine. Once, only once, I remember Gram calling my mother a Bohemian to her face. The name sticks in my head, not the argument if there was one. Probably not. I know Gram thought my mother was low class. Whenever I came back from visiting Mom, Gram had one or two little criticisms about my manners and certain words I used. She blamed it on 'Chicago influences' because that's where my mother came from. Gram allowed that Chicago had some interesting art and architecture but otherwise was mainly hotdogs, Al Capone, speakeasies, Playboy bunnies and my mother's family.

Mom's mother died when she was twelve and left her father with five kids, Mom the oldest. He got married again to a woman with three kids and all ten of them lived in five rooms over the corner grocery store he still runs in Chicago. My mother never liked her stepmother so she left home the day she finished high school and came to New York and eventually put herself through art school working as a part-time model and an art teacher but mostly as a waitress. She still sends Christmas cards and pictures of me to Chicago and other places where her brothers and sisters live but she doesn't see them or phone them. They're all pipe fitters or bus drivers or something. I guess they haven't got much in common.

Gramma told me my mother dragged my dad to rock concerts and baseball games and fashion shows and discos and got him to watch television and do fifty other useless things that wasted so much of his life that he died without finishing his book on gifted kids. I hardly remember any of those years but I sort of remember my dad coming home from the university and saying 'surprise, surprise,' and taking us out. I think he just took us places he never went himself when he was a kid because he thought Mom or I would like it. That's different from being dragged there by her.

My mother told me once, when I asked her, that my dad enjoyed a little 'diversion' and it improved his work and that Gramma was too serious and too organized. I think the diversion included smoking grass because when I tried a joint last year I suddenly remembered the smell from childhood and it was the smell of my parents' bedroom. Gram was dead set against marijuana, so I expect that was the main diversion she objected to, but she never said so. All she ever told me was that my father never smoked cigarettes till my mother got him started and the smoking probably speeded up his heart attack.

My mother was right about Gram being super organized. Just the opposite to Mom. Mom's idea of getting organized is to glue herself to the nearest good-looking jerk and ask what he wants to do. Not that she always picks jerks. Just that she can't tell the difference. Even the ones that aren't totally jerks are vacuum packs with nothing to say so they watch football on TV and start getting chummy with me, acting like they think they're my father or something. My father's dead. That's a permanent condition.

For Gram's funeral my mother looks spectacular as usual, only this time instead of doing it with two or three or more bright colors at once — which is her trademark — she's all in white except for black stockings and black shoes and black jewelry and a black silk scarf that ties her hair back in a bun and trails down her back. At the grave side, even Gloria Steinem stares at her. It's hard not to stare at my mother.

She really looks at me for the first time in two months while they lower the coffin. I know the look says she loves me, but I wonder if she likes my moustache which by now is long enough to twist at the ends. When we walk away, she doesn't even mention it. Instead she brushes my hair back from my forehead as usual. I know she thinks I'm good looking but I'm not very. My chin is so square I look like a cartoon, like Dick Tracy. And I've got ears like Prince Charles, but I'm smart enough to hide them under my hair. That's one good thing, I'm hairy like my dad. Maybe I'll grow a beard like his to hide my chin.

"Lincoln, sweetheart — about Mr. Fenton, James, your new father —"

We're walking out of the cemetery and she has me by the arm. With my free hand I'm twirling one end of my moustache but she's busy looking back at Fenton who's glad-handing the preacher.

In her calmest voice she says, "He's principal of a high school in Toronto."

This is child abuse with dynamite! But I decide to keep cool even though my guts are exploding. It's always best to keep cool with my mother or else she gushes or something. But she guesses what I'm thinking. She gushes.

She says she fell in love with Fenton before she knew he was a school principal. She swears to it. She says it over and over about ten different ways. I believe her. On a cruise ship where everything big is organized for her by the social director along comes prince charming who organizes everything small, and she's so delirious with joy that she has no resistance at all.

"Mr. Fenton, James, your new father . . . he says you'd love his school, Midhill."

"Sure I would. Just like I loved the other three. A school is a school is a school."

Just the word school scares me. Schools are full of bullies, all kinds. I have this recurring vision of bully morons running up and down playing fields chasing balls, and older bully morons making them do it. I can't stand it so they all chase me and trample me to death. I hear old bully bores in classrooms droning on all day about stuff in textbooks that I've already read in other books years before. I can't stand it so the old bully bores put me in solitary and beat me over the head with their textbooks and I die there. I think I should have it in me to fight school bullies but instead I run. Three times I've run for real. Every time, Gram said it was okay.

With Gram gone I know I've got no choice any more about going to school. Powerless. Here I am the same height as Fenton so I look him straight in the eye. Just as strong, probably stronger — he's beginning to sag over his belt. Just as smart. Smarter. Definitely smarter. My moustache is thick and soft and black like a panther pelt. His is motley grey with nicotine stains and prickly-looking, like steel wool that's been used to strip rust.

On a level playing field I could beat Fenton at anything. Including sex. Especially sex. Old guys like him — 47 — take forever to get it up the second time. I read about that. And during the long wait there's nothing for a woman to do but look at fat and wrinkles. That's why men keep boys down. They're jealous. Afraid of competition. And they get away with it because they've got all the power.

It also turns out I'm much richer than Fenton. Besides my education trust which Gram set up years ago, I now own most of what she owned. Iris gets the apartment opposite ours on Riverside Drive (which she's been living in for years while helping Gram) and she also gets Gram's summer house on Long Island and a fund to run both places. The cause gets a million. I get the rest: Gram's Mercedes, her apartment, a fund to run it, her sailboats and the boat house with living quarters upstairs, her bank accounts, her share of a lawyers' consortium that owns rental condos and stuff in Florida, and about two million in blue chip stocks. But I can't get my hands on more than an allowance and school costs till I'm twenty-one, except with the approval of some woman lawyer at a trust company who immediately sides with my mother, who sides with Fenton. The conspiracy against kids is total. Almost total.

Gram was an exception. She started out — so she said — as your typical Vassar woman, except she got restless or curious or something and switched courses, and eventually colleges. Spanish, French, literature, political science, physical education, music. . . . I don't know what all. After graduation — for lack of something better to do, she said — she played violin in an amateur chamber group, taught gym at a girls' school and, because she could afford it, dabbled at graduate courses in physical education at Wellesley looking for something satisfying. What she really liked was marathon swimming and she was good, but her family didn't approve of the notoriety, so she never competed except at the yacht club regatta where she won every year, even against men.

Gram moved on into teaching languages and violin to little kids at private schools till she gave in to family pressure and married your typical bright young lawyer from her father's firm and he made her quit teaching to climb your typical corporate ladder with him. One child — my father — who went to your typical posh nursery school and three of your typical New England private schools and didn't much like any of them even though he was a brain. Make that *because* he was a brain. I inherited my brains and my anti-school genes from my father.

When my grandfather died — just before I was born — Gramma went to a Gloria Steinem seminar, out of loneliness I guess, and curiosity, and became a disciple. She got Iris and some other women interested and set up her own cell. She took over the sailboats and executive car and revolver my grandfather left behind because she said all three were symbols that should be appropriated. Over the years she also took up martial arts, Pritikin cooking, meditation, creative writing, photography, archery, public speaking, and stand-up comedy (which happened to be right across the hall from public speaking at night school and she figured a little humour would jazz up her public speaking).

Her all-time favourite activity — except for swimming and her empowerment seminars for women in poor countries, which came later — was the research project my father did with hothouse classes for bright kids at Columbia. He was a professor of child psychology. (That's how he met my mother — he hired her in her last year at art school to teach the kids art part time.)

Gram taught violin and Spanish and French and exercise games to the hothouse kids as a volunteer. My mother says they took me with them to Columbia when I was a baby and I learned to read at three and to play the violin soon after. I had the feeling then and now that I was the centre of my dad's research, of his interest anyway. But I only really remember the class Christmas parties when my dad played Santa Claus and wore a fake white beard and moustache over top of his real black ones. After he took the gifts out of his bag he always put me in it and swung it up on his back and told everyone he was taking me home because I was his Christmas gift to my mother and grandmother. I was born on Christmas eve.

Gramma was the longest-serving helper in the hothouse classes and I was the longest-attending kid. I was six when the classes ended because my father died of the same kind of heart attack that had killed his father six years earlier.

Mom was so broken up about my father's sudden death that she couldn't even make meals though she'd always been good at whipping up something out of whatever happened to be in the fridge. So Gram came and got us and we went to stay a while with her, and I never left. I still have the same room my dad had as a boy with all his stuff still there including his weights.

Mom moved to a studio in Soho and, what with quite a few guys coming and going, she doesn't want me around. Or maybe it's just because she has to freelance and never has a regular pay cheque. We talk on the phone every so often and go to the zoo or an art show or something once a month if both of us are in town. And every three or four months she makes apple pie from scratch and invites me for dinner and plays mummy with whatever guy is on the scene playing daddy.

I figure she's always intended to get organized, get a bigger place with a room for me, get married, take me back. Meanwhile, she keeps me six years old in her mind so she can take up where she left off.

Gram tutored me at home and taught me how to look up stuff and teach myself according to my father's hothouse methods, and then we taught each other. And we travelled. I never went to school except I tried three when Gram got cancer. I was twelve then. She thought she might get too sick to teach and learn with me, and besides, she said I could use some school credentials for college entrance. The longest I lasted at any school was four days.

While my mother and Fenton are in Soho packing up the studio I'm up at Riverside Drive sorting my stuff that has to go to Toronto on the same truck. I find Gram's note under my old IBM: 'Linc my love, I know it will be a while before you move your biggest computer so here I am waiting for you now that you've had time to get used to everything. Between you and me — *strictly* — (destroy this note because it would upset Iris and might affect the will or insurance or something) the chemo didn't work, and I'm just speeding things up a little. It's what I want. That's all there is to say about that.

'You brought joy to my life, gave me my happiest years. When your dad was a boy I was so busy hosting dinner parties for his father and being his mother according to the rules (which meant teaching him to be dependent — a child) that I didn't teach him to evaluate everything so he could be independent — be himself instead of being his parents' clone. I think I got it right the second time around. Can you imagine how proud I am of me? Of you? How much I love you?

'Keep the faith (in yourself) — and a few dollars in reserve that nobody else knows about. Remember the time all our luggage was stolen from that leaky outboard crossing the Mekong at night from Nong Khai to Vientiane? But I had money hidden in my underwear. Remember? See the envelope inside the longjohns in your under-wear drawer.'

I feel a little power coming my way. I open the envelope and find another note saying about the same thing and $10,000 in new bills. WYSIWYG. A lot of power, which I put in my underwear for the drive to Toronto. During breakfast with Iris I keep adjusting my crotch, which makes me horny and makes it even more crowded down there. I'm not as sure as Gram about underwear as the place to pack your power. In her mind, she must have cut off everybody's dick, so she figured everyone had lots of room. I'm more comfortable with where Gram kept her loaded executive revolver — hidden in the Mercedes, the same place my grandfather kept it in his cars.

Naturally, Fenton has to play daddy and drive my car even though I tell him I've aced a driving course and Gram let me drive as a conscientious objection to ageist rules and also because she pre-ferred taking pictures out the window or playing something on her violin that matched the landscape. I drove from Warsaw to Sofia and from El Paso to Panama and back — through mountains on zig-zag roads, in the rain, at night — but I can't drive from New York to Toronto on the freeway in sunshine on a summer Saturday. My guts are burning up.

They sit in the front seats smoking and stinking up my car, holding hands and mooning at each other. It's disgusting watching old people make fools of themselves like that. And they're listening to my mother's chintzy 60s and 70s tapes. I pretend to sleep in the back. I reach up under the driver's seat and feel the gun in its secret pocket. I imagine pulling it out quietly and putting it to Fenton's head and blowing his brains out if he has any.

Actually, I do fall asleep, because I've been awake all night saying goodbye to New York and Gram, mostly sitting on her bed. Just sitting. And doing something she wouldn't let me do at night — walking around Riverside Park. Nothing bad happened, except I felt like I was inside Grant's Tomb, buried. But I've had that feeling lots of times for years just looking out my bedroom window at the tomb.

While Fenton is having a pee in Utica and my mother and I are looking for something edible on the fried fat menu of a family restaurant — which Fenton has chosen because 'it looks really nice,' — she offers me a choice between firing squad and lethal injection.

"Lincoln, sweetheart, Mr. Fenton, James, your new father — he was saying he thinks you can qualify for college if you take one year at his school. Or else you could do it at a boarding school. But that would break his heart, not having you at home. He's such a family man, and he's always wanted a son."

Well of course I'm not going to be cooped up twenty-four hours a day in some ivy-covered military camp for rich right-wing bullies, so Fenton's school begins to look pretty good by default. The rest of the way to Toronto I lie in the back with one or both bare feet propped up behind Fenton's head close enough to kick his brains out if he has any. But instead I sleep some more.

By the time we cross the border at Niagara Falls Fenton is singing with the tapes. I figure he's in heaven: a year after his divorce he goes on a cruise and brings back a wife who's a looker, the biggest Mercedes they make, and a 'son' who's the smartest kid in his school.

His daughter, I take it, is not exactly Rhodes scholar material.

Fenton keeps turning his head and talking to my feet about Nita while I'm half asleep, till I decide to sit up and check out the twilight ahead because he says we're nearing Toronto and the CN Tower is in sight.

"World's highest," Fenton says. "Isn't that beautiful?"

The tower looks like a hypodermic syringe shooting clouds full of darkness. Fenton shoots me full of more family gas.

"Nita's a day student at a Catholic girl's school," he says. "Her mother thinks it best."

Gram was against anything Catholic, mostly because of their stand on birth control and abortion, and women not being in top jobs. She was against all religions, for about the same reason, I think. That and superstition. She called irrational beliefs superstition and all religions the superstition industry. But she left instructions for her funeral to be in Riverside Church. Her parents belonged there but she never went near the place after she grew up, except to get married and attend her parents' funerals and my grandfather's and my father's. Gram was hard to figure out, not consistent like Mom. My mother is consistently harebrained. At this moment she's hanging onto Fenton's every word about Nita the numby.

You could have better discussions about any old topic with Gram than with my mother. Much better. Except I never told Gram I didn't agree with her on abortion. I think my dad cared the most about me from before the word go so why should he, how could he, have no say about whether I survived or not? I decided any new life that comes from a man's sperm is half his right and responsibility from the time sperm meets egg. I told Mom that at the Bronx Zoo and she said, 'I suppose so, yes. Look sweetheart, that elephant's making a ton of poo poo.' Gram would have had a fit and sat me down and blistered me with a hot compress of acid distilled from her best speeches.

By the time we pass signs pointing to the international airport and

I make a mental note of them for future reference — as soon as you check in always look for emergency exits, Gram said — Fenton has finished with Nita's brilliant academic career and is on about her fascinating domestic arrangements.

"She lives with her mother," he says. "But she has a bedroom for visits at my place. Our place."

Fenton's place on Dundonald Street is a newish row house with a fake-traditional front, a townhouse, which he calls a townhome, a name that nearly makes me throw up. But I know by now that anything Fenton can make hokey he does, so I let it pass. I let everything pass. That's me, all thought, no action.

Dundonald is only a short block long and right downtown, off Yonge Street, which is the main drag for two million people. Very sleazy. WYSIWYG. We drive up Yonge and I can't believe the crowds just walking around and sitting around on Saturday night in front of dumpy looking stores: porno video, surplus, discount, jokes, condoms, pizza, hamburgers, beer. The sitting is mostly at makeshift sidewalk beer joints.

Fenton has no food in the house, just beer, so they both have a beer and I have tap water that smells and tastes like Javex and the pleasure of smelling their boozy breath while Fenton walks us through a quick tour of the house, which is dinky. Only three little bedrooms about the size of the dressing rooms on Riverside Drive. Fenton's whole main floor would fit a couple of times into Gram's old servant's quarters that she turned into the office for her seminar operation. My mother oohs and aahs about how compact and easy to clean 'our new home' is.

We eat dinner in the garden of something called The Dundonald Pub and Parlour which is a Victorian house with petunias a minute-and-a-half away at the Church Street end of Dundonald. Most of the crowd is gay and I get several looks, three smiles, and one wink when Fenton and my mother aren't looking. I just do what I do at the Whitney or the Frick when those guys notice me: nod back just enough to be polite and then turn away fast and get on with my own business, which in this case is second-rate pasta.

The bride and groom are kind of horny or else exhausted from the drive, so they go straight to bed. I wait a decent fifteen minutes and then sneak out to explore. A minute-and-a-half in the other direction, at the corner of Yonge, is Muscle Mag's Muscle Shoppe with Arnold Schwarzenegger in the window looking out at five humongous Harleys parked in a row, surrounded by nine more of the same, and flanked by two monster pickup trucks on gigantic tires. Across the street at the outdoor tables of The Gasworks the owners of all this motor muscle flash their own muscles, mostly tattooed, mostly no threat to me let alone Arnold.

I realize that downtown Toronto neighbourhoods are one-minute long — rednecks at the Yonge Street end of Dundonald and gays three minutes away at the Church Street end. In between is Fenton's one-minute of houses under shade trees.

"No problem," Fenton says next morning when I mention it while we're having outdoor Sunday brunch among the petunias at The Dundonald Pub and Parlour. "Toronto is multicultural."

We walk down Church Street to buy groceries and Fenton seems to know half the Sunday shoppers and all the clerks. They all call him by name, either Mr. Fenton or Jimmy, mostly Jimmy. He stops every two minutes to introduce us and by the time we've finished with the first store I've met eight people. The store clerks ooh and aah at the cheap souvenirs Fenton has brought back for them and which he dispenses from a flight bag like Santa Claus, even to a sickening ho ho ho.

This is bad enough but it also reminds me of my father playing Santa Claus. Maybe all men do it. Maybe dispensing gifts is their idea of giving something.

Halper feels the urge to jump up, as though he might be run over by the Jeep he gave Simon. But he reads on:

It's more than I can stand so I make the excuse that there's no use lugging the first two bags of food around while they buy the rest — I might as well take them home. When I say 'home,' Fenton lights up and gives me a shoulder hug and I'm gassed by a deadly cloud of cheap cologne in which Fenton must have taken a bath.

I take the opportunity of being there alone to really look at Fenton's house which is jammed full of his mother's old-fashioned furniture. He inherited his parents' house but sold it to buy this house when he got divorced and his ex-wife kept their house. Everything is ugly and too big. There are ten chairs, a china cabinet, a buffet, a tea wagon and a table big enough for conferences in a dining room that isn't even a separate room. And Fenton has TV in his dining room — and in his living room, patio, rec room, and den. Probably in his bedroom too, but I can't remember from the quick look in the door last night, and I don't intend to ever go in there.

Gram and I had one TV behind doors in an antique armoire, and tons of books, a library full and more. Fenton has hardly any books except sports books and a stale-smelling 1956 set of *Encyclopedia Britannica*, missing one volume, and inscribed 'to Jimmy from Mum and Dad and Aunt Emily and Grandma and Grandpa.' His den shelves are full of stereo speakers, sports videos and old football trophies. It seems Fenton spent one season on the bench of some bush league pro team called Argonauts. The name Argonaut fits Fenton — an adventurer in search of something rewarding — but I'm willing to bet my $10,000 that he never read about the originals who sailed to Colchis with Jason in search of the Golden Fleece.

Fenton also has hockey trophies. And baseball. Ribbons, pennants, photos, balls, bats, pucks, sticks, medals. A huge faded photo is marked hand tinted and has an imitation brass label on the frame: FENTON'S

ALLSTARS 1960 sponsored by FENTON'S AUTO WRECKING. And there stands Fenton among the debris in his father's junk yard, exactly my age, leering with the rest of the baseball team, all gathered beside one big round gas pump sticking up pinkish gray like some macho hard-on among the wreckage of its victims.

I open the door beside my room and there's a girl in the white fourposter. When I let out a little sound of surprise she opens her eyes and says, "Who the hell are you?"

But before I can answer she says, "You must be Lincoln. I'm Nita. Where is she? What's she like? A prude? My mother's a lush."

The reason I can't get words together is that Nita is a luscious blond with long legs in short shorts and the kind of skin I dream about licking. No shirt. No bra. WYSIWYG!

"What's the matter with you? Haven't you seen boobs before?"

"Yes."

"Then stop staring. Where is she? Where's Daddy?"

"Buying food."

"Figures. He's built his nest and dragged home his mate and now he has to feed his cub."

She sits up and looks me over.

"You're kind of cute. I like your moustache. I thought Daddy said you were only fifteen. What are you eighteen or something?"

"Fifteen, almost sixteen."

"I like older guys. I'm sixteen, almost seventeen. My ex-boyfriend's nineteen. He's in Europe."

"I can pass. I had beer last night at The Gasworks."

"Fake ID?"

"Five-day stubble. Dark glasses, baseball cap. I sat with some bikers."

"You like those guys?"

"Not really. I just like breaking out."

"I can get you fake ID for a price. Also good grass. My ex has connections. We're getting engaged maybe, or getting an apartment or something, if we make up, but don't tell Daddy. You smoke?"

"Not cigarettes. Marijuana once. In Panama."

"I smoke everything. Not here of course. What's she like? Ugly? She must be hard up for men if Daddy's the best she can do."

"She looks great."

"Mom says she must be a rich bitch because Daddy's broke. We're all broke."

"So's my mother."

"What about that big Mercedes beside Daddy's old heap?"

"It's not hers. She can't even drive. It's mine."

Nita explodes off the bed and inside of two minutes we're speeding up Yonge Street. She's got a licence so she's driving my car and waving her cigarette and honking at people she says she knows and everyone driving too slow. She introduces me to her girlfriends as her new kid brother, and eventually we have six of them in the car. I end up in the back seat where several girls feel my muscles, my moustache and stubble and the hair on my chest and legs, and other things, and announce that I'm hung, which Nita says calls for a celebration, just the two of us.

Her mother's house in Leaside is a mess. Beer bottles all over. Cigarette butts. Fast food packages. Beds not made. But Nita says nothing, just that she has some grass in her room. We lie on her bed and smoke up and make small talk. I tell her a bit about Gramma, then a lot — her chemo, our trips, her seminars, the computers she gave me, her executive revolver, our apartment — my apartment — on Riverside Drive. I'm so mellow I'm about to tell about the $10,000 under the mattress at Fenton's place when Nita saves me.

She raises up on one elbow and looks at me and says, "Eighteen rooms? Let's go there, to Riverside Drive." But before I can tell her some agent has it listed for rent she says, "Forget it. You're under age. They'd just find us." And she slumps back down.

She takes a deep drag and stares at the ceiling and says, "My mother lost her job selling dresses. Because business is bad all over, she says. But she's drunk half the time. That's also why they got divorced. She says because Daddy put on more airs every year and thought she wasn't good enough. She was a cheerleader when he was on the football team in high school. She worked at Eaton's selling dresses to put him through college because his father got some kidney disease and went downhill fast and went broke paying for a fake cure in Mexico. And Daddy had to study all the time and even then it took seven years because he mostly blew the finals on hard courses. So he ends up a dumb gym teacher. Then a measly principal. Big deal. At least she could have worked her ass off to make a doctor or something. Some kind of millionaire. I phoned her last week about new clothes for school and she said no. She used to steal me things from the store."

"Don't you wear uniforms?"

"Oh sure. Crummy plaid skirts. You have to have decent clothes so you can switch in a washroom near the school. She says if the money runs out I might have to live all year with my grandmother in Elliot Lake. Retirement city? In the winter? Give me a break. She won't let me live with Daddy out of spite. She hates him. I wouldn't live with him anyway with all his rules. He made me get up at five a.m. for figure skating. I just want to get away from both of them. She expects me to clean the house. This is the mess I found last night when I got back from Elliot Lake. Nothing in the fridge but catsup and vinegar and sour milk."

She pulls a crumpled note from her shorts and hands it to me: 'Gone to a party, sweetie. Back Sunday night. There just might be an advance on your September allowance if you clean up the house. Go ask your father about clothes. You can see his new slut.'

Nita says, " 'Gone to a party.' That means she's gone to get laid.

Wanta get laid?"

"Me? Us?"

"Who else?" She's smiling but it's empty, worse even than Gramma's smile the day she found out her lump was cancer. She feels me up and says, "What are you, a virgin or something?"

"No."

"I bet. You're just a hand whacker. Right?"

"Mostly. But I did it once with a girl. Sort of. In the car. San Antonio."

She keeps on feeling me and says, "What do you mean, sort of?" but while I'm working on an answer she's working on me with some success and she says, "That's more like it. Not bad for fifteen. Leslie, that's my ex, he's really hung. I mean really. But he's bi. Right now he's in Europe with this old guy about thirty-five who deals dope, I think. Anyway, he's a dress designer and owns his own factory. That's what we broke up over, because Leslie wouldn't come to Elliot Lake even for a week. But he says it's only because the guy is paying for his college. What about San Antonio?"

She unzips me and I can't think. I just lie there staring at the ceiling, heaving at the hips but otherwise paralysed, hardly able to catch enough breath to speak, "San Antonio . . . beside the Alamo . . . the cradle of liberty . . . 'Remember the Alamo'. . ."

"I'm on the pill and I've got rubber if that's what you're worried about."

She dumps everything out of her bag on the bed between us and finds three condoms which she drops on my belly while she scoops junk back in her bag. She slides my underwear part way down and kisses me from there up, till she opens my lips and feels around my tongue with hers. Then she pulls my underwear down a bit more and rolls a condom on me. I slip off my jeans carefully so money and stuff won't fall out but she whips off her shorts and kicks them up in the air.

"Wheeee," she says.

It takes a while to use up three condoms what with us both being high and Nita deciding we should run around the house and try a few fancy maneuvers in a wing chair and on the stairs. Fenton is hyper when I phone at 5:25 while Nita is still in the shower and I'm dripping wet — 'worried sick, most inconsiderate, your mother blah blah blah' — but both of them are standing on the patio all smiles by the time we get there for dinner.

My mother sends me to wash my hands. When I get back, Nita is still in the same spot staring. I can tell she's impressed with my mother because she gapes and says hardly anything all the while we're having drinks outdoors: cheap white wine for them and lemonade for Nita and me. I know the wine is plonk because I'm used to having a little of the best with Gram and I sample my mother's while Fenton is busy recording this family gathering by camcorder, Polaroid and 35mm.

My mother is wearing high heels with a lot of coloured straps over bare feet with orange toenails, and she seems about nine feet tall in a frothy dress to her ankles that looks like twelve shades of red, pink and purple cheesecloth. It gets clingy in front but flies in back from the breeze of an electric fan which the great movie director has carefully placed. He instructs her to walk around filling glasses while he shoots crouched. The dress is only prevented from blowing away by the weight of a dozen or so strings of beads and umpteen bracelets and bead-rope belts to match.

The great director's trickiest shot has my windblown mother looking like the Nike of Samothrace in spike heels pointing with one orange fingernail to something compelling off camera which he explains is the penthouse pad of Norman Jewison. Golly gee. I finish my mother's wine while Fenton fiddles with the camera and she holds her pose.

After half an hour of filming, Fenton, who knows every cliché in the book, says, "It's a wrap." We squeeze in among the tea wagons and buffets and Fenton does his daddy routine: says grace, stands to sharpen the knife, and carves the roast while his charming wife and children look on appreciatively. I figure he's arrived in his personal promised land. Nita is a perfect lady in her plain blue dress and flat white sandals. It occurs to me that Fenton can't see Nita any more than my mother can see my moustache.

Nita says, "Your hair looks fabulous like that, Mrs. Fenton, and I really love your dress. I wish you'd help me pick out some decent clothes. I never end up with anything gorgeous like that. But I guess you'll be too busy to shop with me . . ." Her voice trails off into tomato juice.

"I'd love to, Nita. Tomorrow? You can show me the shops. Call me Alma."

With one perfect ploy Nita has herself a new wardrobe and I almost do a barf-laugh on the plate Fenton has handed me to pass to my mother, but Nita throws me a slightly raised eyebrow and a quick kick under the table, so I restrain myself. Did I tell her when we were high that my mother needs someone to organize her, or did Nita figure that out all on her own? She keeps on massaging my mother who fairly moans with the joy of lubrication.

While he saws away standing up, and the women talk to each other, Fenton is raving to me about my mother's apple pie which he says is still warm in the oven and which she made from scratch from an old family recipe especially for him, but he might consider sharing, ho ho ho. He carves his way through the meat, juices flying, and loads everybody up with what I can see is his symbol of success on or off the football field: bloody beef. He hasn't noticed yet that I hardly ever eat meat. Gram said animal fat would kill me if I have the same heart gene as my father and grandfather.

Sitting with the three of them in the living room trying to watch some crummy baseball video of Fenton's called *Field of Dreams*, I'm still a little high, but not happy. Not even neutral. Depressed. I feel like an alien, like I stumbled into the wrong world, into another guy's dream but my nightmare. I wonder how it would feel to stick Gram's gun, my gun, in my mouth and fire. I could do it sitting in the driver's seat of my Mercedes. I could do it without messing up my moustache. A strange noise comes up out of my guts and the others all turn away from the film and look at me. I feel like crying, but I never cry.

I try to think about the computer program I'm working on. I always do that when I need a lift. This time it doesn't work. I just heave up that same sound again and again — a sort of dry cry — and can't stop myself, so I excuse myself and go to my room. I can hear my mother saying, "He's just tired."

The truck comes on Tuesday, and after that for days my mother and Fenton are running around trying to find room for my mother's stuff, and she's trying to set up a studio in the rec room, and Fenton is rushing back and forth getting his school ready to open. I hide out in my room with my computer which I push to the limit trying to build in a backup that's never been done before. I play my violin. And I pump my father's weights to the point of exhaustion. Till Fenton hauls me off to the school board office and leaves me there all day writing tests.

Four days later school starts and the very first day I feel sick and have to leave right after check-in. But Fenton comes home at noon and drags me back with him and parks me in his office where I feel dizzy and suffocated and kind of nauseous. At three o'clock when all the other kids have left he arms me down the hall — him all smiles, me all nerves — to the library, which is jammed full of every teacher in Midhill. Outside the door, Fenton straightens his tie and buttons his jacket to cover his belly bulge and shoots his cuffs so everyone can see his glitzy cuff links the size of Rhode Island. He checks me over and adjusts my collar, which doesn't need adjusting.

He opens the library door and arms me all the way in to the head table and says, "Folks, this handsome fellow is my son Lincoln," and they all clap. I feel like crawling under the table. Then he tells them I've never attended any school before but I'll be taking six Ontario Academic Credits so I can enter university next year in computer science at sixteen. They clap again. Mentally I'm already under the table and all I can think of down there on the floor is I wish I had the gun from my car so I could shoot Fenton in the balls. But I remember Nita has my car because she conned me into letting her drive her mother to the dentist. More likely to drive her girlfriends to school.

Fenton leads me back out the library door with his arm around my shoulder and every teacher watching and clapping and buzzing. He whispers in my ear about how the faculty meeting should be over by five if I want to study in his office and then we can drive home together. But I'm out of there on the run. I can hear him call after me, "Lincoln. Don't forget your books." But I just keep going.

A few blocks from Fenton's house I pace around in some old cemetery reading tombstones till my stomach eases up and I've decided what to do, which is to take my ten thousand and run. Chicago or L.A. or Vancouver. Maybe Honolulu. Why not? Till I'm sixteen. I'll send my mother a note, hide out for three months and a bit, return for my birthday and Christmas, then take off for good with my car. Free, because at sixteen they can't stop me.

My plan is to sneak in quietly and get my money and head for the airport while they're having dinner on Fenton's patio. When I tiptoe in the front door, the living room TV is blasting away as usual. But over the sport scores I can hear a loud argument on the patio. Nita, Fenton, my mother and someone else. I ease along the hall till I can see that the someone else is a woman and she has my gun pointed at Fenton and my mother.

77

Nita is off to one side yelling, "I told you they don't have any money. Lincoln owns the car."

Fenton is standing like a shield in front of my mother who's gushing nonstop, "Now put that down, just put that down, whatever you've got to say, just put that down."

Nita's mother is crying and laughing and blubbering and holding my gun straight out in front of her with both hands. She steps back against the barbecue table and knocks off a plate of hamburgers. I back up and call 911 from the den phone. When I return to where I can see, she's holding the gun with one hand and guzzling wine from a bottle with the other.

Fenton makes a slight move and she shoots. A hanging pot shatters and dirt and red geraniums fly all over the table which is set for dinner.

She fires again and nicks Fenton's arm. Everybody freezes — Fenton, my mother, Nita, three neighbours who are just inside the garden gate, everyone but me. I'm running right at the gun. The third bullet gets me in the left lung but I'm already launched and crash into her and both of us go flying down the steps and smash against the flagstone wall where I break my arm and some ribs and crack my skull, but she — I find out much later — gets only cuts and scrapes and a sprained ankle.

The first part, three weeks or so, I know it's a hospital, not much else. I sometimes see faces in fog. Voices float in and out of hearing but make no sense. Operating rooms. Lights. Respirators. Tubes. Wires. When the fog thins, Fenton is sitting beside my bed smiling.

He says, "The hospital is between home and school so it's easy to pop in and out."

Eight days later, when they move me from intensive care to share a room with some guy who had a bicycle crash, Fenton is standing beside my new bed waiting. When they start giving me solid food,

Fenton is there three times a day to feed me whatever I can't manage with one hand.

Nita comes and goes. She's living in Fenton's house because her mother's in jail. She gives me back my car keys and says Fenton told her in no uncertain terms it's not hers or his or anybody's but mine to drive. Anyway, her boyfriend Leslie is back and has the dress designer's car any time he wants it. Fenton thinks Leslie is a girl so he lets Nita sleep over quite a bit at Leslie's place.

My mother breezes in and out twice a day before and after chasing down freelance jobs that never seem to pan out. She chats up the nurses and Allan, the kid in the other bed, and brushes my hair away from my forehead.

While I'm propped up pecking at my laptop computer with one hand, Fenton sits there reading sports scores out loud, telling Allan his family history, about the season he played bench for the Argos, smelling up the place with his cheap cologne which is stronger than the flowers and antiseptic combined. The nurses adjusting all my tubes and giving me baths keep telling me how wonderful my father is to come so often and bring so many books and flowers and treats and Turkey souvenirs for all the hospital staff. I consider telling them he's not my father and if he came less I'd get to read more of the stuff I like, but I keep my mouth shut. By now I'm used to him forever sitting there.

Allan's father comes once a week on Sunday and stands at the foot of his bed for five minutes holding his baseball cap in one hand and pulling at it with the other hand and asking if the TV reception and the food are okay. Now I know the real purpose of baseball caps.

One Sunday, while Allan's father is doing his baseball cap routine, a new orderly comes to shave me. Fenton tells him to be careful not to spoil my moustache and follows up with a set of instructions that would make even a real barber hyper: mind the bandage, lift up a bit just there, easy now easy strokes, not that direction . . . Naturally this novice nicks me out of nervousness and motor-mouth Fenton takes over and shaves me himself and gives me a stroke by stroke progress report with his tobacco breath.

"There," he says as he combs my moustache. "There. There. Perfect."

He holds up a mirror and it looks okay. He also trims my hair and combs it and, wonder of wonders, manages to get it about right so my ears are covered.

Pneumonia. Critical again. Respirators. Oxygen. When I wake up I'm in a different room and Fenton is not there. I wonder if he's had a heart attack like my father. But when the nurse comes and I ask her she says he's fallen asleep in the waiting room.

Back with Allan. At first I sleep a lot, or half sleep, while Fenton and Allan are busy watching Toronto beat Oakland and then Atlanta to win the World Series. It's kind of dreamlike just lying there ignoring them with my eyes shut and them oohing and aahing and making bets with nurses and doctors and patients all up and down the corridor. Fenton organizes a pool for every game and tries to run it on my computer but screws up so completely that I have to get him to prop me up so I can set it up properly and make all the entries.

November days and weeks are all the same, dull, but not too bad, sort of peaceful. I kind of like Allan but I never had a full-time friend before so I can't tell if he likes me particularly or just sort of. Maybe he only pretends to like me because he has the hots for Nita or my mother or both. I know he likes them because he says so. He even likes Fenton. He says so. But he never says he likes me. It doesn't matter that much.

I work on my laptop and read a lot — all of the English literature books and the other school books Fenton brings, and the novels that circulate around the hospital. My mother finally has her first job illustrating a kids' book and once a day she rushes in with her latest picture to get opinions from everybody. Nita has turned seventeen and plans to move in with Leslie. She whispers in my ear that he lives with the dress designer and that's where she's been sleeping over all along.

They tell me I should be able to go home for Christmas and after that just come to the hospital weekdays for therapy, physical and mental. A resident shrink is already seeing me and using words like trauma.

Late one night in December when Allan is already asleep and the lights are low, when Fenton should have been gone because of visiting hours being over — Fenton is forever late leaving — he holds my hand and tells me not to be too hard on his ex-wife because she's sick and desperate for money. Nearly fourteen weeks and I'm almost recovered and this is the first time he's mentioned anything about the shooting. Once he gets going, he babbles on for half an hour — more — while I stare at little rays of light from the Christmas tree in the corridor flickering on the dark walls of my room.

He says he wants to adopt me if I think it's okay, but first he has to tell me the truth. He's not as successful as it appears. Things haven't gone all that well. He's trying to get another mortgage so he can hire a good lawyer for his ex-wife. And the rear end has given out on his car and it's too far gone to fix. The school board has passed him over for promotion. Nita smokes. She's moving in with her girlfriend. He can't talk to her. He never could reach his ex-wife either. He's just glad he and I get on so well. He needs that — a guy he can trust and talk to man to man. He isn't much good at some things, quite a few things, he says, as he puts my hand down and starts twisting his birthstone ring the size of Rhode Island.

"So many problems. But you don't have to worry about them, son. That's what fathers are for. Just think about getting well and coming home for Christmas. We'll have the best party ever for you, and I'll play Santa Claus."

Fenton takes my hand again and squeezes it in both of his and then lets go with one hand and strokes my forehead, not in a sweep like my mother does. Slower. It reminds me of something, but I can't think what. I can't think, period. Something seems to be leaking from my brain, running down my spine, causing a slight shiver that numbs me. He stands up to go, and fixes his tie, and buttons his jacket to cover his belly, and shoots his cuffs so everyone on night duty can see his glitzy cuff links. They catch the little bit of light from the hall and throw sparkles all around me.

"I've got some money you can have. Ten thousand."

"No. No. You'll need it for university."

"The trust fund pays all that."

"I couldn't. No."

"It's a Christmas gift."

"No. No. Not from my own son. That's backwards. I should be giving you something special, a car or something, since it's also your sixteenth birthday. But I can't. I'm sorry, Lincoln." He picks up my hand again.

"I've already got a car. I've got everything. I don't need anything. The ten thousand is for room and board."

Fenton drops my hand and lets out a sudden burst of breath that has an 'Uhhh' sound with it, and Allan half wakens and moans. Fenton steps back and waves one finger at me.

"Don't you ever say that to me, Lincoln. Don't ever let me hear you say such a thing. I mean it. No son of mine is going to pay room and board in his own home. What do you take me for?"

He squeezes his eyes shut and presses his lips into a tight line like I've never seen him do before. He turns and starts straight out the door, so he's obviously miffed because he usually backs out still talking and saying goodnight about five times. It's no skin off my back if he's riled, but I think I should at least say something polite. I should call after him to make him turn around, but I can't think what to call him because I've never called him anything before.

"Sir?"

He stops in the doorway and stands there half turned while I try to think if I should say I'm sorry or what. But I just hold out my car keys.

"No," he says. "You'll be old enough to drive it yourself next week."

"I've got no place to go. Besides, I've got another set."

He turns around but stays in the doorway and there's silence. I continue holding out the keys.

"I was wondering if you'd get it serviced for me because I don't know that much about cars. And drive it around a bit. It shouldn't just sit there, should it? Isn't that bad for cars? And can I get it insured in your name because wouldn't that cost a lot less?"

"Well, yes. I suppose that's sensible. And it's all in the family."

"Sure."

So he comes back and takes the keys and stands there looking at me. He kisses me on the forehead. His moustache feels a little scratchy. But not too bad. WYSIWYG.

— the end —

Halper is yanked from Lincoln Fenton's hospital room back to his own desk. The shock blows away a wall never quite breached before and suddenly he sees a thousand Lincolns marching every morning into schools that demand all personal lives be checked at the door.

Every kid is yanked from the real story at home into the school story every morning and back again every night. The life kids act out all day long is a fake one that an obsolete institution makes official. Back and forth, real to pretend, ten jump cuts every week. Teachers make it happen. Parents let it happen. Is it any wonder kids act up or drop out? Is it any wonder Jillian ran away and Simon killed himself?

But Halper has *shared* Lincoln's real-life yearning. He feels Lincoln's hand in his. They are leading each other out of dark corridors with closed doors and harsh bells into open light where voices speak softly and people listen.

Twelve thirty. Halper reaches for the next paper to mark. TELL ME WHO YOU ARE.

CHAPTER THREE

Halper's daily blackboard message is inspired by Lincoln Fenton's bedtime habits: 'The only essential human activity for which ignorance is considered the best preparation is sex.' Halper plucks Lincoln from the bodies pouring into senior English and leads him to a corner away from the group already buzzing about the message.

"In a word Lincoln, thanks for telling me who you are and who your father is, I mean your second father, and for that matter quite a bit about who I am."

Lincoln thinks of saying thank you sir, but that seems not quite right. He tugs the neck of his t-shirt with one finger and his words burst louder and faster than intended. "I thought you already told us who you are sir, the first day."

"But you told me lots more. For one thing you told me how fathers see their sons through the scrim of their own limitations and never get a clear picture. Can we set up some appointments after school to talk about all that? And Lincoln, I like your style. Good writing disappears into the story and never draws attention to itself. You've got the knack. Would you mind sharing your story? Just with Gordon Wing and Billy Parr for now because they're working on stories. They'll respect confidentiality and I want them to see your form and frankness. Okay?"

"I guess so."

"Good. And Lincoln, I've got six computers in my grade nine room. I've borrowed a reading-development program from the Institute for Studies in Education but I don't know anything about computers beyond word processing and spreadsheets. Could you possibly come at 7:30 in the morning for a while and teach me and a few kids?"

"I guess so. Okay sir."

"And Lincoln, my law classes are studying abortion. Your abortion position is interesting. I know you're not taking law but would you join us for class discussions? You could do some research the way your grandmother taught you, and present your case."

"I'd be kind of nervous, sir. And the girls wouldn't like my opinion any more than Gram would. Nita says it stinks. I think every guy should withhold semen unconditionally till the law is changed to equalize the rights and responsibilities of both parents. That's it."

Lincoln is overheard by hovering students waiting for a word with Halper. They sidle in — Gordon Wing, Billy Parr, and a beefy girl kids call Bully. The seating plan says Mary Bullman.

Bangs hang over her eyes so that her prominent, drooping nose seems suspended from hair. Her heavy bottom lip is thrust out like a boxing glove about to make a right jab.

Lincoln looks at Bully, tugs his t-shirt collar, and continues, "Only an irresponsible dink would submit to a relationship which requires him, by law, to stand by powerless and see his offspring murdered."

"Right on!" Gordon Wing says. "Give the man a free t-shirt." He pulls from his bag a shirt that reads: COCK SURE. Lincoln accepts the shirt and immediately puts it on. It is, as far as Halper can recall, the first time Lincoln has smiled.

The girl says heatedly, "What's in my womb is mine."

"Not if I put it there," says Gordon. "Which in your case is not bloody likely, Bully."

Billy Parr steps closer and puts one hand on Gordon's shoulder, the other on Bully Bullman's. "God put it there. It's his. You're just his agents."

Gordon holds up a desktop publication and says, "With better sex education there wouldn't be so much unwanted pregnancy. Every girl who's read my sex manual knows there's one, and only one, failproof form of birth control — the blow job."

Gordon has connected abortion talk with the blackboard message and one big discussion evolves. Halper has only to lead the way back to *Macbeth*. If she would pluck her nipple from the boneless gums of her baby and dash its brains out on the floor would Lady Macbeth have an abortion without Macbeth's agreement? A month from now, two months, Halper feels sure, these kids will know enough, be focused enough, to bring any discussion onto the curriculum track without his intervention.

Jillian refuses to budge, has a fight with Liz, and takes off by bus to visit her boyfriend's uncle in Seattle. Liz is so upset that she flies from Vancouver to Bermuda where her mother is living out an arthritic widowhood of bridge and tea in a Hamilton guest house.

Halper lies in bed alone, too tired to sleep, thinking of Liz, her unhappiness, his unhappiness. Twenty years ago they had good sex followed by hug talk about plans, places, ideas, books . . . Books. Current fiction and nonfiction. Two a week, sometimes three. When the kids were small new books were still acquired, sampled, put aside for another time that never came. Two books a week became one a month. Then less. Discussion was replaced by family babble, the sharing of ideas by the sharing of body parts. They had settled for sex. Less and less of that. Lately none.

Halper is adrift in the darkness of night, in the darkness of Simon's death, in the darkness of his heart. He is searching for light and can't find a blind to raise or a door to open. He feels no panic, just loneliness and yearning. He is a good searcher, accustomed to trying, and used to the feeling of guilt for failing. He sits up and turns on the bed lamp and stares a long time at the empty place beside him.

The first Saturday meeting of the early-morning group is thwarted by the head janitor who refuses to let them use the school without a permit. While Halper is arguing with two janitors through the door they have just locked, Becky Kowalski has a word with her father who is the part owner, with his brothers, of the ageing strip mall across the street. He lets them use one of three vacant stores. It was last rented by Green Sporting Goods and there are leftovers: a lot of shelves, some counters, plywood tables, a few balls, cartons, and a box of six dozen emerald-green nylon baseball caps labelled Green. Claudius Ito assumes control of caps, numbers them, and issues himself #1. As he hands out the rest, he suggests they call themselves the Greens.

The Greens ask if they can meet there every Saturday and Sunday. David Halper is agreeable if Mr. Kowalski is. He is. Within days, they are also meeting there at 7 a.m. weekdays and again after school. Halper has the key. Until he gets there, nobody can get in. Every day, he has to stay at school for teachers' meetings, extracurricular activities and meetings with students. It rains two days in a row and everyone has to wait more than an hour in Kowalski's donut shop.

Frank Stringer says if they can get in their own place he will be in charge till Halper gets there and he will break anybody's arm who gets out of line. Mr. Kowalski is dubious but agrees to a trial. It seems to work. Frank is ipso facto assistant director. But Halper realizes he also needs adult assistants. Liz is back from Bermuda but refuses to help.

"I've got my hands full with the junior league, the symphony, the gallery . . . Being on boards, fund-raising, is a full-time job, you know. It just doesn't pay a salary. It costs. Besides I've got nothing in common with those people."

"What people?"

"Those children in the public schools. Teachers."

"You didn't have anything in common with all those human wrecks in the chronic care centre either but they loved you."

"I was visiting your father."

"Twice a week for six years. You hand-fed him treats, trimmed his nails, wiped his drool, talked to him, listened to his endless mumbles, read to all of them. You were wonderful." Halper remembers the the old man slumped in his wheelchair, muttering. Always about Normandy. The beaches. The fighting. Topics he had barely ever mentioned before his stroke. Where were all those memories hidden while his son was growing up? Why? TELL ME WHO YOU ARE.

"I was doing my duty. That's all. You were too busy. He was

our personal responsibility. So was your mother when she was dying, and my father. Those public school kids are not our personal responsibility. That's the difference. Everyone has a station in life. We don't belong in theirs any more than they belong in ours. Why can't you wake up, David?"

"I went to public schools. It was teachers of classes for bright kids in East York that got me thinking, reading, writing, questioning, changed my life, made me want to teach and write."

"Then why don't you teach law at the university and write legal thrillers like Scott Turow or John Grisham. Pay the mortgage instead of wasting time on that journal of yours and street kids in some eyesore strip mall. Wake up, David."

Halper mails a request for volunteer teachers to the executive secretary of the retired teachers' association. The secretary replies that they don't do that sort of thing — organize volunteers — except on occasion for short stints overseas, but he will try to find room for a line or two in a newsletter some months hence. Halper can tell from the sample newsletters enclosed that the association is concerned with pension benefits and group tours, not education.

Maude Fenwick is the first to answer an ad which Halper posts in the variety store at the end of the mall. Miss Fenwick is seventy-eight, thirteen years retired from teaching all elementary grades but mostly three and four. She is rawboned and flat-faced and wears a red canvas backpack full of books. Her grizzled hair is parted in the middle and pulled back decisively to hang like drapes behind both ears, as though that were the main purpose of ears.

While Halper reads her eight-page curriculum vitae, Maude Fenwick lines her white plastic helmet with Kleenex and lays in it half a dozen cookies all different. She tells Claudius Ito and two other students who interview her that she began teaching in 1933 when she was nineteen and taught all eight grades at the same time in a one-room country school a hundred miles from Toronto. Her hobbies are working on her Ph. D. thesis on dyslexia at York University, riding her ten-speed, and baking cookies from scratch.

Claudius takes the last cookie, puts a green cap on Maude and says, "I think we should keep her."

When she swings her backpack to the floor to look for more cookies, Halper comments on the weight of her many books. Maude says, "For exercise you know. With the spin-off benefit of a doctorate. I used to carry a cannonball on my back. And before that my mother, in more ways than one. She was a fatuous old woman given to diaphanous peignoirs and Barbara Cartland wigs even when she was demobilized by osteoporosis and I had to hump her up and down stairs."

"Cannonball?"

"Yes. To add weight for power walking. It's not in my c. v. but the best thing about my genealogy is the pack rat gene. My mother's attic had four generations of junk and I kept all of it. Every day of my teaching life I took a relic to class — a feather boa, a cannonball, a huge hat covered with red silk flowers, a chamber pot with a music box lid that plays Handel's water music, a bustle. I went a two-year cycle without repeating an item except for a few that kids loved. If it was wearable I wore it all day or passed it around for the kids to wear. I rode the velocipede to work once a year. The kids put on shows with relics like that, and wrote stories about them. Well, Mr. Halper, can you use a relic like me?"

Halper hands Maude a key. Within a week, she brings three more retired teachers who receive green caps and keys.

Membership burgeons to forty-two. The Greens decide to stay open till nine p.m. weekdays and ten on Saturdays and have a party to celebrate.

Becky Kowalski asks Halper to dance and while she is leading him around, she says in his ear, "Sir, I mean like — you know — I missed my period." The music is bouncy and Becky jiggles. She is a slightly chubby girl who jiggles easily and keeps on jiggling like Jello once she gets moving. Every time she jiggles past Halper's ear she adds a few words: "You know, like basically, I went to the clinic." "They like, did, you know, the test." "I am. You know what I mean?" "They told me, basically, like I mean, about abortions." "Girls at school say you, like, teach about abortions."

"They just mean we're debating abortion in my law classes and I know about the laws."

The music changes to rap and is so loud Halper can hardly hear. He leads Becky to the side where food is laid out but still covered with tea towels.

While they sip punch and peek at the sandwiches, Becky says, "Should I, like, do it? You know what I mean? Is it okay?"

"It's legal and free if that's what you decide on. The clinic could arrange everything."

"My dad'll kill me and Frank. I mean, it wasn't Frank's fault. I mean, he did it but I mean basically I said it was alright. I said like I wanted him to. You know what I mean? I mean he wanted to but I said you know like I was on the pill and I wasn't."

"You can probably have an abortion without telling either of them. It's up to you, Becky. But I think both should know. I think Frank has as much right and responsibility as you have but that's just my opinion, not the law. You need your dad's support and he needs the opportunity to help you. That's what I'd want if it were one of my daughters. I could explain all that to your dad if you like. Sort of soften him up. Frank's dad too."

"So I mean basically you think I should do it?"

"No. My general opinion is that all people who are sexually capable have the right to decide whether or not to be sexually active. But if they decide to be active it's like signing a contract — they have sex in the full knowledge that a new life may result and if it does, all the rights are with the new life and the male and female who created the new life have no more rights, only the responsibility of nurturing that new life. My youngest daughter might agree with that, I'm not sure, but the oldest wouldn't."

"So like basically you don't think I should do it."

"That's just my opinion, but you have to make your own decision. Whatever you decide, I'll help you all I can. There are strong pro-abortion and right-to-life groups in my law classes and they'll give you all the information they've sifted out on both sides. They could talk to your dad too if you like. If he's willing. And Frank. Anyway, what do you say I start by softening up your dad?"

"Okay. Like, not tonight though. You know what I mean? Okay?"

"Okay."

When Lincoln arrives at the strip mall for the first time, on a Saturday morning, Frank Stringer's father stands in the window like a giant beacon, swinging his red face and hair back and forth, looking at the Greens working individually and in small groups. Maude Fenwick is moving from group to group in an old family kilt with sporran and matching bagpipe which she has been warming up for so long that everyone has forgotten about the occasional snorts.

Lincoln enters and hears Mr. Stringer say to Halper, "I don't believe anything that freak says." He points to his son. Frank has cut holes in his green baseball cap to accommodate his turquoise hair spikes and looks like a prickly pear as he sits hunched over, not looking up, writing on a work sheet Maude has given him. "Why should I? His only noticeable talent is lying. So he says he's studying till nine o'clock every night. Says he's assistant director of some study hall. I'll bet, I say. We need computers, he says. What for, I say, to sell so you can buy cigarettes and hair dye and tattoos? But here he is. Not even smoking. Writing. On a Saturday. Miracle of miracles. So how many computers, Mr. Halper?"

"Five or six if you can spare them. Trade-ins. Anything you can lend us. Lincoln here is our computer expert. He can tell you what we need. And he has a car and could bring them back from your warehouse."

"Six you got. Whatever it takes to keep that jerk off the street a little longer."

Maude Fenwick bursts into bagpipe song and pipes Mr. Stringer to his car.

Frank goes to Halper who is waving goodbye in the window. "See. Like I mean basically that old bugger hates me so I can't tell him about Becky."

"Then you could let me tell him. It'll be worse when he finds out from rumours. But it's up to you, Frank."

"Not yet. Like, what's the rush? I mean I gotta work up to it man. I mean you know basically he's never home and I gotta follow him around the warehouse store, and I mean even when he does like park behind his desk he's always on the phone and he just leaves me you know standing there for hours till he's ready to yell at me again."

Halper imagines Simon working up the courage to tell his father about being gay. Simon would have thought, 'That old bugger loves me. What's the rush? Anyway, he's never home or he's always on the phone. He leaves me standing there till he's

94

ready to put his arm around my shoulder and give me another hug and another pep talk while I walk him to his car.' Halper wishes Russ Haynes had picked up the phone and called him when he was Simon's school counsellor. Haynes was right to respect Simon's privacy, Halper knows, but he wishes Haynes had persuaded Simon to let him call. Parents need an intermediary, kids need one. Halper thinks only teachers are close enough, numerous enough and sensitive enough to pick up distress signals, unscramble them and deliver them to dedicated receivers. He decides to persuade Frank Stringer.

He also decides to persuade Zina the Mexicali Tamale to let him talk to her parents about reconciliation. But Zina doesn't show up for three days, and when Halper checks her rooming house, the owner of the wretched place knows only that Zina has moved to Montreal with a new boyfriend who sells smuggled cigarettes.

Halper is sitting with one of three seminar groups in his senior English class listening to Bully Bullman portray Lady Macbeth as a feminist. Fenton gets on the p.a. and interrupts Bully, "Mr. Halper, could I see you in my office right away, please?"

Fenton is seated behind his desk when Halper walks in saying, "Couldn't this wait. I've got some of my class just at the point of understanding how to move a discussion to the next plateau."

"What the hell's going on? Is this true?"

Fenton holds up a memo and slides it across his desk to Halper who is standing before the principal like a recalcitrant boy. Halper is reminded of standing across a desk from his own late father, and of Frank Stringer in the same position. He has a vision of fathers with desks permanently attached to their stomachs. Fenton is all fathers. In loco parentis.

"Jerry Duchok hears from that troublemaker Frank Stringer

that you're tutoring him after hours in some storefront school. That's conflict of interest."

"It's free so how can it be conflict of interest?"

"Free! You're moonlighting for free? You're undermining everything the union has fought for all these years salary-wise. They're talking right this minute about the next strike and you're saying let's do more for free. And how does it make us look? Like we can't teach them here."

"We can't. There isn't time. The school day is too short. The school year is too short. Nobody here teaches reading. Nobody knows how. Nobody here knows how to use, let alone construct, diagnostic tests. The curriculum is wrong. The model of schooling is wrong. The union is wrong. They should be agitating for a new model of schooling."

"And you're the expert in your first semester. Well let me tell you something, Halper. Midhill is the best high school in the country by anyone's standards. Best academic. Best technical.'

"Then all schools are on the wrong track."

"And you're on the right track."

"Yes. Maude Fenwick — my assistant — knows a lot."

"I've heard about your assistant. Some crazy old woman with a ten-foot boa constrictor around her neck."

"A boa, not a boa constrictor. A red feather boa."

"Right. That makes all the difference. The latest educational innovation."

"Maude knows a lot about language, remedial work, testing. Already we see progress in reading, writing, speaking, listening, organizing, evaluating, self-propulsion, self-esteem."

"I'm not here to argue. I'm telling you to stop whatever the hell it is you're doing."

"Come and see. What I do mostly is mentor the kids, listen, suggest. I help them organize, evaluate. We should move the whole operation over here and call it a home room and I'd just stay there with them all day and send them out and back to other rooms for science and math and things when they're ready."

"Everybody's got a warm and fuzzy solution. I don't need to see yours to tell you it's dangerous. The minute there's an accident some parent will sue you and us. You're a lawyer. You must know what litigious cranks are like. Any place our students gather with one of our teachers, people are going to hold the school responsible."

Halper is in the school parking lot at dusk depositing an armload in his car before crossing to the strip mall. It is another of those moments of uncertainty that have bumped him like icebergs since childhood. He feels himself standing on the deck of a ship holding back a great wall of ice with his bare hands. Every confrontation with Fenton leaves him with cold hands.

This time the ice looms because he has had a stand-up argument in front of the office with Fenton and Duchok and the other staff adviser to the student council. Halper opposes selling chocolate bars to raise funds for any purpose because it promotes junk food. And a mascot costume is the worst of purposes. His counterpart is intensely proud that Midhill student council raised more money last year than any other high school by selling a ton of chocolate. Duchok wants a mascot. Fenton favours chocolate sales to buy a mascot. Halper stands in the parking lot pushing on the cold metal of his car trunk long after it has clicked shut.

Gordon Wing emerges from shadows with a paper in his hand, reading aloud: "Gordon says, 'Once a week or so I wake up to loud knocking.' That's how my story starts. Does that grab you?"

"Yes."

"Good."

Gordon thrusts the story into Halper's hand. Halper sits on the car seat with his legs outside and reads aloud:

Gordon says, "Once a week or so I wake up to loud knocking. I wait for a second knock which never comes. Sometimes I get up and look out at the empty street. Usually I just lie there wondering: maybe it's vocational retards knocking on Chinese doors for kicks."

Gordon pictures himself lying there alone in bed and notices tears. Just a few. No sobs. Seventeen and crying.

Counting Dr. Ashman's bedside visits four years ago when Gordon was in hospital with burns, this is their thirty-sixth meeting, but the first in nearly four months. This is the only time Gordon has ever asked for an appointment. All of their previous meetings at the psychiatric out-patients' clinic have been routine, always at four o'clock the last Wednesday of every month except December and July. The sessions are follow-ups, part of Dr. Ashman's research on heroes. Gordon participates voluntarily.

The clinic receptionist thought it unusual enough when Gordon appeared at the office on a Monday demanding an appointment — it was noon today and the director was out — that she called Dr. Ashman at home and he offered to come to the clinic if Gordon wouldn't mind missing his afternoon classes. He wouldn't. If he would wait or take a walk till two. He would.

Halper looks up at Gordon pacing back and forth and says, "How come you didn't write this in first person, Gordon?"

"Because I wanted to step back and see myself the way I see other characters. And I wanted to get inside Ashman's head. I know what he thinks."

Halper reads aloud:

Dr. Ashman is thinking, as he has for some time, that Gordon's expressed exasperation stems from other sources, particularly home and school, and that Gordon shows little or no emotional scarring attributable to the fire. The recurring dream, if it is a dream, may or may not be fire-related.

"Nobody else hears knocking?"

"I told you umpteen times. My dad works nights. One of the roomers — Len, the floor mopper, the old black guy I told you about who just grins and mumbles and mops — I have to wake him up for work because he takes so many sleeping pills. What could he hear? The other one upstairs is new — always bombed out of her mind on drugs. She hears voices so I'm not about to ask if she hears knocking."

"And the woman in the basement. Is she still there?"

"Mrs. Raffferty. Ida. She'd say she hears knocking fifty times a day. She agrees with everything I say just to have somebody to talk to. She's so cagey she just eats toast and tea unless I take something down. She cooked forty years on lake boats for godsake. She's got enough giant size pots and pans down there to open a restaurant. Which is what she talks about doing. She's eighty-two for godsake. She pulls her toast and tea routine every time she hears me cooking so I'll bring down something decent to eat. 'You hoo, Gordie love, I'm just making a nice cup of tea.' I hate eating down there. Not because of Ida. She's sort of interesting. I hate the basement. But Ida hates climbing stairs."

"What about your brother?" Dr. Ashman glances through his notes for the name.

"Arlix," Gordon says. "He's been gone nearly two years."

"You never mentioned that before."

"You never asked." Gordon stands up and walks once around the office. He does that when he feels agitated. He slaps his hand on an empty shelf. "What happened to your books and stuff?"

99

"In boxes in the bathroom. The clinic assumed I wouldn't return."

"They thought you'd die from your heart attack?"

"They assumed I'd retire. A misunderstanding. I'll have them put the books back on the shelves. Is Alex living with your mother and sisters?"

"It's not Alex. It's Arlix. Did they pack your brains with your books or what? I told you about that years ago. I used to think my mother was trying to spell Alex but Arlix was as close as she could get. Till last month. Arlix turned sixteen and she took him and me to Sutton Place for dinner. That's where she goes to see movie stars now that the Windsor Arms is closed. She had three martinis and told us Arlix is named for some famous old movie actor her grandmother had a crush on in Shanghai, an English guy called George Arlix. I looked him up. George Arliss. My mother can't pronounce or spell English for beans. I suppose you don't remember how she spells my name either."

"Gordian."

"Your memory's improving, Doc. Gordian's knot. That's what my head's in all the time and my gut half the time, when I have to sit every day while teachers talk like textbooks I've already read. You know my theory, Doc? The reason teens do dangerous things — play hero, drive too fast, take drugs, get pregnant, play football, rob stores, quit school — it's for relief. It's subconscious rebellion. Because we feel worthless, and that's because schools keep us powerless. Teachers keep on dishing out data instead of teaching us how to take charge of our own lives, dig up our own data, teach ourselves and each other, run our own schools with teachers as backup . . ."

Halper looks up at Gordon leaning on the next car cleaning his nails. He asks, "Did you really hold that opinion of schools and teachers last spring or put it in now for my benefit?"

"Last spring. Long before that. You're not the only one who

thinks school stinks. I told you, everything in that story is true. Just mined and refined. Cut and polished."

A chilly wind blows misty rain across the parking lot. Halper swings both legs inside his car and opens the opposite door. Gordon walks around and gets in. He slumps in the seat, leans his head back and closes his eyes while Halper reads silently:

Gordon slides so low in his chair that he is almost lying down. "How come you never made any Freudian hay with Gordian knot? Or did you?"

"What do you make of it?"

"You know something, Doc? Just for once. Just for bloody once, it'd be nice if you'd answer a question with something besides another question. I need some answers. At least some opinions. I listen to what you say, you know. I do. Even if I don't agree with it. I listen. You owe me. How many of your case studies listen to you?"

"I'll consider that. I always consider what you say, Gordon. You told me once that you changed your name to Gordon from Gordian when you started school because you could already read and spell so you knew — in your words — that Gordian was stupid spelling."

Gordon tires of reclining and tries sitting up almost straight and staring at his feet. His heels are held together while his toes swing apart and back together beating the rhythm of heartbeats growing weaker and slowing to nothing. Thump. Thump. . Thump. . .

"I never told you — when I was in that gifted learner class in junior public school — I researched hell out of all the Roman emperors called Gordian. Sometimes I feel like a dead emperor. Gordian I — Marcus Antonius Gordianus Africanus — he committed suicide. Every time I think about suicide I think maybe I'm his reincarnation. Not that I'm suicidal. Just that I wonder how I'd do it if I did. Don't say I never mentioned suicide before. You're right. But I write about it. You never ask to see my writing — except for those dopey assignments you give me to write once a year to see if I've got that burning house on the brain. I could see through that when I was thirteen. Anybody really interested in me would ask to read my current writing, real stuff. Because my writing is me. Nobody asks. Not the school. Least of all you."

"I'll read anything you bring."

"Sure. Now that I've brought it up. But you never thought of it yourself because you don't care about me. Piss on you and teachers, all adults. Wait till it's published and pay for it."

Gordon pops up and walks around. While he walks, he says, "Whoever cuts the Gordian knot rules Asia. But am I Asia or North America? It takes a bold stroke to solve a puzzle like me. Alexander the Great used a sword. Why shouldn't I? Is that Freudian enough for you Doc? Or do you even know what I'm talking about?"

"Yes. I read a lot. Even before my illness."

"You never told me that before. Now that's interesting. So do I. I used to hate Gordian but now I'm using it, except at school. Gordon is perfect for school because it's as phoney as school is. Gordian Wing is perfect for a writer and it's my real name. Now I realize, Gordian is the biggest favour my mother ever did me. Guess who I'm named for? I found that out last month too. Not Flash Gordon."

"Gordie Howe."

"That's gross. Why did you say a dumb thing like that?"

"Immigrant parents might pick a Canadian hero."

"It's even grosser when you call a man a hero for not growing up, for playing boys' games. If you want to be an expert on heroes, get your head straightened out, Doc. It was Chinese Gordon. I suppose you've heard of Chinese Gordon?"

"A general. I seem to —"

"General Charles George Gordon. British. Died 1885. My mother says her great great great grandfather was Gordon's top Chinese aide in the Taiping Rebellion. Her grandmother told her all this stuff.

Her grandmother smuggled herself and my mother into Hong Kong at night, covered with fish, in the bottom of a junk, in 1950 when my mother was still a baby and had to be drugged. No wonder she's crazy. Her grandmother wasn't exactly ordinary either. She owned a vaudeville house in Shanghai with movies and live shows, dancing girls, jazz, booze, for honkys — foreigners. When the commies took over, she blew up her own theatre with a time bomb because they intended to commandeer it to show propaganda films. It took her nearly a year, dodging around dragging a baby, before she got to Hong Kong. She ended up managing a movie theatre there."

"Remarkable. Commendable, wouldn't you say?"

"Except that when she blew up the theatre her own daughter — my mother's mother — was inside."

"A communist collaborator?"

"Or staying behind with a honky lover. Who knows. Her granny told my mother nothing about that or about her father, and my mother didn't ask. Chinese are like that. There were still Americans and other foreigners around Shanghai in 1949. My mother could be Eurasian. She's tall, white-skinned. She's the most beautiful woman I've ever seen. Look."

Gordon opens his wallet and shows two pictures of a lithe woman dressed like a fashion model in a shimmering red gown: crimped black hair, full red lips parted and glistening, wide-open almond eyes like closed doors of shining black marble.

"Yes. Exquisite. You look like her."

"We all do. Look."

Gordon flips to a family picture with banquet food in the foreground.

"Your father's good-looking too."

"He thinks so. He struts around like one of those little fighting roosters. He wears elevator shoes that he gets sent from Hong Kong and he's still shorter than my mother and me. That bugs him. He never walks right beside us so nobody'll notice he's shorter. I don't think of him as good-looking."

"How do you think of him?

"Mean and mighty and fake. A ceremonial dragon. Just like his father. My father and aunts and uncles brought my grandfather here from Hong Kong after his second wife died, when I was twelve. I was so excited. But he couldn't even see me in the fog of self-importance he generates. Another loud-mouth loser like my father. I'm just glad he lives with my uncle, not us."

"Does it matter if you're one-quarter white?"

"No. Except it might help explain why none of us fits in. My youngest sister is eight and hyper and suspicious of people and doesn't make friends. The oldest is fourteen and passive and eats too much and then starves herself and she's an easy lay. The middle one is twelve and goes to Salvation Army services and steals from stores on the way home. Arlix is a compulsive worker and laughs all the time and loves everybody even old bag ladies on the street and he lives with a man, a guy he met at the Y, an architect. I never mentioned it because you would have called the cops. But now he's sixteen. He can leave home legally."

Gordon is leaving legally, walking out the front door alone, with two suitcases, down four steps to the sidewalk. He doesn't know which way to turn so he just stands there. He picks up his bags and returns to the house and does the dishes his father left on the kitchen table. He goes to his room and lies on the bed and looks at the ceiling and cries a little. What the hell. Some other time.

"Would you have told me about your brother if I'd asked?"

"No. Not likely. Maybe."

"Your dad never objected, never reported him missing?"

"You should get the picture by now. We don't talk at home. My dad chops veggies in an all-night restaurant and gets back after we've gone to school. He watches his Bruce Lee videos or works out at some martial arts gym. Forty-three and still thinks he's the next Bruce Lee. When we get home from school, he's asleep. When he wakes up and leaves, we're out making a living, working part-time jobs. Weekends he's got another night job as a lookout for a fun house down around Spadina. Gambling I think, not whores. Or else he's out with one of his girlfriends getting laid. My brother came and went for a while then moved out completely. He still comes to see me and get help with essays. He shows up for family gatherings. We're all programmed to do that. That's all my old man cares about: appearances. Maybe it gradually dawned on him that Arlix isn't home. Maybe not."

Dr. Ashman has been leaning back in his swivel chair with his elbows on the chair arms, his fingertips pressed together in a steeple to keep them from trembling. He eases himself forward and writes a note on his pad. He speaks as he writes.

"Is the architect he lives with Chinese?"

"You're a racist, Doc, you know that? Just like the rest. You have to categorize people by something superficial like race. What the hell difference does it make what colour a friend is? Why didn't you ask me is he smart? Is he interesting? Is he kind? Is he dependable? Is he honest? Is he well-informed? Is he creative? He's all of the above, also white."

"What makes you think I would have called the police about Arlix?"

"By law you have to report child abuse if you suspect it."

"Do you suspect child abuse?"

"Hell no. I suspect love. Why don't they require guys like you to report love? Most of the accusations would prove false but you'd find some cases of blatant love. Imagine the headlines. Father found guilty of loving son. Six Christian Brothers admit loving orphans. Woman math teacher sentenced to three years of vocational classes for loving boy."

"You often mention vocational students unfavourably. I take it you look down on them."

"Not me. Live and let live. I can tolerate short exposure to dimwits who watch TV with laugh tracks. But I'm not too crazy about stupid people as close company. My friend Moose is about as thick as I can stand and he gets seventy-five percent in academic. It's *you* who look down on vocational classes, Doc. And teachers do. Most North Americans won't respect vocational schooling till there's a Nobel Prize for plumbing. That's from the editorial I wrote for Careers Day."

Gordon is watching the king of Sweden hang a two-foot gold pipe wrench on a gold chain around the neck of a plumber in a tuxedo. The image dissolves into a school auditorium full of chained students which the Nobel plumber is addressing by waving his golden wrench and rattling his golden chain.

"How much more time do we have? I didn't come here to rap about my brother or the school system unless it's relevant to you, shrink-wise."

"You're my only patient today so we've got as much time as you want. Can you tell me why you made this appointment?"

"Because I felt guilty about the times I had to cancel last year. Because I felt sorry that you were sick again. Because you're a dealer who got me hooked and now I have to keep coming for a gut-spill fix. I was bored at school. Every time I come here it gives me story ideas for the next month. I've got the hots for the redhead out front. I was lonely. I was fed up. My sex life was dull. One of the above. All of the above. None of the above. Take your choice. And don't call me a patient. I'm not sick. You're sick. Look at you."

"It was good of you to send me roses. And I enjoyed your get-well card, especially the poem. The only card I got that was hand made."

"I was broke. I got the yellow roses half price if you want the truth, from Moose Matkowski's mother. She sells flowers at a subway stop. You were asleep so I just left them. I saw you though. With all those tubes attached. Scared shit out of me."

" 'Up above the world so high/ You won't find heaven in the sky/ Kinky wrinkled little shrink/ You're still too young to die I think.' Wrinkled yes, little yes — except around the middle — but I never thought of myself as kinky."

"Researching heroes is kinky. Especially for a teddy bear like you. I figure you for a meek little kid who was a hero-worshiper and never got over it. Right?"

"My only hero was the father of a roommate who took me home for vacations from the time I was eight."

"Why him?"

"He was a jolly man, a small-town doctor who read a lot and retold the stories to us. He went through river ice and drowned while I was there one Christmas. He was trying to get to a child who was choking on a Christmas ornament."

Ashman sticks his finger in an ivy plant on his desk and, finding it dry, takes it into the bathroom and holds it under the tap.

"Why didn't you go home for Christmas?"

"No home. My parents were divorced. I grew up in second-string boarding schools and summer camps during the depression and the second world war. My mother travelled with a man she was then married to who had something to do with shipping. Port facilities I think. Mostly in Africa judging by the postcards."

"Why didn't you stay with your father?"

"He was a career army captain, always moving, always gone. Distant in other ways too. Killed overseas when I was fifteen."

"That's interesting. You wish you were like the doctor who drowned, I suppose. You stuck your finger in that pot the way he would have stuck his finger down the kid's throat. But heroes are nothing, Doc. I figure most heroes are like most murderers — we do it only once, without thinking. Big deal. The only difference is everyone remembers the murderers. Except you. You remember the heroes. That's kinky quirky. Your antique Rolls Royce is kinky classy."

"Twenty-four years old is hardly antique."

"It is when you're seventeen."

"The Rolls belonged to my mother's fourth husband, deceased. It's her legacy to me. I keep it because it was her crowning achievement. It's her memorial."

"Who left you those vintage sport coats? Mackenzie King? They're kinky crummy. Also your haircut, especially that long grey strand plastered sideways across your whole skull. It looks like the trans-Canada highway crossing Saskatchewan in winter. Face it Doc, you're bald. And your brown suede Hush Puppies are kinky corny. I wouldn't be caught dead in those things. How come you remembered that poem? Have you got it in your notes there?"

"No. On my desk at home. The card's a work of art. I collect art."

"Do you? So do I. Mostly my brother's and his architect friend's. Arlix is a super painter, especially of people. His architect welds beautiful sculpture of people from scrap. Arlix drew the people on that card but I coloured them. I'll get him to do a real picture for you. Did you almost die?"

"No."

"What'll happen to me if you have another heart attack, a big one?"

"You'll be informed. You'll be referred to another psychiatrist if you want one."

"Just like that. The redhead out front calls me up and says Ashman snuffed it so your new shrink is Dr. Blank. Forget it. Dr. Blank won't know me."

"He or she will get to know you."

"No thanks. I'm not going to start over. Piss on it. Thirty-six appointments with you. Thirty-six hours. That's the most I've ever talked to any adult. You've been at it four years and you still don't know me. Nobody knows me. I don't need a shrink anyway. I just come as a favour to you."

Gordon walks his circuit but stops at the bay window and looks out at late-March snow falling heavily on budding bushes. The clinic is beside the hospital in a Victorian mansion which Gordon likes. He sometimes jokes that Dr. Ashman should get a top-floor office so they can sit in a cupola with Uzis and pick off yellow bulldozers that make the mansion garden smaller every year as they make the hospital parking lot bigger.

He is in a cupola alone looking out at the swirling snow, shooting at — exploding — persistent snowflakes trying to bury him.

"What would you like to tell me? What's relevant to you, Gordon?"
    "You're the expert."
    "You looked at your wrist just now. You've lost your watch?"
    "Sold it. I sold a shipment of knock off's at school — my uncle imports stuff — and I kept a gold Cartier for myself but somebody offered me forty bucks. What could I say? Everything's for sale if the price is right."

He is standing on an auction block in the snow, chained, with no clothes on, and yellow bulldozers are bidding for him but not much, not enough.

"So now you're selling watches instead of working at the super-market?"
    "Both. I'm a hustler, Doc. Which reminds me. I brought you a welcome-back gift." He digs in his backpack and pulls out a box. "Genuine imitation Chanel for men. Spruce up your image, Doc. Throw away your Old Spice. You smell like Fenton, my school

principal, and he smells like Woolworths." He slides the package across the desk. "Just be grateful I sell knock-off watches and perfume and t-shirts instead of drugs or my ass. I'd make a hundred times as much selling either and I've got bills: food, clothes, books, rent, phone, dates, wheels, dentist, contact lenses, allergy drugs. I had to buy a computer. I need a printer . . ."

"Thank you, Gordon. This is very thoughtful of you. Wheels did you say?"

"Bus, subway, ten-speed. I aced the Pro Driver course a year-and-a-half ago but I've never driven my dad's car. Not once. And he's a lousy driver, the kind who guns it from stop lights and goes too fast and then squeals the brakes so everyone will notice how spiffy he looks talking on his car phone in his Hong Kong Italian suits. He gets tickets and fender dents and his insurance premium deserves delivery by a Brinks truck. But his self-image says he has to zoom everywhere in a new car, even if house bills aren't paid. I came home and found the phone cut off so now I pay it."

"You never mentioned before that you pay rent, just that you buy your own groceries."

"I say rent but it's the mortgage I have to help with. And taxes, lights, heating, water, repairs. When they bought the house six years ago there were five kids and two parents' pay cheques. Now there's just my dad and me left. Imagine if we lose the house, him and me in some little apartment? This way, I never have to see him. He lives in what used to be the living room — with the doors closed. The other three rooms are always rented unless somebody moves. That's my job too. Advertising. Collecting rent. Cleaning up. You should see the trash. I mean the trash they leave behind, but some of the people are trash too."

The back-bedroom door is half open, the radio blaring. He knocks and she says come in. She lies there on the bed nearly naked, propped up on cushions, one arm behind her head, grinning. He feels sad, emptied out.

"The woman in the back room leaves her shitty panties in the bathroom, hair in the sink, bottles, crap, even her crummy drugs and needles. She knows I'll dump it all back in her room and she waits there with her bathrobe wide open puffing smoke from her shitty cigarettes. The ad said no drugs, nonsmoker. Everybody lies."

"Including you?"

"Well naturally. What kind of dumb question is that? If you don't know everybody lies, you're in the wrong business Doc. Schools should teach people how to do it properly. Selectively. Ethically. I lie ethically. Moose Matkowski was so scared of lying he never got laid till he was sixteen, so I gave him lessons and now he lies fairly well and gets laid about once a week on my bed. I taught him how to do that too."

Moose is shunting back and forth on the bed. Gordon is in the closet, on the air mattress, looking out, making notes, wondering what it's like for Moose.

"I read all the sex books and wrote a manual with pictures by Arlix for dolts like Moose. Jake uses it too and he's not stupid. *The Art of Sex for Teens.* Costs me ninety cents to produce. It's a best seller at school for three bucks, mostly to grade nines and tens. Sort of *The Joy of Sex* meets the *Kamasutra* in the age of AIDS. There's nothing else on the market that assumes sex is good and the right of teens and an art to be learned. That's what schools should teach if they want kids to make informed decisions about sex. Jake says he's considering postponing any more penetration sex because of my book. Jake's the math whiz, the one on the swim team. Jake Zimmerman. You probably forgot that too."

There is a tap on the door and a pretty young woman with red hair enters. She smiles at Gordon and says, "Pardon me, Gordon." Gordon thinks he sees her cheeks flush. His breathing quickens. To Dr. Ashman she says, "You said to remind you." She steps into the bathroom, fills a glass, deposits the water in front of Dr. Ashman and exits still smiling slightly, professionally. Dr. Ashman takes his pills.

Gordon loosens the red hair from its bun and lets it cascade. He slowly removes all her clothing and she keeps on smiling. He takes off his own clothes and she laughs. She leaves the room laughing.

"How about Wilkins the swim coach. How's your conflict with him, Gordon?"

"Same. I tell him I'm in training to be a writer not a fish. I swim from 7:30 to 8:30 every morning. I do whatever he says. I swim my ass off for one hour. Wilkins wants three or four. But one hour a day for humans is all swimming deserves. All any sport deserves. Hockey and football deserve about five minutes. Let's get our priorities straight. I spend the other three hours writing. You could use an hour of exercise, Doc. No wonder you had a heart attack. Too much flab. What you need is low-fat Chinese cooking and regular exercise. I could get you in shape. You shrink me and I'll shrink you."

Gordon takes a turn around the room while Dr. Ashman allows himself a slight smile as he concentrates to steady his hand and jot a note.

"Last year you told me your friend Jake won the national mathematics olympics, but he still has time to swim four hours a day."

"It keeps him away from Luba — that's his mother — and his grandmother. They sell dresses on the Danforth, for matrons with bad taste. Buttons and bows and swags. Arlix breaks up every time he sees the store window. Nobody buys what they really know about: hats. They still make women's hats in the back room. Not many buy their dresses either. They're going broke bitching because nobody wears hats. Two crazy old ladies, mad hatters. Jake's father took off years ago, disappeared. Naturally, Jake wants to get away too, out of town, so he needs a big scholarship, all expenses for four years, and he'll get it for swimming not math. Nobody scouts for top mathematicians. Not with really big bucks to buy you off. But splash up and down a pool faster than the next guy and they fall all over each other trying to get you on a plane."

"Once before you said swimming didn't get much respect."

"Compared to football. Money-wise. Scholarship-wise. Chase a ball up and down a field and American universities send emissaries bearing frankincense, myrrh and pots of money to bow down and kiss your ass. Moose is eighteen and has sixty-eight football scholarship offers as of this morning — I'm not kidding about that number — all four-year, some for $150,000. His old man hasn't had a pay cheque since the freight yard closed. He's trying to figure how much of Poland Moose can buy. I'm not kidding about that either. And Moose's mother just keeps stuffing him full of sausages, cabbage rolls and prayers because it's worked so far. She never says anything to Moose except, "Eat, eat. Pray, pray." Moose just wants to be a dentist so he can lean on tits all day. What the hell has that kind of education and career got to do with football? It's all so sick."

"But you need a scholarship."

"I need an education. I've got principles. Jake and Moose haven't. Universities should be lined up from here to the airport to sign me up for a writing scholarship. I'm bloody good. Nobody gives a shit if I'm the next Dickens or Dreiser. The University of Toronto may give me one of their five national scholarships. Worth a measly $5,000 and one year in residence. But that's only because my average is always ninety-eight percent or more. They just want a machine that grinds out high marks. They don't give a shit about my writing.

And they won't bother to let me know if I've got a scholarship till May next year. If I haven't, all I'll have to live will be the $2,500 I got for being hot stuff when I was thirteen."

Gas explodes. Windows shatter. Doors blow off. The house bursts into flame. Across the street, in the arena parking lot, classes from several schools and four finalist hockey teams are being marshalled in front of their buses. The last day of the winter carnival, the hockey tournament. A thousand students, fifty teachers, coaches, bus drivers, carnival organizers.

A woman runs out of the flames carrying a baby. She is on fire and yelling, "Help me. Terry's upstairs. Help me. Help me." She rolls in the snow. "Help me. Terry's upstairs." Smoke rises from her. "Help me." The baby is screaming.

Because the street bends there, the parking lot is like an amphitheatre and the carnival visitors are an audience curving around the flaming stage.

"Help me!"

Gordon happens to be off to the right farthest from the stage with the rest of his team, but he drops his hockey equipment and rockets across the street with what is later described by witnesses as superhuman speed. He passes the woman wailing "Help me," enters the house and comes out again minutes later in a cloud of smoke with his hair and clothes on fire carrying a small boy who is alive and crying.

There are hero stories in the papers for three days and the chairman of the school board leads a delegation accompanied by television cameras to visit Gordon in hospital. They bring a basket of fruit — which rots before Gordon can eat any because of bandages — and a white azalea which perishes before he can take it home in the ambulance three months later. The following year a small item in the *Toronto Star* lists six Canadians, each awarded a hero medal and $2,500 by the Carnegie Hero Fund Commission. Gordon is one of them.

All this is nearly forgotten by everyone except the plastic surgeon who prevented Gordon's burns from disfiguring his face, and Dr. Ashman whose concern is internal scarring. The surgeon thinks one more minor operation to eliminate marks around Gordon's ears will do it — leave his surgical artistry no more detectable than the stretched creations favoured by ageing celebrities. Even before the final operation, Gordon's thick, neck-length hair tumbles over his ears and forehead covering the few slight scars that remain. His colour is good, not blotchy. Gordon thinks he looks a little older than he would have without surgery and perhaps less oriental. He tells the surgeon, with a little irony in his voice, that there's some advantage in both.

Ashman asks, "How come you keep Jake and Moose as friends if you don't approve of their principles?"

"Nobody I know has principles worth a damn except maybe my brother and his architect. You haven't. You only talk to me because you get paid for it and because you're researching heroes. You're paid to do what all the books say older men are supposed to do free for younger men, mentor them. Who are my mentors? Coaches so dumb they actually believe that bullshit about sports building character or else know it's bullshit and work like hell to shore up the myth so they can get more pay? Teachers who see me three periods a week on the run and can't remember my name without a seating plan? You're all part of the problem not the solution."

Gordon sees himself talking to a crowd of men who smile and nod but they have no ears, just scars where ears ought to be.

He walks once around the room and drops back into his chair with a sigh before he continues. "I don't hold it against people because I don't approve of their principles. I'm here in your office aren't I? And I hang out with Jake and Moose in spite of their principles. Jake has other qualities — enough brains to have something to say. And he's a good listener. He's creative. We're inventing a computer program together, a thinker's game, better than Nintendo."

"And Moose?"

"He can barely play our game let alone understand writing the program. I told you. Moose and I were neighbours in Regent Park. Ten years in the same subsidized slum, till both families got out. So we're friends. He listens but he's got nothing to say worth hearing. Like you. Except you've probably got something to say if anybody could ever get it out of you. Just today you've said more than in four years and that wasn't much. But Moose's got no brains. He's not a vocational clunk but he's got no ideas, no imagination, no curiosity, except about sex. He can't even get a fix on the mindlessness of his own family. You'd be surprised how many people can't do that. I'm an expert at figuring out families."

Gordon is with his father and mother and forty relatives — his grandfather, his father's three brothers and two sisters, their wives and husbands, cousins, kids — all smiling, all talking, taking pictures of each other — at one of the family gatherings that happen in the banquet room of some restaurant three or four times a year. Whatever the occasion, the purpose is to prove how prosperous and proper everybody is. The pictures prove it for posterity. When the photo opportunity is over, his mother goes one direction, his father another.

"I have to go to Moose's house and eat sausage and listen and put it all together for him. Jake can figure out his granny and Luba on his own. Moose gets seventy-five percent. That's like sixty-five when you went to school. Peanuts. And he works his ass off to get that. I tutor him. He's a six foot six, 286-pound machine that anyone can program up to his capacity. Nature programmed him to follow his cock. The system programs him to follow a ball up and down a field. So now he's the best offensive lineman, the most offensive. Except for what I teach him, Moose would be entirely offensive by now."

"Is tutoring one of your businesses?"

"Only a mercenary like you would ask that question. I'm a hustler, not a mercenary. You wouldn't understand. Moose is my friend. I'm not about to charge for saving him from death by exams. You know what exams do, Doc? Exams test your ability to memorize for short-term retention. Most people who pass can't remember enough to pass the same exam a year later. Anybody who can remember the stuff two years later obviously didn't need an exam in the first place. I program Moose to pass exams even though he doesn't know what the hell the information really means and forgets it right after the exams."

"You consider that principled?"

"The school system does. And you know me, Doc. I'm into saving people."

"Why is that?"

"You tell me. Earn your keep for a change."

"Perhaps it boosts your ego."

"Right. I said to myself, well looky here Gordie-boy, a house fire and a lady burning outside and screaming about her kid burning inside. Now's the time to get a big dose of feel-good. Why not run into all that smoke there and look for the kid and see if you can burn too?"

His mother is in the kitchen still in high heels from work, lighting up with a Bic flame-thrower, in a perpetual cloud of smoke, lighting her way with that butane torch, tossing Chinese ingredients together on the run. No measuring, no recipe book, no sampling. It's not just cooking. It's the rhythm of life. Everything tastes right. On the rare occasion when she takes out a Western cookbook, life comes to a halt. Deliberation sets in. Measuring is suddenly invoked. She's in uneasy country. It tastes wrong.

Dr. Ashman says, "I meant only that your self-esteem may have needed bolstering after your mother left without you. That was only two months before the fire."

"Is that what you've been thinking all these years? That I was looking for approval? And I suppose the four hockey teams, the thousand people who stood there watching, had all the approval they needed so they let the kid in the house burn. Piss on you, Ashman. Take that back or I'm out of here."

Gordon is on his feet and pacing his usual path. He feels hot. He pulls his red plaid shirt out of his jeans and unbuttons it. The t-shirt underneath says SCHOOL SUCKS. He swings into the bathroom which was once a little vestibule with a door to the side porch. He yanks the outside door wide open and sits on the toilet lid gulping cold air. He whacks his hand repeatedly on the cardboard boxes full of books.

Dr. Ashman waits, making notes, till Gordon returns to his chair. Ashman speaks while he adjusts his glasses by pushing on the nose piece of the colourless plastic rims. "I wasn't talking about conscious needs and actions but rather subconscious. And it's not uncommon for children of separation to feel abandoned, worthless. Maybe you even felt to blame."

"Ah, blame. Now you're onto something. I was always an unpredictable shitter. My mother said she'd sit me on the pot for half an hour and I'd grunt seriously the whole time. Nothing. But twenty minutes later in the car I'd suddenly shit my pants. The feel of it coming is my earliest memory. My father was never a good-tempered man and the smell of shitty pants would trigger a day's worth of yelling and slapping. That's what caused the family breakup.

Why didn't I think of that before? And me a writer."

"The recollection is useful but you must know the conclusion is false."

"And you must know my self-esteem is okay. This isn't the old days when you had to be a WASP — and a jock, or a preppie or a rocker — to make it socially at school. I've got a following. And not just the Chinese tong either. I'm well-built, five ten. Taller than you, Doc. I'm considered cute, you know that? How long since you've been considered cute, if ever? You look like Dustin Hoffman in *The Rain Man*, only older and dumpier. Same schnoz. Only yours is redder. I can recommend a good plastic surgeon, Doc. Which reminds me, Jack Palance didn't look the way he does in movies till he had just as much plastic surgery for burns as I've had. More. I like my face if that's what you're digging for. I'll take it over Moose's or Jake's any day, and girls say they're both good-looking. I'm the only Chinese in town that nobody can peg for sure. Sometimes they're surprised when they hear my name's Wing."

A familiar thought skips through Gordon's head, that his real father is a white man. His own skin is light. But his mother and lots of northern Chinese are whiter than whites. He's the oldest. They must have been doing it with each other that early in the marriage. He has the same body as the Wing who is supposed to be his father. Still, a white man is looking for him, finds him, talks to him, reads his stories, understands them. No Chinese father could ever understand his stories.

Dr. Ashman looks over top of his slipping glasses at Gordon. "You'd rather not look Chinese?"

"Right. And not because I've got anything against looking or being Chinese. Just because I like being free of bloody ghetto mentality. I'm Canadian. North American. Period. No hyphens. Who gives a shit where some ancestor came from? Nobody should. They all came from one place: earth — one little earth spinning around in endless space. That's all that matters. And just for the record, the reason my family broke up is because my old man is a shit who beat up my mother and my mother is a shit who screwed around with white guys. She wouldn't dream of doing it with Chinese guys."

Another tap on the door and the redhead looks in. "Very sorry. The director. He insists. Line three."

Dr. Ashman picks up the phone. "I'm with a patient — And I refused — No — No — Half days at least — That's not true — I'm with a patient." He hangs up sharply.

Gordon says, "I get the impression I'm in the way around here. If you don't have time for me just say so."

The phone rings. Ashman grabs it and says, "The answer is no — That was one occurrence — That's personal — No." He hangs up. "I'm sorry, Gordon. That should never have happened with you here."

Dr. Ashman searches his drawers one at a time. They have been emptied. His hands shake. His whole face is red. His eyes are watery and blinking. Gordon stands up and digs in the pockets of his bomber jacket. He holds out a pocket pack of Kleenex. The doctor takes one and murmurs thanks as he turns away to wipe his eyes and nose. There is silence for a moment.

"Are they trying to make you retire, Doc?"

"It's nothing. Just that this is my first time back and some were surprised to see me walk in."

"When I came at noon they told me you were home writing your hero book. How's that thing coming?"

"Oh, well, you know. My illness. It's been on hold."

"What you need is a good ghost like me. I could jazz it up. You're a lousy writer, you know that? I read that hero article of yours. Turgid stuff Doc, even for a medical journal. Your eyes are still runny. Have another Kleenex. Keep the pack."

Gordon leans forward and shoots the pack across the desk. He flings his leg over one arm of his chair and that foot beats up and down bass-drumming his feelings. Dr. Ashman wipes his eyes and blows his nose and clears his throat several times.

"Well. Now then — you never told me that about your mother before."

"You never asked."

"I didn't ask now."

"Yes you did. You said I might blame myself for the family breakup. That amounts to an accusation or else a question about who was to blame if not me. Don't play games with me, Doc. I'm not some naive nerd."

"I'm not looking to blame anybody for anything. I was just concerned about your self-esteem."

Gordon sighs. He removes his leg from the arm of his leather chair, presses down with his hands on both arms of the chair and stands up decisively. He takes one arm out of his shirt and makes his exposed arm and chest muscles bulge.

"Take a look, Doc. Do I look okay?"

"Yes."

Gordon drops his sweat pants to his knees and lifts his t-shirt. "Do I look like the elephant man? Are the scars repulsive?"

"No. Barely visible."

"Then get off my case." He pulls up his pants. "Stop trying to twist everything I say to make it look like I hate myself, like I'm holding back stuff so you won't know how fucked up I am." He sits down with one arm still out of his shirt sleeve. "And spare me the self-esteem bullshit. Adults don't want kids to have it. Self-esteem means self-authority. Schools are scared shitless of kids developing self-authority. The whole rotten model of schooling depends on us looking to teachers for authority. Same thing with parents. Chinese are the worst. That's why there's never been a real Chinese democracy.

Everybody just keeps bowing to higher authority. Singapore has daddyocracy."

"You mentioned years ago that your father's violence caused the breakup but you never said anything about your mother in that regard."

Gordon stands up and shoves his arm back in his shirt sleeve by flinging the arm in the air while he walks.

"My dad was in Hong Kong for a month when his stepmother died there. I came home one day because I forgot my skates and found my mother on the basement floor with the guy who reads the gas meter. On a red blanket, the two of them. Playing the rec room radio. Not a stitch on. The guy's dick was slithering right over his leg like a big wet snake with a red head dribbling. Pecker tracks on the blanket. With the baby watching too, my sister. Both of them just lighting up with that olympic torch of hers. You know, a nice smoke after a satisfying fuck. That's all. Case closed." He falls into his chair.

"How old were you then?"

"Old enough to know an easy lay when I saw one. But it's not her fault she's that way. She was only thirteen when her grandmother died and she was left on her own in Hong Kong. She told people she was sixteen. Got a job sewing. Then some woman took her in and got her a job at a spa. I think they were all whores."

"But how old were you?"

"When the gas man came? — you'll excuse the expression — barely twelve. I was still a little kid. You know, crotchwise. But I knew what was going on. Moose was a year older and already six feet and horny. He had lots of girly magazines and showed me pictures. That's another thing I never told you. I still keep Moose's and Jake's sex magazines — they keep them — at my place. I'm the one that never buys those dumb magazines but I'm also the one that has a safe place to keep them. Luba snoops in Jake's room. Moose's mother even looks in his wallet. At least my mother never snooped."

Gordon jumps to his feet again and paces once around the room before dropping in his chair with a plunk. "She was too busy changing shitty diapers, shagging pickups, selling bloody cosmetics — she still manages that paint shop in Yorkville by the way — changing her own face or somebody else's every ten minutes. Just why the hell is it that boys have no privacy except if their parents don't give a shit about them? Tell me that. I've got all the privacy in the world and I'm the one willing to spill my guts to any adult who cares to listen."

"I'll listen."

"But you don't *care* to listen. There's a difference. You don't care, except professionally. You make me feel like statistics. Who are you anyway? Some data gatherer. I don't know anything about you. Till today when you mentioned your parents I didn't know for sure you were even born. You might have just accumulated out of medical waste in some lab. I've had to invent you like one of my characters so I'll know who the hell I'm talking to. I've made you a working drunk because I could smell gin or something when you sat on the bed when I was in hospital. And your nose is always red."

"That's perceptive. But I've been dry for three years — since I had hepatitis — except for one recent slip."

"Is that what the guy on the phone was mad about?"

"That and my age."

"You let people push you around. Don't be such a pipsqueak, Doc. Be more aggressive."

"There's a policy. I'm sixty-five next month."

"I'll make you a birthday card. How's this for my Ashman scenario? You're a bookish boozer with a wife about two inches taller than you and very smart. Also better looking than you. Three kids, two girls and a boy. One dog. A collie. Lassie. The boy's a dud. You can't communicate with him either, from your academic fortress with its moat full of gin. How'm I doing?"

"He's a gynecologist."

"A rich dud."

"Quite successful, I hear. The dog was a spaniel. Taffy. Only one daughter, in Vancouver, divorced, remarried, alcoholic, recovered. My ex-wife lives there too, also a physician, remarried." Ashman looks past Gordon, out the window, at turbulent dark gray clouds breaking apart leaving bars of flat gray underneath. "Yes, very smart, better looking than I ever was, but the same height as me, except in heels. Four grandchildren I've never seen. My son is on his third marriage. He lives in Los Angeles as far as I know."

"That's where my parents wanted to go. Hollywood. They met working as extras on movies in Hong Kong. Always extras and bits. Couldn't make it big in Hong Kong and thought they would in Hollywood. Really dumb. Both of them speak lousy English. Toronto was to be their first stop on the way up. Instead it's their last stop on the way down. I'm sorry about your family. Was it because you were a drunk?"

"Partly. Mostly."

"I bet you never told a patient before."

"No."

"See. I got it out of you. That means I'm a good writer type. Observant, inquisitive, persistent. Yellow stains on your fingers. Right now you want a cigarette but you gave that up too. Right?"

"Yes." Ashman looks back at his notes and leans forward toward them. He picks up his pen. "You just referred to yourself as a patient. I thought you hated being called a patient."

"That's what gets me about you guys. Adults. Teachers. You especially. You lurk around the edges of my life trying to find a weakness to pounce on."

"Maybe that's because you hedge, so people have to be observant, inquisitive, persistent."

"Since when did I hedge? Tell me once."

"You hedge about sex."

"I told you years ago I jerk off every night and I think it's no big deal, and my cock's kind of small but that's no big deal either, and I played doctor and nurse with the little girl down the hall when we were both eight or nine, and that's no big deal, and I've got the hots for blonds and redheads. What else is there?"

"Fantasies, for one thing."

"I listed half a dozen for you. All I could think of. I told you, my favourite fantasy is some day I'll find a Chinese restaurant that serves brown rice."

Gordon grins and twists around so that both legs are over one arm of his chair and his toes are tapping on the front of Ashman's desk.

"And I said you were either pulling my leg to change the subject or making a cultural statement not a sexual one."

"And I thought about that later. I told you, I listen to what you say. I think it's just a nutritional and a culinary statement: brown rice is healthier and tastier. But maybe it's cultural — Chinese like that inferior white crap because it's white and they're not. I, on the other hand, don't eat it because it's white and I'm not. Or else I eat brown because it's not white and I'm not. I suspect Chinese eat cultural crow by eating white. How'm I doing, Doc?"

"You're hedging the sexual question again. Last September I asked you a second time, specifically about sexual fantasies, and all you said was 'girls, of course.' What do you think about every night when you masturbate?"

"Girls, of course. I imagine fucking some redhead."

Gordon jumps up and tramps around his usual circle twice before continuing. "Okay. Alright. I imagine I'm some white guy with a big cock fucking a redhead who loves it. I'm always somebody else. So what? I'm a writer. I'm always playing the characters I'm writing."

"And when you're actually making love? Do you imagine you're doing it as someone else?"

"No. Yes and no." He turns and paces the opposite direction one full circle before continuing. "Alright. Okay. If you really want to know. I'm a virgin. Go ahead. Have a laugh on me. Gordian Wing is a fucking virgin."

Unexpectedly, tears well and Gordon searches his jacket pockets for Kleenex. Dr. Ashman picks up the package from his desk and stands to hand it to Gordon. Ashman says, "Half the people your age are virgins."

"Not my half." He begins walking again.

"It's not a bad half to be in."

"Oh shit." The tears begin to flow. "Shit." Gordon stops walking and presses his lips together and looks up at the ceiling and down again. "Shit." He draws a deep breath that escapes in small shudders. "I can't do it with a girl. That's it." He strides around the room crying, saying shit, wiping his eyes first on Kleenex, then, when it runs out, on his shirt sleeve. "Oh shit. Shit. I'm so horny I get a hard-on when your redhead comes in the room but when I get a girl's pants off in my bedroom I can't do anything but sweat. I've had a million chances. It happened last night. She laughed at me. She laughed at me."

Gordon wheels into the bathroom and slams the door and presses his forehead to the cold window and closes his eyes. He clutches the sash with both hands. After a moment, he opens his eyes and sees that heavy snow weighs down forsythia about to blossom. He pushes the window up, reaches out, and shakes the bush so hard all the snow flies off. Some hits his face and melts into supplementary tears. Spring thunder growls and tails off oddly into three little taps.

There is a pause then one more tap. The bathroom door opens a crack and Dr. Ashman says, "You alright, Gordon?"

"Yes."

A moment later, Gordon hears the office door open and close. He thinks Dr. Ashman has stepped out. But instead, the clinic director has stepped in.

"You're a fool Ashman. I've just spoken to cardiology. You're supposed to be at therapy right now. Pennington says you're not fit to work or drive. And in this weather. If you want to make an issue of this —"

"A patient needed me."

"That's nonsense. We can handle your former patients."

Gordon yanks the door open and explodes from the bathroom yelling, "You can't handle me so fuck off! Leave him alone!"

As he bursts through the doorway roaring, he grazes Ashman's shoulder knocking his glasses to the floor. Gordon meets the director for the first time, head-on. Dr. Chong is thrown backwards into a wine-leather wing chair where he sprawls motionless, wide-eyed, blank, like a mannequin purposely slumped by a trendy window dresser. The mannequin's jaw drops. Chong is in his mid forties, smallish, wiry, dapper, silk-tied. Before he can rally, Gordon grabs him by his impeccably tailored navy-blue pin-striped lapels, lifts him from the chair and pegs him to the wall with a thud. Gordon raises one knee in front of Chong's well-pressed groin.

"Say the word Doc and I'll make him a soprano."

"No. No. Don't!" Ashman cries in the loudest voice he can muster, hoarse and breathy.

Ashman is on his knees retrieving his glasses. He puts them on and struggles to his feet while Gordon yanks the speechless Chong from the wall, turns him around, seizes him by his Hong Kong–custom-made collar, marches him to the door and shoves him into the corridor, hard. Gordon slams the door, opens it, says 'Pick on somebody your own size,' slams the door again, opens it and says 'Your own age, pick on somebody your own age, runt.' He slams the door again and locks it.

"Now where were we, Doc?"

There is loud pounding on the door and Chong shouts, "Open this door!"

Gordon yells back, "Fuck off, chink-face!"

Dr. Ashman leans — red-faced, breathing hard — against the desk, gripping it on both sides with white-knuckled hands. He clears his throat and tries twice before he can say in a choked whisper, "You'll have to go out there, Gordon, apologize."

"It's okay Doc. Us chinks can call each other chink."

"Not just that. Your whole rescue operation."

"What? Oh, I get it. I did it again."

"Yes. But from his point of view, you attacked him. Assault. Right this minute he's calling orderlies, security guards, police."

"I'll plead insanity."

There is a muffled rumble. Gordon thinks the thunder has returned. But the sound transforms to little grunts and then nasal snorts. Ashman is laughing. Gordon has never heard him laugh before.

Between snorts, Dr. Ashman says, "You're as sane as anybody I know."

"That's not saying much. You're a nut dealer."

Suddenly both are laughing and for a moment they are as helpless to stop it as they are to control the sun which has just thrown a bright path across the rug and into the bathroom.

"Nut dealer, knot dealer," Gordon says between laugh bursts. He is thinking up a birthday poem. "Head peeler, faith healer . . ."

Ashman gets toilet paper and wipes his eyes and blows his nose. He says still smiling, "Go. Apologize."

"How can I apologize if I don't feel sorry?"

"You'll feel it later. Chong's all right. He just stands for the wrong things for both of us. I'll help you think it through. Meanwhile, pretend you're sorry. Lie a little — your way, properly, selectively, ethically."

"Why don't I just duck out the side door and you can have a word with him on my behalf."

"Because Gordian Wing, the writer speaks for himself. And he uses the front door."

"Yes."

"Apologize."

"Okay."

"And after, would you be so kind as to fetch my car from the hospital parking lot?" He holds out the car key like a sword pointing the direction. "I'd be most grateful if you'd bring it around to the side and pick up those boxes of books and take me home."

Gordon accepts the key.

— 30 —

Darkness has closed in around his car and Halper has been reading by the map light. The iceberg he was pushing half an hour ago has melted away. He folds the paper slowly, wondering about being so touched again. First Lincoln, then Gordon. They have confided so much more than his own children ever have. Their openness eats away his own varnish of protection. The car is a bubble of warm light that floats in the black mist of night. Simon seems to be there. Halper looks at Gordon asleep in the seat beside him or pretending to sleep. On an impulse, he leans over and kisses him on the forehead the way he used to kiss his sleeping son.

With his eyes still closed Gordon says, "You liked it."

"Yes. Terrific."

"The yellow peril strikes again."

Both know a bond has been struck.

"We have to make time to talk about everything in this story. And I want to read all of your writing. All. What happened to Dr. Ashman?"

"Fell off his deck last month. There's a visiting nurse and I go two or three times a week. I drive him around. We've got his book almost rewritten."

"Then you might not have time for what I'm thinking about.

Interesting that Lincoln's story also ends with car keys handed over. I'm not suggesting you copied him. My story has car keys too, the hidden ones I gave Simon. Billy Parr tells me the story he's working on has a car symbol. And there are other parallels. Suicide. Schools. Parent problems. And Billy told me his story deals with a gay brother. My son Simon was gay. Your brother Arlix."

"And Lincoln's grandmother I guess."

"When Billy's is in I thought we might all read the stories for deeper meanings. Not the short story club. Just the four of us, starting with the car and key metaphors. We could meet across the street with the Greens. You might find some Greens interested in working with you on that computer game invention now that your friend Jake has graduated. Claudius Ito could do it. And Lincoln, of course. But you might not want to get that involved what with your home chores, swimming, supermarket job, t-shirts, editing the newspaper, Ashman . . ."

"I'll think about it."

"We've got fifty-six Greens and counting. We've spread into two stores. We could use the experience you got tutoring your friend Moose. Seems a shame to waste that ability now that Moose has graduated. And I'm responsible for the spring revue so I've got to get a theme, get people writing material, do auditions."

"No thanks. Last year the theme was multiculturalism so we had about fifty folk dances and sixty skits about togetherness and then everybody left the auditorium in ethnic gangs as usual."

"I wonder if we could do a show called The Rights of Spring. R-i-g-h-t-s. About kids' rights. Nice chance to satirize parents, teachers, punishments, examinations, sex, censorship, arbitrary rules. Claudius Ito is interested."

"Who is this Ito?"

"Grade nine. Very bright. Looks a bit like you come to think of it. Could be your brother. Claudius could use a big brother. Of course it's up to you. But it's a chance to run things the way you think schools should operate. You say your best-selling sex book appeals to grade nines. Lots of Greens are in grade nine. They could use some seminars on sex in the age of AIDS."

"First you better take a lawyer's look at *The Art of Sex for Teens*. I kept it underground last year because I knew Fenton would ban it. This year the government might jail me because of that stupid new pornography law."

While Halper is talking to Gordon in the school parking lot, Keiko Ito arrives across the street in her red Supra to collect Claudius and see this Halper person she hears so much about. Ms. Ito is as much a media celebrity as an interior designer. The Greens, especially the girls, are excited because they have seen her on the fashion pages, on TV cooking and talk shows, on one crusade or another. Today she wears a dusky lavender leather sheath with a red belt and pumps and dangling amethyst earrings.

She is told Halper should arrive soon, so Keiko Ito perches like a tiny perfect porcelain lamp with swaying pendants, lighting up the lid of a wooden packing box. She says, "Call me Keiko or Kay."

Maude Fenwick sits opposite, on an orange crate full of books, wearing her green baseball cap, brown slacks, a pink fuzzy cardigan, jogging shoes and a ceremonial sabre left over from the Crimean War. Maude recites "The Charge of the Light Brigade" and they have a nice chat and tea in cracked mugs, with cookies on paper serviettes, while Claudius and Lincoln finish supervising a computerized reading lesson for Frank Stringer.

Keiko says, "The cookies are divine Maude, but this place is a mess. Claudius, get my tapes in the car."

When Halper walks in, Keiko and Maude have four students measuring and four more drawing a floor plan to scale. Keiko invites Halper to come with her and Claudius for a bite to eat so they can discuss furnishings. He accepts. Three days later she arrives at the wheel of a rental truck with an assortment of furniture she has commandeered from the back rooms of the trade. The Greens have sofas, television, VCR, folding chairs, computer tables, lamps, rugs, microwave, dishes . . .

They also get a phone which Halper pays for. He feels he needs it so the Greens can call home and he can try to establish regular contact with Jillian. He gives the new number to his youngest daughter, Alison, and asks her to give it to Jillian. Jillian phones to say she is back in Vancouver and wants her clothes but her mother has just refused to ship them. Halper agrees to send five hundred dollars and will try to send her clothes.

As soon as Halper finishes the incorporation, a small sign is placed in the window: THE GREENHOUSE: an incorporated nonprofit learning centre — MAUDE FENWICK, DIRECTOR, assisted by FRANK STRINGER. A list of directors follows. To avoid conflict of interest it does not include David Halper. It does include Keiko Ito and three other adult volunteers, one a retired judge married to a teacher, and two retired teachers. A little later, the Greens will elect three of their number to the board and will vote the chair into office.

Fenton's ears are red and moving in sync with his nostrils as they flare. The long hairs growing from his ears are more noticeable than usual, waving, as though dancing, energized by the extra blood of repressed rage. This time Halper is seated in Fenton's office and Fenton has come around his desk and is standing with his hands on both hips. Halper recalls the time his father came around his desk at the bank and stood like that and said, "Understand me, boy. Law or business administration. No Ph.D. in English. Got it?"

Halper almost answers 'yes sir' to his father and is about to stop himself when he realizes the answer will do also for Fenton. "Yes sir."

"Abortion!" Fenton says once more in disbelief. "You admit that? You're debating abortion in law classes?"

"Yes. But I don't admit it. I proclaim it."

Fenton wheels, walks the length of the room smacking his fist into his palm, wheels again, walks back and looms once more over Halper. He gulps breath, controls himself, speaks through his teeth.

"Miss McCubbin is new. The family life teacher. New, Halper. Twenty-five years old. She knows better. She says nothing about abortion except the exact words in the course outline which isn't much. But you Halper, forty-five, you choose up sides and make a game of abortion. And it isn't even on your course. You've got screws missing Halper. Miss McCubbin tells me you've even had a pregnant girl and her boyfriend and her father as contestants. Are you giving prizes? Who won the refrigerator? Who's next, that abortionist Morgenstall?"

"Morgentaler. No, I don't think anyone has invited him yet, but he's been quoted."

Fenton's secretary pops her head in the door to say the director is on line three. Fenton answers, all smiles. Halper considers telling Fenton that his son Lincoln is next, but decides not to. Lincoln has already told Halper that he makes his own decisions about which people to discuss his opinions with and that Fenton is not one of them.

Halper wonders which teacher is Miss McCubbin. There are a dozen or more new recruits, not counting the army of substitutes that come and go filling in for casualties. Regulars who report to the library for meetings are deployed by department at crowded tables, behind the counter, and strung around the perimeter writing on their knees. There has never been a meeting with all present, not even the union meetings about salary which are the best attended. Halper knows maybe twenty-five teachers by name, none well. Most of the ones he nods to in corridors are as nameless as the legions of kids. TELL ME WHO YOU ARE. He wonders if he will ever know McCubbin. He wonders if it matters. Fenton hangs up and his smile wilts like flowers in frost.

Halper continues, "Abortion is a rights issue and human rights is on the course. And it's dead right when it comes to moral and ethical considerations in law, and relevance to these students."

"And dead wrong when it comes to community relations and common sense. Look at this."

Fenton grabs a letter from his desk and thrusts it at Halper. Reverend Ben Gambell, president of the Christian Rebirth Society, objects to tax money being used 'to pay Halper to teach sin.'

CHAPTER FOUR

Gordon, Lincoln and Billy converge on Halper as he hurries along the hall toward his senior English class.

Gordon Wing is fresh from an encounter with Matsushita, the union leader on the faculty. Matsushita has refused student reporters admission to a teachers' meeting about changes in teaching roles that will accompany changes in curriculum just mandated by the government. And Matsushita has vetoed a story about the meeting which Gordon based on interviews with a few willing teachers and his own reading of the new regulations.

Lincoln Fenton is fresh from an encounter with his father

about his ban on publication in the school newspaper of Lincoln's comments on abortion to Halper's law classes. James Fenton has also censored so much of Lincoln and Gordon's report on computers (called Computer Illiterate Teachers Mean Computer Illiterate Schools) that what remains is, in Lincoln's words, just the wrapping paper.

Billy Parr is fresh from an encounter with Duchok, the vice-principal, who refuses to let the author of *Future Schools* address a student assembly on the topic of students' rights and responsibilities, or the student council on student government, or the newspaper staff on freedom of expression and information in high schools, or even the Christian student club on sustainable sex and other essential values which the author thinks young people worldwide should be developing jointly in global studies programs.

Gordon says, "We want to publish Billy's TELL ME WHO YOU ARE story."

Lincoln says, "Desktop. My printer, my paper, my staples."

Gordon says, "We'll give it away with the next *Midhiller*. I'll make it a theme issue, a student council special — who's who and what's what. With a literary supplement about and by the president."

"Sounds good," Halper says. "But why release Billy's story when we agreed that yours and Lincoln's should be read only by the four of us and Claudius?"

Gordon says, "Because our stories are too hot. They skewer Fenton and this school. Billy's is about another school and principal but makes points that apply to all schools. And it's right on the mark about minority group awareness, which is the topic of next week's assembly."

Billy says, "If you don't like the newspaper and student council connection we can call a meeting of the short story club and let it emanate from there, just hand out copies at lockers. That's been done before."

Halper has not yet read the story. He says, "Why don't we see what the class thinks?"

Two minutes later Billy Parr is sitting on the front of Halper's desk facing the senior English class. He says, "I started out writing about my loneliness since my girlfriend and her family moved to Calgary in August, and about the misery I see on my weekend job at the hospital, everything that's going on right now. But I realized I had to write about my brother Arnie instead because I can't yet see myself except in relation to the two most important people in my whole life, Arnie and Jesus. They make me whatever I'm becoming. You've heard me talk about Jesus lots of times but never about Arnie because I couldn't. But it's time. And it's the only way to tell you who I am. This takes place northeast of here where I lived till I was in grade ten:

They could have reopened the school after a few days but that would have meant having some kind of assembly, saying something, so they just kept it closed till after Christmas. By then they had the rotunda cleaned up and sheets of drywall painted green covered the hole where the display case used to be.

On the first school day in January, the principal got on the p.a. at nine o'clock right after 'O Canada' and said, "Happy New Year everyone. In view of the tragedy last term, extracurricular activities will be cancelled this week and, instead, the board is providing special counselling sessions every day at noon and after school. Any student wishing to participate should sign up in the guidance office at noon today."

That was it.

Special counselling. As if that would make everything okay. Even after four years I can hardly bear to think about it. In all that time I haven't changed a thing in Arnie's Museum. I just sit there every time I visit and try to remember happier days, the way you remember summer — oriole songs — in the middle of winter.

I found out my brother Arnie was gay the summer he was thirteen and I was eleven, long before Dad knew or the principal or anybody else (except Arnie's best friend Dave Bond), before I even knew what gay meant exactly. I knew you weren't supposed to be that way or even talk about it. Twice I heard men who worked on the township road crew with my dad tell dirty jokes about faggots while they were helping Dad drive his hockey teams around to other towns. When they did that, my dad pressed his lips together hard and cast his eyes upward for a second, like he did after any dirty joke. My dad is a religious man but too nice to ever say anything except maybe, "Shhh. The boys might hear."

I found out about Arnie in his Museum.

I'm in the loft looking out the little window at baby swallows learning to fly, when Arnie and Dave Bond come in.

Dave is a rich doctor's son from town, very Ralph Lauren and Benetton-looking and always happy, also generous — he gives me lots of stuff when it's nearly new, even expensive downhill skis and boots which he buys new every Christmas when he and his mom and dad go skiing in Switzerland. Dave is home for the summer and rides his Italian ten speed out to our place every day. He's been away in Toronto all winter in grade nine at Upper Canada College, which he likes, especially the wrestling team.

Arnie knows Dave from way back when they were both in a special class for smart kids. That was in town, and Arnie went to Dave's house every day for lunch and they played games of chess or dungeons and dragons that went on for days, weeks I guess.

I decide to wait a bit and then jump down from the loft and scare them.

Arnie says to Dave, "You wanta do something?"

Dave says, "Okay."

"Sixty-nine?"

"Okay."

Arnie locks the doors. Next thing I know they fling off all their clothes and do it to each other lying on their sides facing each other on Queen Victoria's bed, Dave with his feet to the head and Arnie with his feet sticking off the foot of the bed. Arnie is tall, nearly six feet I think, taller than Dave and nearly a foot taller than me.

Queen Victoria is also on the bed, in her usual place, staring up at me and bouncing slightly due to Arnie's activity. Arnie is facing my way and sees me up there, paralysed. He just pauses for a second and grins and winks and puts his finger over his lips as a sign to keep quiet. He picks up Queen Victoria's hand and waves it at me. Then he gets right on with what he's doing.

Whatever Arnie had in mind, he got on with. Arnie's Museum, for example. The log cabin used to be Dad's workshop but Arnie gradually crowded him out with treasures he brought home from the dump and junk shops and other people's attics. Arnie talked his way into attics and basements.

Some people said Arnie must have inherited that trait from my dad's father, Grandpa Parr. It stands to reason. Arnie was the only one of us that was tall like Grandpa Parr with the same laughing eyes. My parents never mentioned Grandpa Parr but Arnie found a picture of him in somebody else's attic and when he showed me, I thought it was Arnie.

Grandpa Parr was a country auctioneer and a horse trader and ran off to the States with a horse and a sulky driver leaving Grandma Parr with eight rocky acres, an old farmhouse and my dad to raise by herself from when he was two. She survived by praying a lot and walking three miles into town every day, pulling the baby on a sleigh or wagon, to clean the church and other people's houses. Once my dad turned fifteen, he quit school and worked odd jobs till he got on the township road crew and made enough digging ditches so Grandma Parr could stay home.

Before Arnie was twelve, my dad moved his work bench and tools to the barn and Arnie painted and hung a sign over the front door of the cabin — ARNIE'S MUSEUM, Arnie J. Parr, Curator — and got my dad to wire an old ship's lantern beside it on one side and a revolving glass barber pole on the other side. At night you could see Arnie's pole all the way to the concession road, spinning upwards toward heaven.

Arnie's Museum is the log cabin where the original settlers lived, two big rooms downstairs and a loft upstairs barely high enough to stand up in and only over the back half. You can sit in the loft and look down on what used to be the living room and kitchen.

The Museum is on a hill slope beside our house. It's surrounded by lilacs and boulders of rose and gray granite, some as big as a car, scattered around an old orchard of tangled apple and cherry trees which Arnie said were authentic and couldn't be cut down. Nothing has been cut down and the orchard is exactly as Arnie left it except for the visitors, the wildflowers and the sculpture. Some visitors come to see the orchard full of wildflowers but most come to see the sculpture. I know Arnie would like the flowers and sculpture and declare both authentic.

Arnie said practically everything about his Museum was authentic. He said his Queen Victoria was the original one from Tussaud's, sold off when they made a fresh replacement. He said her clothes came from Queen Victoria's own boudoir and he lifted her skirts to show visitors her authentic knickers. He said the queen's bed was authentic nineteenth-century bird's-eye maple. He got it at an auction for twelve dollars because it was so huge nobody else wanted it and it had a post missing. My dad made the missing post on his lathe out of red maple and Arnie stained it to match, including several authentic imitation bird's-eyes.

Everything was for sale — except Queen Victoria and her bed and one war medal — but Arnie never said so. There were no price tags. Arnie just attached to every object an official-looking file card with a typed description that included the estimated value. 'Authentic 19th century butter bowl hand carved from Peterborough County pine. Note the exquisite black markings and the delicate slope rising from the gently curved bottom to the flaring rim. Estimated value $75.' Arnie found that bowl in the township dump full of tar and paid me to clean it up.

The medal not for sale and actually authentic was the Victoria Cross which Mr. Townsend gave Arnie. Mr. Townsend was old and poor so my dad cut firewood for him and Mom and Grandma Parr went to his place once a month to scrub and sent Arnie with food every Sunday. Otherwise, Mr. Townsend ate mostly bread and tea and beans from cans.

Mr. Townsend was no relation to us and not very clean or even friendly. I was always afraid of him and none of us kids ever went near there, except Arnie. Grandma Parr said we had to help Mr. Townsend out because it was the Christian thing to do. Arnie went every Sunday night and stayed a long time. He told me he stayed so long to escape family scripture reading which was going on at the same time in our living room.

Arnie took his guitar and sang and he took his own books and read to Mr. Townsend who was nearly blind and had only one leg from when he was shot up in the first world war and won three medals. Arnie liked to read out loud and put on all the different voices. My first memories of Arnie are of him reading me bedtime stories and whipping on and off funny hats and other things which he kept in a trunk. When Mr. Townsend died, everyone was surprised that he had a will and left Arnie his war medals and all his money, $912, and everything else he owned, which wasn't much.

From the summer he was twelve and I was ten, Arnie's Museum was open to the public Saturday and Sunday afternoons and I was assistant curator. Arnie ran a small ad in the town paper and we were in business. The way he got away with Sunday opening — our grandfather being a minister and our family being religious — was to say his museum was a cultural establishment not a commercial one. It wasn't his fault if some visitor made him a quiet offer he couldn't refuse. He said, "Us curators have to cut deals with itchy collectors, Panther."

My name is Bill but Arnie called me Panther because of my jet black hair which he liked and always trimmed for me the way he liked it. Once in a long while he called me Billy Boy.

The summer Arnie is fourteen he says to me, "Hey Billy Boy, wanta get laid?"

I'm barely twelve and just starting to change.

"I don't think so Arnie."

"Do me a favour, Panther. Pretend."

How can I refuse Arnie anything since he always takes me places and jokes around with me and teaches me guitar chords and his best moves in hockey and buys me fifty-pound bags of seeds at the co-op for my bird feeders? Not like our older brother, Fred, who says to leave his stuff alone and won't even let me touch his animals.

So Arnie gives me lessons how to act like I want to get laid. By this time Arnie knows something about acting. Dave Bond's mother is a sculptor and every time she takes a statue to her gallery in Toronto she takes Dave and Arnie along and they all go to some play, which Arnie loves, especially musicals. He also has under his belt one production of the high school drama club, not to mention the Christmas concerts he starred in at Sunday school and public school.

The purpose of my acting is to divert attention from Arnie who is really the one who wants to get laid. Arnie is famous for his diversionary tactics in hockey and football but is just as good at diverting my mom or dad or, in this case, a girl who likes him.

Twins from Ottawa, a boy and girl, thirteen, are visiting three farms away for two weeks and Arnie can't get the boy into the barn without the girl tagging along. Arnie is always over there trying. Time is running out. He tells her I'm thirteen and crazy about her type, which is small and blond and cute. He tells her I'm better looking than he is, positively handsome. This is not exactly true but hardly anything Arnie says is exactly true, except according to him.

Six or seven rehearsals later, Arnie gels my hair and hangs an earring on me and puts my Blue Jays cap on me backwards and arranges it just so. He shoves his pack of cheroots in my shirt pocket and unbuttons my shirt almost to my belly button. He puts one of his condoms in plain sight behind a plastic window in my wallet opposite the picture I'm supposed to show her of me in hockey uniform. He pads my underwear with a pair of wadded socks to add what he calls a 'touch of maturity' and off we go on our bikes, me sweating buckets, Arnie singing.

This actually works. I remember all my lines. She agrees to go to the woods with me and look for deer while Arnie shows her brother how to swing in the hayloft.

"I'll show you the ropes," says Arnie.

The brother ends up staying a month at our place but his sister goes back to Ottawa. Meanwhile, Dave Bond is at a cottage in Muskoka with a friend from Upper Canada whose grown-up brother teaches orienteering and takes the two of them camping every weekend in Algonquin Park. Arnie and Dave are still best friends but don't do it with each other any more because by now Dave goes exclusively for older guys and Arnie only fools around with boys about his own age.

Dave reports to Arnie that every night after his friend is asleep, he gets in the older brother's sleeping bag and they do some fancy orienteering which he describes in detail. Arnie reads Dave's letters to his new friend and to Queen Victoria who is sitting out the summer in an authentic nineteenth-century cherrywood rocker, estimated value $275, so Arnie's new friend can have her place in bed. I get to listen since Arnie lets me sleep in the Museum loft on hot nights right under the 'authentic Somerset Maugham fan circa 1920 reminiscent of Raffles Hotel in Singapore, estimated value $185.' It's cooler there than our bedroom in the house.

Now that I'm eighteen, our old house with three bedrooms and one bath seems too small for nine people — six kids and my parents and Grandma Parr. Back then, it seemed big, mainly because of the huge attic where Arnie pitched his giant tent.

All four of us boys slept in the attic, even Arnie in winter, for two reasons: it was hard to heat the Museum with the wood stove; and besides somebody had to get him up for school and especially for early morning hockey. It had to be me because his tent had a sign in front BY INVITATION ONLY and I was the only one with a permanent invitation. I slept inside the tent except once in a while when Arnie had company in which case I slept just outside like a guard. I *was* a guard. Arnie said so.

Arnie got his tent for nothing from the lawn bowling club in town where it was used for years in case of rain at the annual picnic, till one end caught fire and they decided to get rid of it. Even without the burnt end, it took up one entire side of the attic. Arnie did a lot of cutting and sewing and painting and trimming and finally pronounced it the authentic headquarters tent of Lawrence of Arabia.

It contained a sideboard with shelves and doors above, an oak wardrobe, a huge low table with ram's heads for legs, three folding screens, and so many hangings, pictures, lanterns, steamer trunks, cushions and rugs that there was hardly room for the really neat stuff: a copper samovar, a hookah, a travelling bathtub of hand-painted tin which Arnie kept full of hockey equipment. My favourite was the camel saddle which Arnie let me sit on to watch his TV. Arnie liked to sit on Lawrence's authentic motorcycle circa 1922.

I doubt if Lawrence fed birds in his tent but Arnie said why not and cut a hole exactly the right size where his tent came up against an attic window. I built a feeder on the sill and every morning at dawn a cardinal came and waited for me. Chickadees flew right inside and ate from my hand while I filled the feeder.

Arnie slept on the floor in different places around the tent but usually on a low platform covered with a feather tick, which in turn was covered with a tapestry showing pilgrims, which in turn was covered with cushions of many colours. This was the authentic reproduction bed of the authentic Lawrence of Arabia from Tussaud's. Arnie found Lawrence in some basement at the same time he found Queen Victoria.

Lawrence came with two complete Arab costumes so Arnie wore one outfit most of the time he was in the tent and always when he slept on the platform with Lawrence. Sometimes at five in the morning, when I was hardly awake myself, I tried to waken Lawrence by mistake. When he slept in the Museum with Queen Victoria, Arnie was usually bare because of summer heat but if it was chilly he wore his Prince Albert outfit. Arnie never owned Prince Albert though, just his authentic clothes.

I'm sound asleep under the table with ram's-head legs, which is one of my favourite places. Arnie crawls under and shakes me and says, "Wake up Panther. We need a cheroot."

I know something is up because we only smoke in emergencies. This is when Arnie is fourteen and me twelve and he's had the same package of cheroots for two years and it's still nearly full. I look after

Arnie's cheroot package and his condoms and his magazines with nude guys — everything like that which somebody might look for in Arnie's stuff but would never dream of looking for in my stuff because I'm such a quiet kid. I even look after Arnie's secret bankbook for the account he keeps in Toronto. My parents don't pay much attention to the Museum so they have no idea Arnie has $4,628 in addition to the account in town which they know about, $1,376.

Arnie sends me to make sure Fred and Donnie are asleep. Fred is seventeen and Donnie eight. They sleep in bunk beds on the other side of the attic. (My sister Jean who is fifteen and Alice who is six have one of the bedrooms down on the second floor.) I take the flashlight and pick my way across the middle of the attic which is full of Arnie's barbells and dumbbells and benches that all four of us use to get stronger for hockey.

Fred has his side of the attic fixed up with 4H Club posters and a Norman Rockwell picture that Arnie describes as some rube leading a calf around or vice versa. Fred raises calves and wins 4H prizes. He wants to be a vet so he studies hard all the time and goes to bed early so he can get up early and look after his animals before school.

Arnie hardly ever studies or does any homework and he stays up all hours writing his journals and drawing and reading books that have nothing to do with school. When I get back from checking on Fred, I notice Arnie is writing in his secret journal as well as puffing his cheroot.

"Have a drag, Panther. Tonight, I did it with a girl."

"How come Arnie?"

"Mrs. Peck."

"You did it with your math teacher?"

Mrs. Peck is the high school vice-principal but she teaches one math class.

"With one of her daughters. Nancy. Have another drag, Panther."

This is six months after the episode with the twins and in that time I've developed more of what they call in health class secondary sex characteristics. I'm all ears.

"How was it, Arnie?"

"Cold."

"Your thing or hers or both, Arnie?"

"The couch on her back porch. We got caught. Mrs. Peck is gonna tell Dad and Grandpa and the principal. Have another drag, Panther."

Grandpa is the Reverend Frederick Smothers, my mom's father, who is the minister of our church which is the same one where Mrs. Peck leads the choir and the principal, Mr. Bark, sings tenor solos and leads the men's Bible class. Mr. Bark knows my dad well because Dad attends the men's Bible class, which Arnie says is just Sunday school without crayons.

I'm not in high school yet but I know Mr. Bark and Mrs. Peck and Nancy from church. I also know Nancy has always liked Arnie and Mrs. Peck has always not liked him because she says he's too big for his boots and needs to be brought down a peg. Mrs. Peck is full of phrases like that which she lets out in little bursts like she was spitting darts. But other times she can be quite smiley if she feels like it. When people are congratulating her after an organ solo, she can hold a smile throughout an entire conversation as though it was carved in her face. She smiles at me when she arrives at the last minute for choir practice and gets me to hang up her black fur coat which smells of perfume and has a red silk lining.

Every time Mrs. Peck reports Arnie to Dad or Grandpa for showing off in choir, Arnie tells me she's just frustrated because nobody does it to her since her husband died. Arnie says Mrs. Peck has the hots for Mr. Bark. Arnie says he can tell by the trendy way she fixes her hair and mascara and then looks at Mr. Bark like an ad for ladies' underwear while she plays the organ and he sings 'Because you come to me with naught save love,' and stuff like that for weddings.

"How come you did it to Nancy, Arnie?"

"Rupert Bark."

Rupert is the principal's son. He's a year older than Arnie but in the same class because Arnie skipped a grade. Rupert is on a hockey team that Arnie plays against and Arnie once broke Rupert's tooth in a dressing-room fight and another time broke his collarbone on the ice. Both times Arnie was just getting back at Rupert who makes up for being a bit too short and stocky by being a bit too under-handed. Arnie has a quick temper which he appears to get over right away, but he also remembers for a long time till exactly the right opportunity for getting even comes along.

"You did it to Nancy Peck to get even with Rupert Bark for something?"

"Sort of. Rupert asked Nancy to go steady and took her to the Girls Athletic Association dance tonight to suck up to Mrs. Peck so she'd give him the lead in *Guys and Dolls*."

"So you took Nancy away from Rupert at the dance and took her home so she'd break off with Rupert and be your girlfriend to help you suck up to Mrs. Peck till she gives you the lead, but Mrs. Peck caught you doing it on the back porch."

"That last part was Nancy's idea. She said she was gonna do it with Rupert anyway to seal their engagement to go steady."

"How was it, Arnie?"

"Nothing. Have another drag, Panther."

Arnie loved to sing and dance and entertain. It wasn't that his voice was so great, just that it was so loud or soft, happy or sad, whatever he wanted it to be. When Arnie played his guitar and sang "Four Strong Winds," he sang softly and sadly and he felt it so much that you could see tears in his eyes and it made you cry just listening. Even Grandma Parr, who didn't go in for anything but hymns, wiped her eyes. When Arnie sang "Hey Look Me Over" at the scouts' concert, I looked around and every single face was smiling, even Grandma Parr.

Arnie was the best dancer in the whole county, the same fast and fancy footwork he used for hockey. He did a tango with Queen Victoria for museum visitors every Saturday at three. He used to grab my mom or my sister Jean — even Grandma Parr who didn't believe in dancing — and dance them around the kitchen. They always said, "Stop that, you silly thing." But you could tell they liked it. Most girls and women liked Arnie a lot. And he liked them a lot — to dance and joke with.

I think Arnie was my mom's favourite. Not that she ever said so or did anything that was unfair to the rest of us. It was just the special way she looked at Arnie after hockey games when we sat around the kitchen table and she fed us pancakes and cocoa while my father recapped every play and told us our mistakes. Mom always stopped what she was doing whenever Arnie spoke and stood by the sink or the stove or the fridge, on one leg, with the foot of her bad leg hooked around the ankle of the good one, and turned her head around to look at Arnie.

Arnie got five times as many lectures from Dad as the rest of us put together but he was Dad's favourite too. Now that I'm older and have been through therapy I know a bit about psychology and I figure Dad was reconstructing his own life through Arnie. My dad thinks hockey is the closest thing to heaven on earth, but he wasn't big enough as a kid or good enough or rich enough to play much hockey — just shinny with old skates and sticks people gave his mother when she cleaned their houses. But he played with the road crew team for twenty years, from the time he was sixteen; and everybody said he was the best coach around in the kids' leagues. So when Arnie came along and was the best player around, my dad's black-and-white life started over again in technicolour.

Dad was fair, though. He displayed Fred's prizes for calves and Jean's for needlework, or whatever any of us won; but he was always busy making frames and shelves for Arnie's press clippings and news photos and trophies. He also framed the letter signed by him and Arnie and my grandfather saying Arnie would be sixteen when he finished grade twelve and that would be the earliest time at which Arnie would discuss hockey contracts with NHL scouts. Arnie's stuff is all gone now but back then it was displayed all over the house and Dad gave visitors a tour with running commentary that was total recall and went on and on till my mom said, "Come along now, Dad. Tea's ready."

The rest of us liked Arnie best too, even Fred and even before Arnie gave him money to go to Guelph University. When Fred was sixteen and fell in love for the first time, his idea of a date was arm wrestling and playing monopoly on the kitchen table. Arnie gave him what he called chatting-up-chick lessons, cut his hair a different way, bought him new clothes and taught him to dance. It worked.

Arnie was forever carrying Donnie or Alice around over his shoulder like a sack, to and from the van, up and down the stairs, around and around the pond when he put on his figure skates and got going like a rocket and then did his whirls and twirls while the kid over his shoulder giggled and screeched.

The only one not that fond of Arnie was Grandpa Smothers. When I was little, I thought Grandpa Smothers must be the next thing to God in perfection till Arnie told me, "You gotta see through people, Panther." I began to think Grandpa's problem was that *he* thought he was the next thing to God in perfection. Now I think he was scared of his own weaknesses and the front of perfection was his way of faking it, getting by. Even now that he's retired he still spouts scripture to cover his ignorance and he won't read the books I give him to help him understand Arnie.

Arnie had lots of run-ins with Grandpa but never took him too seriously and always called him 'the rev' even at Sunday school. When he was sixteen, Arnie told me the rev thought all of us Parrs were below par, beneath him, but he accepted us because our dad was the only one who dated his oldest daughter, our mother, after she fell off the wagon during a church hay ride and crushed her leg leaving an otherwise pretty girl with a bad limp.

We're at the hockey banquet in the church hall and the church ladies are catering. Arnie is ten and I'm eight. We're both starved. Meat is already on the tables and my mom and the other ladies are standing over by the kitchen door with their aprons on waiting to serve vegetables. The aroma of scalloped potatoes with cheese, his favourite, drives Arnie crazy. The sight of hot juices running down glazed hams is more than he can bear. The rev is saying one of his boring prayers that goes on forever. Christ this and Christ that. Arnie leans over to me and says, "Christ, I'm hungry."

Grandpa glares at us but carries on and eventually gets to, "Lord, bless this food to our use, and us to Thy service, for Christ's sake. Amen."

Arnie says, "For Christ's sake pass the ham."

Grandpa descends on us and says, "What did you say?"

Rupert Bark who is sitting opposite beside his father says, "He swore."

I knew Arnie was joshing Grandpa not Christ. I never ever heard Arnie swear even when he hit his finger or something. Maybe an occasional four-letter word on the bus with the big boys.

Arnie heaves a whole jug of tomato juice and gets Rupert but also gets Mr. Bark who is in his best blue pinstripe suit because later he's going to sing "On the Road to Mandalay" and other manly songs that he always sings at hockey banquets. Mr. Bark lets off one of the bursts for which he's famous at school. My grandfather plucks Arnie up by the back of his collar and marches him out. Later, while Mr.

Bark is singing in his wet suit, 'Give me some men who are stout-hearted men,' I sneak up to where Arnie is locked in the vestry and take him all the food I can stuff in my pockets. But Arnie is gone, out the window.

Arnie never said anything when Dad and Mr. Bark teamed up with Grandpa to lead the fight against ordaining homosexuals in our church. Dad was forever practising what he would say at some meeting: keep perverts from the pulpit of the Lord; don't invite the wolf to tend the flock; protect family values by keeping molesters away; unspeakable acts of indecency; depraved sodomites . . .

When Grandpa Smothers roared from the pulpit about degenerate abominations, I glanced sideways at Arnie and wondered what he was thinking. He never let on. But when he was fifteen, Arnie read me a headline in the town paper, 'Smothers, Parr and Bark win congregation vote to ban gay preachers.' Arnie said, "Aw shucks, Panther, I'll have to give up my dream of being a preacher man."

Actually, I was the only one in the family that dreamed of being a minister. I always just knew that's what God wanted me to be. I never knew why He wanted me because I wasn't as good at anything as Arnie but my mom said God works in mysterious ways and I should just follow my heart.

I never heard Arnie dream about being anything in the future, not even a hockey star. He was too busy being Arnie in the present. Arnie could have been lots of things besides a professional hockey player: an actor, movie director, museum curator, antique dealer, executive, politician, professor, lawyer, salesman.

There were only a few things Arnie wasn't good at: doing chores around home, telling the simple truth without what Grandpa Smothers called embellishment, mathematics, composition, anything mechanical. He was good at math in public school but lost interest after Mr. Bark got on his case and kept putting him in Mrs. Peck's classes as a punishment after the Nancy episode on the back porch.

Mr. Bark taught one English class every year and he kept putting Arnie in it for the same reason. Arnie wrote a lot of stuff, almost as much as I did, and we read our stuff to each other so I know his was good, more exciting than mine, but Mr. Bark didn't appreciate his stream of consciousness, his mix of fact and fancy, his sudden changes of topic. Arnie refused to use quotation marks and Mr. Bark took off so many marks Arnie's results were artificially low.

Arnie said, "People don't talk in quotation marks, Panther, so I don't write in them. If it's good enough for James Joyce, it's good enough for me." He showed me in books where James Joyce wrote without quotation marks. He also showed Mr. Bark but it didn't do any good.

Arnie scraped and painted and patched stuff for his Museum but never touched clocks or motors. Anything mechanical, even his bike, he brought to me or Dad to fix. His first year in high school, Dad insisted Arnie take one basic tech course called Fixit to find out about repairing household appliances and motors. Arnie drove the technical director nutty and vice versa. Mr. Karp was a fussy man who wore white smocks over his wide ties and polyester suits — about twenty years out of date, according to Arnie who read GQ and was a stylish dresser.

Arnie is jazzing around with the big kids and forgets his lunch on the school bus. I notice it and keep it all morning and run over to the high school with it at noon. This is the first time I've ever been there while school is on and it scares me, so big and so many people.

Mr. Bark is standing with his arms folded over his barrel chest in front of the trophy case in the rotunda growling orders at kids passing to and from the cafeteria. He sees everything so he sees me, but he just looks up timetables and points me straight down a corridor, about a mile long, which leads to the tech wing. I find Arnie in one corner of a shop so big it makes me feel like a midget. He's being kept in at noon because he can't get his small motor back together. He's pacing around, stalking the motor.

I say, "That piece goes on over there, Arnie. Watch."

Sure enough, it works, and Arnie buys me a coke and shows me off to his friends in the cafeteria as a genius. He also shows me Black Lightning which is a souped-up Firebird, the pride of Mr. Karp. Mr. Karp and his favourite students keep working on Black Lightning to make it the most perfect car in the world. The outside is gleaming black with a ton of chrome including the name Black Lightning in fancy letters like in Grandpa's best Bible. The entire interior is tufted in blood-red glove leather. The engine is so hot that no car in town has been able to match it when Mr. Karp has his Zero-to-Sixty contest on the football field every year to raise money for extra shop supplies. Black Lightning is sitting like a jewel on a red velvet platform which is up a ramp a foot above the shop floor.

Nobody is around so Arnie says, "Come on Panther, climb in."

Arnie is thirteen and doesn't drive but pushes pedals and gears and says, "Vroom, vroom," and turns the key. Black Lightning flashes straight ahead off the platform and strikes a concrete wall.

Mr. Karp was also the person in charge of student council and Arnie had just been elected representative of his grade nine class. The second year Arnie was student council secretary, the year after that vice-president, and the fourth year he was president. Arnie could have got elected just on his fame as a hockey player but his campaign speeches were sensational too. He took Queen Victoria to school and danced with her on stage while the entire school clapped and whistled. Mr. Karp banned dummies and Arnie asked — for clarification — if that meant Mr. Karp would resign.

For the next election campaign, Arnie dressed in his Lawrence of Arabia clothes and when he walked out on stage his supporters started to chant Arnie, Arnie, Arnie the way they chanted Lawrence,

Lawrence, Lawrence in the film *Lawrence of Arabia*. Pretty soon the whole school was chanting Arnie, Arnie, Arnie and the big boys were carrying him up and down the aisles on their shoulders while Arnie threw kisses. When Mr. Karp banned costumes, Arnie asked — for clarification — if that meant Mr. Karp would stop wearing his present wardrobe of period costumes.

Arnie called Mr. Karp, Mrs. Peck and Mr. Bark the gang of three. Every time Arnie got in a bind with one of them, Mr. Bark chewed him out and then phoned my father and Arnie would be lectured and then grounded for a few days from everything except hockey. Supper the night of a call from Mr. Bark would be unusually silent and right after, Mom would take the rest of us into the living room and leave Arnie with Dad at the kitchen table. Mom stayed in the front hall straightening pictures. Dad lectured Arnie about what was expected of him and Arnie said hardly anything except, "Yes sir," because all Dad ever asked him was, "You know what I expect from you, don't you?"

You could tell it was nearing the end of a lecture when you heard Dad and Arnie together reciting the Lord's Prayer. You could tell it was the end when Mom went almost to the kitchen door and said, "Come along now, Dad. Time for scripture reading."

If it was Wednesday or Sunday night when Arnie got a lecture, it took longer because Grandpa's housekeeper had those nights off and Grandpa came to our house for supper. He stayed in the kitchen to help lecture Arnie and said several prayers. Mom never interrupted when Grandpa was there and sometimes the lecture went on till nearly eight.

One Sunday night in September the lecture took till after nine o'clock and for the first time Dad closed the kitchen door. For the first time, Arnie talked back. He yelled. But we couldn't make out anything except, "Dave — school — Bark," a few words like that. Afterwards, Arnie ran out the kitchen door to the Museum. I ran out the front door after him.

Arnie is sixteen and in grade twelve and president of the student council and he's crying. I've never seen him cry before. He's sitting on the bed beside Queen Victoria. I sit beside him and say, "Don't cry Arnie." I think of saying I love you Arnie but we don't say things like that in our family so I just start to cry too. I'm fourteen and in grade nine and I don't even know what we're crying about.

After a while Arnie tapers off and finally says, "We need a cheroot, Panther. Dave Bond has AIDS."

I take that in while Arnie lights a cheroot so dry it breaks and he has to light half.

"Will he die, Arnie?"

"Yes."

"How soon?"

"A few months, a year. Depends."

A terrible thought strikes me.

"Do you have it too, Arnie?"

"No. Dr. Bond got me tested."

Arnie shows me the report. Negative. I feel better till I think of Dr. and Mrs. Bond. They're so sophisticated and so nice, especially Mrs. Bond. She always makes a fuss over me when Arnie takes me there and she kisses me just like she kisses Dave and Arnie. We don't go in for kissing at our house except for Arnie who must have got it from the Bonds.

"Have a drag, Panther."

Arnie has been at the hospital and at Dave's house every day all summer. But everyone thinks it's just a bad case of pneumonia.

"How come you didn't tell me before, Arnie?"

"They were going to keep it a private family matter. They only told me. But Dave's feeling better and he wants to start school tomorrow, here. They decided to go public to educate people. Bark doesn't want him in school. Bark told Dad and Grandpa. They agree with Bark."

"Because Dave's gay?"

"No. Just because of AIDS. They don't know he's gay. Dr. Bond told Bark about the blood transfusion Dave had when he got hit on his bike. That was before they tested blood."

"Is that how he got it?"

"Possible. Not likely. Dave's friend, the guy who taught orienteering — he died of AIDS."

Dave Bond went to school and everything changed at our house in the next three months. There was one terrible fight in September, at our kitchen table, when Arnie threw back his chair and thundered around the room, "Can't you get it through your head that nobody at school will catch it from Dave?"

Dad said, "Look at you right now. Three football scrapes that I can see. Most kids have cuts and scrapes. David Bond too. Not to mention washroom waste. Put the two together —"

But Arnie was gone out the kitchen door.

Every meal was tense. Even hockey and church talk were strained. Nobody asked any longer, "What happened at school today?" Everybody already knew. The school was split in two, on one side Arnie and most of the student council executive and quite a few outspoken students and some teachers willing to stand against the principal; on the other side the gang of three and all the teachers interested in good reports from the principal at promotion time and a lot of strong-minded, conservative kids.

Arnie took on any kid who dared say anything against Dave. He had several skirmishes and two big fights, one at football practice and one in the locker corridor. Both times he won and both times several people had to hold him to stop him from pulping the other guy. Mr. Bark wanted to suspend Arnie but he didn't, partly because Arnie was essential to the football team, but also because my dad was on Bark's side and asked him to give Arnie another chance.

All of this was going on while I was in my first term in high school and feeling kind of lost and scared but at the same time proud because people were slowly finding out that I was Arnie's brother.

I'm at my locker and Marilyn Dewey is right behind me and I'm so nervous I can't undo my combination and I drop my jacket. Marilyn is the most beautiful girl in grade nine and the one I can't get out of my mind especially at night when I'm doing what Arnie says all boys do before going to sleep, what Arnie describes as the world's favourite sleeping pill — Arnie says sleeping pull — the only one that's free and has no adverse side effects.

Marilyn isn't in any of my classes and I've never spoken to her but I've followed her in the halls close enough to smell the perfume of her hair. I've watched her from behind the potted plants, darting around like a dazzling humming bird when the table tennis club plays in a corner of the rotunda at noon.

Marilyn picks up my jacket and says, "Are you really Panther Parr?"

I drop my books! Pencils and stuff fly all over. My heart pounds and my forehead breaks out in sweat. I'm unable to speak and barely able to stand. I grunt something which I hope sounds like yes and squat down to pick up my stuff. People are milling around. The warning bell rings. She squats down to help me, very close.

She says, "I was wondering if you like table tennis —"

All of a sudden I'm so wild to join the table tennis club that I topple over from my squat and brush against Marilyn taking her with me which is embarrassing but no big deal; but Mr. Bark comes rushing through the crowd roaring, "What's going on? What's going on there?" He yanks my collar at the back and snarls, "Leave her be."

Just then Arnie comes along and sees me being dragged by Mr. Bark and Arnie grabs me away and shoves Mr. Bark so hard he ends up on the floor. Arnie ends up suspended from school but only for a week since Mr. Bark is on shaky ground blaming me for something I didn't do on purpose. I end up going steady with Marilyn.

Dad said the suspension was justified because Mr. Bark was just doing his duty and made an honest mistake which would have been straightened out easily and Arnie had no business interfering and pushing his superiors and no attack on a teacher is ever justified. Arnie had to stay in the house for that week and couldn't even phone Dave Bond who was home feeling sick because of flu that was going around town. So I went to Dave's house every day at noon and took notes back and forth. That wasn't too risky because the main one who might see me was Grandpa Smothers and he was also sick with flu.

Things settled down slowly and by mid-October, it looked as though Arnie and Dave had won. Mr. Bark and my dad and Grandpa Smothers had fallen into silence. The town paper and the Catholic and Anglican priests had come out in favour of Dave going to school and the physical education teachers were doing AIDS awareness in health classes. In spite of Mr. Bark, they invited Dave and his father to speak.

All the grade nine boys are crowded into the big room beside the library. Dave is so thin and pale I can hardly imagine he is the same person who used to ride his bike out to our place. There are big dark spots on his face. Dave and Dr. Bond do a presentation taking turns. Dave sits down while his dad is speaking but drags himself up when it's his turn and Dr. Bond stands beside him and looks at him with an expression I've never seen before. I think it must be love and pride and grief mixed together.

The presentation is sensational. Words like anal sex, oral sex, penetration, ejaculation, climax. Tension pumps up in the room till it feels like the roof will blow. Dr. Bond pulls a plastic penis from his bag. Some boys catch their breath all at the same time and you can hear it; some titter. Dr. Bond shows how to roll a condom on the penis and the room is tomb quiet. The head of physical education stares at the floor. Dr. Bond recommends free condoms in school. A few boys stage whisper, "Yeah!"

But one kid blurts out, "What for? There's no queers here."

Dr. Bond says, "As time goes on, more and more heterosexuals will get the disease. Protect yourself."

Dave says, "Besides, about ten percent of any school is gay, including this school, including me."

That night my dad forbade Arnie to speak to Dave ever again. He made me gather up and return all the clothes Dave had given me. Dad said AIDS was the wrath of God on Dave for his sexual sins. Grandpa and Dad and Mr. Bark got their anti-gay committee from the church back together and demanded that the school board give Dave special education in a room by himself to protect the innocent from moral contamination.

What Grandpa described as 'voices of Christian charity reaching out' told Dave Bond to repent and renounce his sinful ways. A delegation of ladies, which included my mother, called on Mrs. Bond at home and delivered that message in her living room.

The next day Dave showed up at school wearing a t-shirt saying Proud To Be Gay and began slipping bits of gay rights information and facts about famous gay people into his answers in every class. In history, when they discussed great generals, Dave said, "Alexander the Great was gay and a general at sixteen, Julius Caesar was gay and the greatest general of all time, and Bernard Montgomery, the famous second world war field marshal — he loved a Swiss boy."

In English, when they discussed The Wars, the teacher said Timothy Findley won the Governor General's Award for it and Dave said, "Yes and gays like me are proud that Mr. Findley's gay too." Remarks like that spread around the school faster than rumours about the latest pregnancy.

There was an early snowfall and some kids threw snowballs at Dave on his way to school. A few hissed him in the halls. Once in a while, people called him names but he just went on as though they weren't there. Someone tripped him. I saw some big boys block the washroom so Dave couldn't get in but he just said, "Watch out fellas or I'll have to pee all over you." He started unzipping his fly. "Feel free to hit me. I'll just bleed on you." The boys parted like the Red Sea in one of Grandpa's sermons.

Somebody spray painted 'KILL QUEERS' on Dave's locker at school and on Bond's house. They slashed the tires and top of the Jeep Dave got for his sixteenth birthday. There were several nasty phone calls, all anonymous. When a threatening note came in the mail, Dr. Bond hired off-duty policemen as guards and one of them went to school with Dave and walked the corridors with him and stood outside his classes all day. Mr. Bark tried to bar the guards from school property but Dr. Bond went to the police with his lawyer and demanded protection at public expense and in the end the privately paid guards were allowed to stay.

Dad got the gang of three to watch Dave and make sure he stayed away from Arnie and vice versa, so Arnie got me to take notes back and forth. Days when Dave was home sick it was almost impossible to do safely in daylight because of Bond's house being so close to my grandfather's. I did it at dusk — this was mid-November — when lights were on inside and Grandpa wouldn't likely be looking out his study window.

I told Mom I was going to Marilyn's house to do homework after school (which was true) and that her mom or somebody would drive me home in time for supper (which wasn't exactly true). The 'somebody' was always Dave Bond's mother. I would take Arnie's letter or tape to Dave and wait for his answer while Mrs. Bond showed me her sculpture and stuff. Then she drove me home and let me off in the dark, behind the evergreens, down at the end of the lane. She kissed my cheek and said something like, "We appreciate what you're doing Panther. It means so much to Dave."

I was the one who carried all the messages back and forth planning the famous video.

Mrs. Bond drops me off in the dark as usual down at the gate only this time Dave is with me and I help him up the hill because he's so weak. We can see Arnie's barber pole and ship's lantern and I keep pointing to them saying, "See, it's not that far Dave," and I keep praying my dad won't come driving in and see us. I get Dave safely through the orchard, into the Museum and beside the stove, and then I run to the house just in time for supper. I wink at Arnie who winks back.

This is Friday night so after scripture reading Arnie and I go out to the Museum as usual to get it ready for Saturday opening. Only this time we spend the whole two hours making a video and several still pictures. Arnie has a gold throne rigged up in front of purple velvet curtains. In the first shot, Queen Victoria sits there in her royal ruby-red robe, only I'm underneath her so when I get up, she gets up. We've rehearsed this about a zillion times so, what with her width and her queen-size robe and with Arnie as cameraman, I'm never seen.

Arnie has removed Queen Victoria's arms from her dress and my arms are in there instead reaching around from behind. Arnie being Arnie, he has me rehearsed to do a few little things like wipe the Queen's nose and scratch her belly. She lifts her skirts and adjusts her knickers.

When she's finally ready, the Queen holds out her arm and Dave walks into the shot wearing his Proud To Be Gay shirt. Queen Victoria pins the Victoria Cross on him. Close up of Dave's chest slowly zooming right in on the medal. Cut to a sign saying 'The Victoria Cross, for acts of conspicuous bravery in the presence of the enemy.'

The video played continuously in the window of the town paper. There were always videos playing there — local sports, township council meetings, visiting dignitaries — but Arnie's was the only one that ever drew a crowd and stopped traffic on Main Street. The paper ran a front-page picture of Queen Victoria pinning the cross on Dave Bond right beside the word Gay in his motto Proud To Be Gay.

Copies of that picture made into flyers appeared all over town. As soon as they were torn down, new ones went up. The school was papered with them.

Arnie was grounded till New Year's and forbidden to play his guitar or watch TV or even play hockey. He wasn't allowed to ride the school bus. My sister Jean drove him to school and home again in the van. Fred was in university by then but Donnie and I went along in the van even though we could have gone on the bus. It was strange. Nobody talked. Jean was a nervous driver. Arnie was a super driver — better than Dad who was a professional driver of snow plows and bulldozers and dump trucks — but Arnie wasn't allowed to drive or do anything except go to school and church.

Rehearsals had started for the church Christmas concert but Grandpa cancelled Arnie's number, and instead Mom taught Jean and Alice to sing "Whispering Hope" because by then all the Christmas songs she could play on the piano were taken by someone else. She took Jean and Alice one at a time in the living room and played the piano and drilled them for hours because they had never sung harmony before. Alice had to learn the alto part and Jean the soprano. The house was full of the words: 'Wait till the darkness is over, hope for the sunshine tomorrow . . .' When they were finally able to sing together, the words were even stronger floating up to the attic: 'Then when the night is upon us, watch for the breaking of day . . .'

The double gym is open and the entire school is packed in for an assembly on the United Nations. My class is seated next to Marilyn's and by a little seat switching we're able to sit beside each other and hold hands. Arnie sits on stage beside the gang of three. As president of the student council he gets to thank the main speaker who is the local member of parliament just back from New York and quite enthusiastic about the UN Declaration of the Rights of the Child.

Arnie says, "And I've got just one suggestion about children's rights, sir. Give all the kids in the world who are naturally that way, the right to be gay. Including the hundred or more in this auditorium. I'm one of them. I'm gay. And just like Dave Bond, I'm proud of it. The only difference between Dave and me is I'm lucky and he's not. Oh yes, one other difference: I'm top, he's bottom."

By this time Mr. Bark has reached the podium and is fighting Arnie for the microphone. He is joined by Mrs. Peck who is flashing one of her cement smiles to the audience while flailing her arms trying to grab one of Arnie's; but Arnie's footwork is too fast for her. Mr. Karp runs off to the right to close the stage curtains. The member of parliament is frozen in his seat. It's Arnie against the gang of three.

Arnie yells into the mike, "Gays in the audience, stand up and shout, proud to be gay."

Mr. Bark cries out, "Assembly dismissed."

They grab the mike back and forth and each repeats the same message louder every time. Mrs. Peck, still smiling with her teeth clenched, has ahold of Arnie by one arm and he's shaking her off. The curtain is closing.

Dad padlocked the Museum and took down the tent. I was ordered to sleep in Fred's bed and Arnie was moved to the sofa bed in the living room. My grandfather and Dad were in there every night after supper on their knees with Arnie praying that he would be forgiven and cured. They told him he had to start seeing a psychiatrist in Peterborough and if he cooperated, the doctor and God together would heal him of being perverted.

Arnie was suspended, possibly expelled, pending investigation by the school board of five charges including inciting a riot, choking the principal with a microphone cord and swinging on a stage curtain with the vice-principal in tow.

Mr. Bark removed all of Arnie's trophies and pictures from the display cabinet in the rotunda. The big cabinet formed the entire wall between his office and the rotunda, glass on the rotunda side and sliding wooden panels on the office side. He opened the panels in his office and removed all traces of Arnie at noon while there were lots of students in the rotunda. I was one. It was like watching Arnie disappear.

Two janitors were in the school on a Saturday afternoon putting up the big Christmas tree on the far side of the rotunda. There had been a group in rehearsing with Mrs. Peck for the school Christmas assembly but they were gone. The janitors were just listening to "Hark the Herald Angels Sing" on the radio and talking over it, kind of joking, they said, about how the tree got bigger every year as they got older.

Down the long corridor from the tech wing came Black Lightning, full throttle, Arnie at the wheel, Dave Bond beside him, one singing "Hey Look Us Over," the other yelling "proud to be gay," Dave wearing the Victoria Cross, Queen Victoria and Lawrence of Arabia in the back seat. The car hurtled past the janitors, crashed through the display case as though it wasn't there, demolished Mr. Bark's desk, and imbedded itself in the far wall of his office, solid brick.

I get up in the middle of the night when Donnie starts to cry again. I take my pillow to prop against the wall and lean on to hold him till he goes back to sleep. I find Arnie's letter under my pillow.

Dear Panther,

By now you know but don't cry for me Panther it's okay just do me a favour and get them to cremate me and Dave and give our ashes to you to spread in the orchard when summer comes and you say a prayer or something and maybe sing us a song and play my guitar if you can remember the chords and say goodbye to everybody for me including Marilyn and my hockey team and yours and everybody at home and church and school and give some of my stuff to Donnie and Alice or somebody else if you want to because it's all yours now except Queen Victoria and Lawrence of Arabia who are going with me and I hope you use the money to have some fun including becoming a preacher because I like the idea of Panther the rev.

Well I have to go now to meet Dave.

    Your brother,

    Arnie

P.S. I never said it before but I should have because maybe you never knew I love you Panther.

I planned it for the Saturday of the church picnic so everyone else would be gone and just Dr. and Mrs. Bond would walk out in the orchard with Marilyn and me and find some nice places to sprinkle the ashes mixed with fifty pounds of assorted wildflower seeds. I would say a prayer I made up specially and try to get through the last verse of "Where Have All the Flowers Gone."

The Bonds arrived in their Mercedes followed by a flatbed truck followed by a crane, and now there stands in the orchard beside Arnie's Museum the most beautiful sculpture I've ever seen, one huge boulder twelve feet high of rose granite, just its natural shape and texture at the bottom but turning into people at the top.

On the left is Queen Victoria, on the right Lawrence of Arabia. Between them are Dave Bond and me. In the middle, taller than everyone, is Arnie smiling his biggest smile with one arm around me and the other around Dave. And imbedded in Arnie's chest right over his heart is the authentic Victoria Cross.

The inscription carved in granite reads: Arnie J. Parr 1973–1989 for acts of conspicuous bravery in the presence of the enemy.

. . .

Billy Parr is able to read the last lines of his story but just barely. He slides the story into his notebook and keeps looking down at it. A girl at the front hands him a tissue which he accepts and holds squeezed in one hand while he grips the edge of Halper's desk with the other. There is a long silence. Halper sits among the students and waits.

Bully Bullman claps lightly. One or two others join. The ripple rises. And then something happens that Halper has never seen before. The whole class stands up and applauds.

Gordon Wing says, "Let's hear it for Panther Parr." He begins a chant, "Pan-ther, Pan-ther, Pan-ther." The others join in.

After half a dozen questions by students, Halper comments, "Your brother's death must have had profound effects on your family, besides grief."

"It fell apart, more or less. My dad went to work on the roads miles away, down east, Renfrew, because he couldn't face people at home. He sent money but didn't visit except once in a while in and out on Sunday. Mom just clammed up, stopped going out except to some church things with my grandfather. Then she moved to Renfrew too, but just my sisters went because their

167

apartment only had two bedrooms. Donnie and I stayed with my grandfather. I was sort of okay for a few months, prayed a lot, but then I started having visions of Arnie. He spoke to me. He told me to put his school trophies in the new display case they built. They wouldn't. I decided to smash the display case. Dr. Bond realized I was cracking up and got me into therapy. The Bonds sort of adopted me. When Dr. Bond moved here to head family practice at the hospital, I came too. And he bought our old place and fixed it up as a weekend retreat. He says it's mine. The Jeep I drive was Dave Bond's."

Within days Billy's story is all over Midhill in gossip and hard copy. In class, then in the locker room, then everywhere, Billy Parr, Preacherman Parr, becomes Panther Parr. The student council president, the person and the office, have new stature. For the first time in his life Panther experiences what Gordon Wing refers to as 'the humiliation visited upon generations of children: arraignment before the star chamber.' Panther stands in front of the principal's desk while Fenton flicks through several pages, pulling each from its staple binding and discarding it like toxic waste.

Fenton says, "Mocking law and order. Ridiculing school administration. Glorifying queers. Sex and more sex. Violence. You wrote this rubbish?"

"That's not rubbish, sir. That's the truth about my brother."

"Then why wash your dirty laundry in public?"

"Arnie is not dirty laundry."

"Filthy might be a better word for gross perversion. What's got into you, Bill?"

"Truth, sir. Truth and the information necessary to find more truth. And the know-how to look for it. And the confidence to look for it and fight for it. And others to search with me. And someone to guide us."

"Well I'm giving you better guidance so listen. I'm responsible for the moral tone of this school and I want damage control. You understand? I want circulation halted. I want this trash recalled. You'll make an announcement on the p.a. Say you regret and withdraw."

"No sir. I can't do that. I won't."

"Then I'll do it for you and you'll sit out the next two weeks in the detention room before school, at noon and after school every day. No student council, no hockey, no Christian student club. Nothing but classes. Let's hope that brings you to your senses. Dismissed."

CHAPTER FIVE

Liz, in long black velvet slit to the knee, enters the den fastening a pearl ear ring and saying, "Why aren't you dressed?"

Halper waves their VISA bill and says, "For godsake Liz, $1,937.85 for clothes, extra clothes, for a fourteen-year-old. I tell her no but you take her shopping."

"She needs decent clothes for school. Besides, I saved far more than that by shaving my own clothing bill. Everybody but you will notice this is last year's dress."

"We don't have that kind of money for anybody's clothes, and we don't need private schools."

"You're the one always complaining about your typical high school. Get dressed."

"Private schools are the same model, just as bad. But the point is I want my last child at home with me, not being boarded in some posh stable like a thoroughbred in training."

"When would you see her? You're never home. I'd be stuck with all the responsibilities."

"She could go to Midhill, ride there and back with me, jog with me, have breakfast and dinner with me, help with the Greenhouse, be a Green."

"Never. I'll beg school fees from my mother and brother before I'll throw my daughter in with those losers. We owe it to Alison to give her a decent start in life."

"The same start we gave Simon and Jillian and look how well they turned out."

"You bastard. My mother was right about you, David. Brains and looks but no class. Class is bred in, and you haven't got it. Your father never got past managing a little bank branch on Danforth Avenue. Imitation classical columns in front. That's what's bred into you. And you've got your mother's school-teacher smallness. And her lack of mettle. Now get dressed. Your tux is on your bathroom door."

"You go. They're your friends anyway."

"They're our friends."

"Our friends means your friends. I have to see if I can make some winners of those losers."

Keiko Ito is the unopposed choice to chair the Greenhouse board. Gordon Wing, Lincoln Fenton and Panther Parr devise and present a thirty-point program proposal that gets all three elected to the board:

The Greenhouse may not be used for hanging out, except on

Saturday night or occasional nights designated as special events. Greens will not segregate according to age, sex, race, religion, etc. and instead will join various project teams according to individual interests, abilities and needs. Every Green must be working on at least one individual and one group learning project at all times. All projects will be reported at Greenhouse seminars as scheduled well in advance. All Greens will give high priority to attending all seminars. All Greens will adhere to the testing programs in reading, writing, speaking, listening, group skills, conflict resolution, mathematics, science, and such other tests as are added from time to time; and all Greens with test scores below expectancy (as defined by Maude Fenwick) will give priority to remedial tutorials and remedial computer programs. All Greens will participate in making decisions about management of the Greenhouse . . .

The same night, there is a party but it is only partly to celebrate the election. Claudius Ito is turning thirteen and Frank Stringer sixteen.

Many of the Greens have brought friends. Several of Halper's senior English and law students who are not yet Greens are there to look the place over. Halper has invited his wife and Alison but they have declined. His wife said, "I won't have Alison in a place like that especially with that flashy Ito tart."

Halper is dancing with Bully Bullman when Claudius Ito bursts onto the scene from the back room and grabs Halper's arm. "Sir. Sir, come quick and see! I just saw. In the washroom —"

Halper runs behind Claudius expecting to find a dead body, a rape in progress, a fight, a drug deal, someone guzzling liquor. But when they reach the washroom Claudius drops his pants and underwear in one swoop and shouts, "Look!"

"Where?"

"Right there!"

"What?"

"Can't you see it?"

"I don't know what I'm looking for."

"The hair. Right there. It's my birthday present from God. I've got pubic hair!"

"So you have. Well done, Claudius. Congratulations."

"How long do you think before you can really see it, sir?"

"Not long. A few weeks. By spring anyway."

"Then I'll be able to go to gym. Wow!"

"Don't you go now?"

Claudius looks down and pulls up his underwear and jeans and fusses with the belt until Halper puts one hand on his shoulder and uses the other to lift his chin.

"The other guys would laugh at me, sir. I wrote a note from my doctor to excuse me. You won't tell Mr. Duchok or my mom will you?"

"No, I won't tell anybody. But I'll try to persuade you to change your mind. Meanwhile, for exercise, I was thinking — I jogged a lot in the summer and I want to get back to it. You and I could jog every morning or night and see if some others want to. You could organize it. Is that okay?"

"Okay. But not tonight. Okay?"

"Okay."

Halper wonders if Simon agonized about pubic hair. He was a late maturer too. Halper realizes he never saw Simon's private parts. He was always a very private boy. Always at private schools. Alone. Halper hugs Simon. But it is Claudius Ito who hugs him back and says, "Thanks sir," and runs off to dance. He turns and says, "Sir, you think it's okay if I tell my mom about the hair? She's a girl."

"Oh sure. Nowadays you can tell girls just about anything, especially moms, especially yours."

"Wow, will she be surprised. Oh sir, Mom says she's sorry if she's late or maybe can't get here at all because she's hung up with some big hotel client, and she says I can invite you to dinner for my birthday Sunday. She's cooking all my favourites. You can bring your wife and daughter."

"I'd like that. Thanks Claudius. Just me though."

Lincoln parks his Mercedes in front of the Greenhouse. He and Gordon, in the front seats, are listening to quotes on kids' rights and responsibilities which Panther, in the back seat, reads from the manifesto he wants student council to send Fenton, the school board, and the government: 'Freedom of information is so important to children and to society that high school students have a moral responsibility to challenge and defy school boards and administrators when they are the oppressors.' 'People can be educated only to the extent they have the rights and responsibilities of self-determination. Subjugated people can only be indoctrinated.'

Halper steps out of the Greenhouse to help unload dim sum dishes the boys have brought for the Sunday morning meeting of the Greenhouse board. Panther opens his door but keeps on reading: 'Teachers should lead the discussion that will redefine children's rights and hence our models of childhood and schooling.'

Halper is about to agree when Lincoln gets out and says to him over the roof of the car, "I had a bad argument with Fenton at dinner last night. My mother sided with him. They said I can't go near the Greenhouse. So I took off for good. I slept at Gordon's."

"You should try to keep your family together. That's conventional wisdom." His own words sound hollow to Halper as they reverberate down the tunnels of memory. He recalls the togetherness of his own childhood, his father pronouncing on every topic at every family dinner, his mother's frequent 'yes dear,' his own silence.

"He's not my real family. And I don't approve of him." Lincoln slams the car door. "Oh, I kind of respect him in a way. He goes all out for whatever he thinks he should do. He was good to me when I was in hospital."

Gordon gets out, saying, "Fenton's good to anybody who plays his game by his rules and to nobody else. He thinks he's got the only game in town. That's the mark of a redneck like Fenton or an ethnocentric chink like my father."

"Or a Christian bigot like my father," Panther says.

"Or a gray rock like you were to Simon," Gordon says. "Why the hell doesn't somebody tell fathers that their kids are not supposed to be clones. That should go in our kids' rights declaration. Everybody knows fathers should never teach their kids to drive because they transfer their bad habits, but everyone thinks it's okay for fathers to force their lousy beliefs on sons who don't match them intellectually, emotionally — every which way."

Panther reads, " 'Children don't belong to parents, they belong to life, to life's yearning for itself.' "

When the others have gone inside carrying food, Lincoln says to Halper, "Fenton and I just don't mesh. Do you think I'm going to change to match him or him to match me?"

"No."

"I'm not giving up the Greenhouse. I've got my own money and I can live at Gordon's. He invited me. He likes me. He said so. And I want to end this adoption thing before it's final. I want my own name back. And I want to make a will or something so Fenton can never get my money. I feel kind of excited but also kind of shaky. Could we talk after the board meeting, just the two of us?"

Panther has finished his detention sentence and is on stage with Fenton, Duchok and six candidates in the federal election. As president, he is emcee, and for an hour has been remembering the day his brother Arnie was president and emcee. Gordon Wing, as editor, and four other student leaders, have asked the approved questions on employment, the economy, the environment, and national unity and have received the usual political replies.

Gordon asks one more question, "How many of you candidates agree there is and should be such a thing as a Canadian culture that's worth keeping, and that multiculturalism is a divisive abomination which should be replaced by multiracialism within a Canadian culture?"

Silence. A ripple of applause. Fenton shifts back and forth in his seat and frowns. The first candidate to answer takes what he thinks is the safe ground of minority rights rhetoric, but turns it to sentimental ooze and sinks in a slough of political correctness pulling each successive speaker after him. While they wallow, Panther Parr says a silent prayer, 'Dear Jesus be with me. This one is for you, Arnie.' He loosens his tie, takes off his jacket, and jumps in.

"Minority rights," Panther says. "Let's devote the rest of our time to the rights of the minority group in this audience: teens. Most of us are denied the right to vote in the coming federal election. What will you do about the franchise for all teens?"

Panther pauses, the audience applauds, the politicians puff up with platitudes and lean toward their microphones. But Panther continues, "November 19 has been declared Children's Day. Which of you will stand up that day and declare that kids are exploited because of labour laws and attitudes originally intended to protect us from exploitation. The economy would collapse without our cheap labor in sectors such as food, health, entertainment, transportation and retailing, but we are denied even the minimum wage people over eighteen get for the same work. We are denied the right to make contracts, join unions, get unemployment benefits. That's modern slavery. What will you do about higher pay and a fair share of the economic pie for teens?"

Cheers from the audience. Politicians glance at Fenton and Duchok who shake their heads no and point at their watches to signal time is short.

Panther takes his microphone from its stand and crosses to the politicians, "Scores of kids in this school and every school live on their own in appalling conditions. What will you do about decent housing for teens?"

More cheers. Fenton and Duchok stand up and point again at their watches. Panther raises his voice over the cheers, "We have no say in running this school, no say in decisions about our own education. We should evaluate teachers. We should participate in decisions about everything: budget, discipline, curriculum . . . How come our curriculum never includes children's studies? We have black studies, women's studies, environmental studies, every kind of studies except about us, the kids. I'll tell you how come. Because you adults know if we the kids found out who we are it would empower us, and the last thing you want is for us to have any power. The student government of which I am president is a sham entitled to make decisions up to and including which brand of chocolate bar to sell for fundraising, but nothing more. What will you do to democratize schools so that kids have a say in running them?"

Every politician looks at Fenton. He crosses to Panther, puts on his biggest smile and reaches for the microphone in Panther's hand. Panther yanks it back and says to the candidates, "We are denied freedom of speech and expression in school and are subject to arbitrary detention and punishment. I just did two weeks in the Midhill slammer without a trial for a crime no adult could even be charged with. What will you politicians do to liberate us?"

Cheers, clapping, whistles, foot-stomping and the chant, Panther, Panther, Panther. Fenton grabs a politician's microphone and says loudly, "I regret time is running short and we have to thank our guests."

Panther shouts, "No wonder kids are angry. You politicians and school administrators are in cahoots to keep kids powerless. Let me hear from everyone in this audience who demands rights and responsibilities for kids. Let's hear it: Kids' rights! Kids' rights! Kids' rights!"

Half of the audience is standing and yelling, "Kids' rights!" Fenton is grabbing at Panther's microphone and hollering into the one he already holds, "Assembly dismissed!" Nobody leaves. The politicians are paralysed. Duchok is yanking at strings trying to close the curtains.

Diane Lemon, chic in a dark blue dress and pumps, is perched on her battered desk holding a cigarette and pouring coffee for the two invited guests squeezed into her cubbyhole office. Intermittent roars from the final football game drift through the open window which vents her smoke. Head of guidance, Brenda Sprung, is eating a fourth cookie and smiling. Traces of icing sugar and tiny beads of perspiration cling to hairs on her upper lip. Her massive body overflows the folding chair and presses against David Halper. Her musky odour mixes with the smell of cigarette smoke.

Halper tries to think only of what Brenda is saying but finds himself counting the cookies she consumes and imagining that each one goes directly to her bulging thigh, causing it to press harder against him. Five. He wonders if the students she counsels have as much trouble listening to her.

"Meetings?" Brenda says as she offers Halper the cookie tin and then takes another one herself. Six. "You mean detentions."

"Meetings. Entirely voluntary. One private meeting with each of my students will take eight months at one meeting per day. That kind of meeting takes an hour, usually a lot more. And I have to schedule all of those meetings before or after school or on weekends. And that gives me an hour a year with each student! Ridiculous. I need at least an hour a week one-to-one with each of my students."

Brenda pinches crumbs from her lap and pops them in her mouth. She says, "The guidance staff feels we can handle counselling."

"But you can't handle detailed review of academic work. You can't diagnose academic problems. You can't handle remedial work. You can't handle specific academic and leadership challenges for gifted students. Besides there's no way to separate academic from personal counselling. When I run into something that needs further action I report it to you provided the student in question agrees: abusive parents, drugs, all-night jobs, cult brainwashing, ethnic gangs, rotten teeth. I've sent you several memos."

"Twenty-nine," Brenda says as she helps herself to another cookie. Seven.

"Look David," Diane says, "Other teachers wonder what's going on. These student disturbances. We had some trouble with the school paper last year, Gordon Wing being editor, but the short story club and student council were peaceful. Now they're raising hell too. Even Billy Parr, the prince of peace. Jimmy would have suspended Wing and Parr by now if they weren't our top honour students."

"What's going on is democracy, students' rights, children's rights and responsibilities. I tried to get it on the agenda for discussion at faculty meetings but Fenton refused, the union refused. Now Gordon Wing and Billy Parr have taken the initiative and are miles out in front while the teachers haven't even discussed it. Back in September when he thought children's rights meant free vaccinations in Ethiopia Fenton approved a children's rights assembly for November 18, but he's cancelled it now that he knows rights means human and civil rights here at Midhill."

"You should talk it up informally with the staff. Mingle. You're not the only one who thinks our attitude to kids needs rethinking. I'm kind of intrigued with your ideas. My son thinks they're right on. Quite a few teachers might agree with you. But you never play cribbage or go bowling or drink beer with teachers."

"I don't do those things with anybody."

"Sports then. Watch some games with teachers. Get together at each other's houses. At least talk about games in the lounge. Get into Jimmy's lotteries. The Leafs have won nine straight and the Jays are about to take the World Series again."

"If that's what turns you on, enjoy it. But I've got other things to do, better things from my point of view, and not enough time to do them."

"It's the way you make friends in this profession."

"I did the golf thing for twenty years and won the odd trophy, quite a few deals, and some clients. But no friends. I never cared for golf so how likely is it that I'd care about somebody who does? I played golf because I had to. With decision makers. But teachers aren't decision makers in this model of schooling. Art Wilkins is right about that. So I no longer play social games that bore me. It's part of being who I really am. To thine own self be true."

"Union committees then. With your background you could

do salary negotiations, get a following. You could make time. You're here all hours. Twelve-hour days. Seven-day weeks. House calls."

"The school day is too short. Should be seven hours. That would allow time for one-to-one meetings with students. And the school year should be at least 220 days of regular classroom operation for every student and teacher. In Japan it's 240, in China 250, but here the union draws the line at 185 and, you said it yourself, the real figure is more like 150, even less in years with strikes. What have I got in common with that kind of union?"

"Kids are talking about your one-to-one meetings," Brenda says as she plucks the glazed cherry from her shortbread cookie. "Parents are concerned. I had a parent phone about the early morning detention you gave her daughter which disrupted breakfast and transportation arrangements." She transports the cherry to her mouth by pinching it between her thumb and forefinger. Halper is reminded of a lover squeezing a nipple even though Brenda extends her pinkie in a gesture of dining room etiquette that has no place in the bedroom.

"I never give detentions. I offer meetings. Some refuse. Not many. Usually we find a time."

"Jerry Duchok says a parent phoned him to complain about a detention set for six weeks from now and at night."

"That's a voluntary meeting schedule for the year. Students fill in the appointment time they want."

"And the place is that empty store across the street."

"Yes. If a student chooses a night or weekend time we meet at the Greenhouse because school rules make the school building off limits."

"You look tired, David," Diane says. "Exhausted. More coffee? Why don't you try my shortbread. Brenda loves it."

Eight.

Lincoln has moved his computers to the room he shares with Gordon and they are either there or at the Greenhouse at all hours creating a computer program that teaches reading. It has a game approach that springs from the computer game Gordon invented, but Lincoln spends the most time at it because Gordon has so many other obligations. Claudius is so much involved that his mother is as likely to find him at Gordon's house as at the Greenhouse or Midhill. Maude Fenwick is also part of the team. Almost daily, Lincoln, Maude, Claudius and sometimes Panther try out variations on the Greens they tutor.

Panther is part of the project whenever he isn't tied up with student council, hockey, the Christian student club, or his hospital job. Halper moves in and out of the computer team as he does every other group, listening, questioning, evaluating, encouraging, stretching. When Halper is busy at Midhill, Maude jogs two or three miles every night discussing progress on the reading game with whichever team members are available to run.

As he drives away from a school board meeting, Fenton sees three joggers slightly separated from a dozen or so other runners in green caps. He pulls his new little Geo into the entrance of a gas station and calls "Lincoln" as they pass. Maude and Claudius veer to one side and hang back running on the spot while Lincoln bends down and Fenton leans out the window.

Fenton says, "Come home with me Lincoln. Your mother wants that. So do I. You've made your point. I'm sorry we've had this misunderstanding."

"It's not misunderstanding on my part. It's understanding. I understand you. I feel sorry for you. I feel sorry for my mother. But I've got my own life to lead. And that's the point I haven't made clear to you yet because nobody can make it clear for guys like you. You just don't get it."

"You're letting that smartass Gordon Wing pull you down to his level. He's got Billy Parr under his spell too."

"That's really stupid. Nobody's under anybody's spell. Gordon and Panther and I disagree — all of us disagree, about lots of things. We discuss, listen, read, discuss some more. That's where truth comes from, not from your storehouse of rules. Mr. Halper knows that. Maude Fenwick knows it. She's right over there. You want to meet her?"

Fenton rolls up his window as he drives away.

Liz is going alone to meet Princess Margaret at the opening gala of the Royal Winter Fair. She is having her hair done by Robert Gage in his grey-and-white salon and telling him about her husband who prefers ill-bred kids to purebred horses.

Meanwhile, David Halper and Keiko Ito sit on the white loveseat in front of her rose brick fireplace going over numbers. For nearly two hours Claudius participates, standing on the floor behind them with one arm around each and his head between theirs. To make for himself this perfect parking place, he has moved the antique parson's table which belongs behind the loveseat.

Maude Fenwick sits on the white hardwood floor on a Persian cushion made from two silk prayer rugs sewn together. She is beside a coffee table of inch-thick glass on top of an ancient Japanese door. As Halper and Keiko call out numbers, Maude enters them on grant applications. The Greenhouse is applying for foundation funding.

While Keiko and Maude are in the kitchen, Claudius sits on the arm of the loveseat running his fingers lightly over the crown of Halper's hair. He says, "It's a bit thin right there, sir. I guess you're getting kind of old."

"Kind of. Forty-six in January."

"My mother's thirty-five. That's kind of old too."

"Not compared to forty-five."

"She doesn't care. One of her boyfriends was forty-eight. Oliver. But I didn't like him much. He didn't want me to go to Mexico with them, but my mother took me anyway. He had a stroke at Chichén Itzá. Now he's back with his wife. Are you going to be my mother's boyfriend?"

"I'm married, Claudius."

"That doesn't matter. You could sleep over anyway, like Oliver did. I know all about that. Making out."

"I don't make out, Claudius."

"Why not?"

"Oh, well, I just never did. I think I'm too shy. When I was young in the 60s lots of kids were making out but I never had the nerve, the confidence."

"Why not? Was your dick too small?"

"Not really. Just regular. But I thought everything else about me was too small to be interesting, especially things like my conversation, talent, ideas, personality, income . . ."

"Gordon says he can't make out yet either and his psychiatrist thinks it's partly because he can't trust women because his mother makes out a lot which has made Gordon think deep down that making out isn't such a great idea. But my mother makes out a lot and it doesn't bother me."

"Well, you read Gordon's story so you know there's a lot of difference between your mother and Gordon's. For one thing your mother isn't cheating on a husband and father. And she's honest with you about what she does."

"Lincoln says his mother never tried to hide her lovers either and she wasn't cheating on anybody, so maybe I'll be more like Lincoln. He makes out every chance he gets, but that's hardly ever. Even though he's got a Mercedes and lots of money and he's hung and hairy and six feet tall. Sex is weird. Do you think I'll get as tall as Lincoln?"

"Not likely. You know about genes. But tall isn't everything. Look how handsome you are. And bright. And interesting. And everything. If I had to design a perfect boy I'd design Claudius J. Ito with no changes."

"Couldn't you design me a bigger dick?"

"No. The one you've got is exactly right. You can't stick a great humongous fountain in a nice little park and expect it to look good. Besides, the one you've got will grow along with your pubic hair."

"How big?"

"Oh, I don't know, four or five inches. Big enough. Any size will do the job."

"That's what Gordon says in *The Art of Sex for Teens*, provided you know how to use it and how not to use it. But he also admits he's seventeen and hasn't done it yet, so it's all theoretical. Except that he taught two other guys his method and it worked for them. Lincoln says the only girl he ever did it with more than once is Nita and she likes guys well hung. Panther says there's nothing in the Bible about dick size so it must not be important. Becky says it doesn't matter, but you notice she goes for Frank Stringer who has a great humongous one. I think I want a great humongous one."

"Well, that's not in the cards so you just have to accept what you've got."

"How about if I go to that doctor in Yorkville who does dick extensions. I could ask for a few inches for Christmas."

"I'd say, forget it. Use the money to extend your brain by reading. Buy books. A cock is just a cock Claudius, a dumb tool controlled in every way by one brain function or another. I'd rather have a small cock controlled by a big brain than vice versa."

"I'd rather have both big," Claudius says laughing as he slides off the sofa arm into Halper's lap.

"I'll tell you one thing for sure. Lots of girls, the very best, will accept whatever you've got, Claudius. Girls will burn up the phone lines to date Claudius Ito. Hello Claudius, this is Angela Gorgeosa speaking and I was wondering if you'd like to do something on Saturday."

"Well I don't know Angela, my big brain says yes to Saturday but my dumb little dick says right now."

In the kitchen, Maude Fenwick tosses salad and says, "Listen to those two laughing. That man has a way with kids. They trust him even when he disagrees with them, which is often. Even when he tells them he's uncertain, which is also often. Maybe that's it. He reflects their own uncertainty like a mirror, but he's solid as the wall behind the mirror. I was always too certain, too stiff-upper-lip content, even when I was neither. Kids know David isn't content, just like them. They know he's trying to find out who he is, as much as they are."

"He seems lonely," Keiko says while she sticks a toothpick in a casserole.

"All the best teachers are lonely. There are good ones who aren't, but I've noticed the very best ones, the trail blazers, are always lonely. Not conspicuously. It's like a subtle seasoning." She sprinkles coriander. "They're available to kids but near loners otherwise. Adults never quite know who they are. Only kids peek through their keyholes to see treasure and slip in when the door opens a crack."

"I just meant lonely in the man-woman sense. I'll bet he defines himself by his work, not his woman. He never mentions his wife, does he?"

"Rarely. Only to say she's gone some place. Vancouver.

Bermuda. The horse show. I've never met her."

"I have. Once. Five or six years ago. In a TV studio. One of those local daytime shows. I was filling in for some ethnic cookbook author who had flu, and Liz Halper was plumping a benefit for the symphony. I sort of liked her. Let me tell you she wasn't playing second fiddle to a workaholic husband. She was in virtuoso concert. Sabre slim and sabre sharp. Not a great beauty but striking. Glitter-girl charming. So well bred and coiffed as to be almost indistinguishable from a poodle. I bet she wears Chanel suits to get an oil change."

"I get the impression she goes her own separate way running those charities."

"I get the impression the marriage is on cruise control with two people along for the ride and nobody steering. If so, he could be had. But I'm not sure I want him. I admit I'm attracted but there's something so committed about him. I'm not sure I'm into commitment. Commitment never lasts even when you commit to it. Does that make sense? That's the kind of thing I say on talk shows and they think I'm kidding for laughs, but I'm not. David's only ten years older but he reminds me of my father, and my father died on me. I think most of the kids see a father in David. Have you noticed how father hunger is an epidemic? Claudius looks over every man as a potential father and this time he's found one he likes."

"So Claudius is committed. At my age I shouldn't commit to anything longer than five minutes, but I do it all the time. Habit. I like commitment."

"But not to men."

"Men too, if you mean like David. But I only got one chance of the coupling kind. I was never much to look at but my father found somebody to court me. Lionel. That was 1940 and I was no chicken, twenty-five, and no fool, so I knew that Lionel knew he would get my father's hardware store along with me. But while Lionel was away at the war my father died and my mother went to pieces. She was a fluttery woman who had no idea how to run a hardware, so she sold it. When Lionel returned in 1945 there was just me, age thirty. I was teaching in Belleville and mother was living with me. Lionel came to dinner once. He got a job in Peterborough making Ovaltine. Sent me a case. Never came back. Since then I've gone to bed every night with a cup of Ovaltine."

"Just as well. I'd rather be put to sleep every night by a hot Ovaltine than by a cold grunt-and-shove routine with a jerk like Lionel."

"I just realized something — my father died on me too."

Claudius dances into the kitchen, literally. When he is especially happy he does a little dance crouched over with his elbows flapping, his knees together and one knee after the other shooting out and crossing over in front.

Fenton barges into the librarian's work room where the school newspaper is put together. He thrusts a picture in front of Gordon, and says, "You've got an erection!"

"You need one for sex," Gordon says looking up with a final tap at the computer keys. "It works better that way."

"Don't get smart with me Wing. This is obscene."

"No sir. It's sensuous. Sex is supposed to celebrate sensuality. That picture's erotic. Erotic means pertaining to sexuality, and sex is what my book is about. Tasteful erotica is never obscene sir. Violence is obscene. Violence as in hockey, football, boxing, hunting, war, rape, pornography." Gordon pushes a dictionary toward Fenton.

"This is full of child pornography." Fenton is waving *The Art of Sex for Teens*. "This photo is you and these drawings are you, and you're only seventeen."

"Sixteen when my brother made those pictures and I wrote the book. And he was fifteen. And the pictures are erotic, not pornographic."

"Don't play word games with me, Wing. The law passed last June by the government of Canada says it's illegal to make or show sex pictures of anyone under eighteen."

"Foolish law. Draconian, ageist and child abusive. One of the many I'm targeting for a special issue called Children as Chattel. The editorial I'm writing here for you to censor out of existence is headed, 'The law is an ass and kids should be ass kickers.' Just think of it, sir. According to law, the age of criminal capacity is twelve but the age of sexual capacity is eighteen! Mark Twain or Stephen Leacock couldn't dream up anything more ludicrous. *The Art of Sex for Teens* is a book by teens about teen sex. Think how silly it would look if Arlix had used models who clearly were not teens. If it was you jerking off in that picture instead of me that would make it unobscene by your definition."

"So you admit it! You weren't merely holding your member, you were abusing it sexually."

"Sir, that old self-abuse lie was made up by big bosses of the religion business. All the lies that make people like you think sex is sinful were made up by religion executives like Augustine as a marketing strategy. They figured correctly that if they got control of sex they'd have control of people, thereby insuring a clientele for their product, which is hocus pocus. The rotten remains of those old lies pollute your mind and my world. Listen sir, my body is not obscene and I won't let perverted people say it is. And my sex activity isn't obscene. It's beautiful. At seventeen guys are at the very peak of sexuality but pious perverts try to castrate us. That's sex abuse. What teens need is to have our sexuality validated, not denied by idiotic laws and stupid adults."

"Don't get rude with me, Wing. My job is to protect you from sex. All responsible adults do that. That's why our laws were made."

"And meanwhile the God those lawmakers claim to worship made us sexual at thirteen or before. Who are they to contradict God? God intended us to start practising at thirteen, not eighteen, or he wouldn't have turned on our hormones for another five years. You can't expect gifted lovers to emerge miraculously at midnight on the eighteenth birthday if every kid's sex equipment has been mothballed for five years and we've been bombarded with negative messages. What emerges from that is a world of sexually dysfunctional adults full of guilt. They hate their own sexuality and take out their anger on kids by denying that kids are sexual. Or by raping them. Often the same folks do both. We should be learning sex as teens the same way we learn everything else — by instruction, by research, by practice, by learning all the facts, by honest discussion."

"Get this straight, Wing. If one more copy of this trash arrives on my desk I'll call the police."

"Your choice, sir. Good publicity for my book. Bad publicity for you as the principal who only found out about it eighteen months after every kid in his school. Anyway, my lawyer says my book will stand up in court because it has artistic and educational merit. Besides, it's not a school matter. I'm going public. The same government that passed the stupid child pornography law passed another law declaring a Children's Day, which is Saturday, November 19 this year. You cancelled the children's rights assembly on the 18th but I'll have about fifty kids on the street selling my book. Greens as sellers. Profits to the Greenhouse. A tag day for children's rights with my book as the tag. A good sex manual is a healthier thing to sell than chocolate bars. And we'll use the proceeds for a better symbol of kids than a plastic mascot. We're raising $5,000 for a flea-powered radio station so we can broadcast the views of kids to the neighbourhood from the Green-house."

Other years, the gardening company would have collected all the leaves on Halper's seven landscaped acres north of Toronto but this year even the long curve of driveway is leaf-covered and in the car lights, with early snowflakes swirling, it is hard to tell driveway from lawn. As Halper passes in front of the house heading for the garage, his headlights pick out luggage between porch pillars. His wife's car is parked sideways blocking the garage. He backs up.

Three bags are Jillian's. A note stuck on with tape says, 'If she wants anything else, she can come and get it herself.' Five suitcases and sixteen cardboard boxes contain some of his clothes and books. His journals are in a green plastic garbage bag. Suits and coats on hangars are piled on top. A note pinned to his black trench coat says, 'If you want anything else, see my lawyer.' The lawyer's card is attached with tape.

Little spits of wet snow catch him in the face. Halper has a passing thought of his wife spitting on him which changes to her spitting him out. He feels himself lying there on the paving bricks like spittle that will disappear with the melting snowflakes.

He drives to the airport in a daze, ships Jillian's things to Vancouver, and then phones her. A male voice he has never heard before says she is in the valley on a shoot. So he leaves the message and adds, "Tell her I love her." Beyond that, he seems not to feel anything, just empty, depleted, mechanical, numb. He considers buying a drink, one drink. Instead, he buys a paper and stands in the emptying airport looking at apartments to let. But he is unable to concentrate and it is almost midnight, too late to phone landlords.

He drives back in a stupor, through blinding snow, following a huge truck, changing lanes obediently when the truck does. He imagines following it through the whiteout to the end of the earth, free of decision-making. But some little soldier of self-respect comes to attention in his mind and marches to the rhythm of the windshield wipers. He pulls away on his own and doesn't stop till his lights are reflected back at him by darkness behind the Greenhouse window. He will sleep there. He sits behind the wheel for ten minutes watching snowflakes dissolve the moment they hit solid objects.

Frank Stringer is asleep on a sofa. His turquoise spikes are askew like broken lances. Halper thinks of boy soldiers killed in battle. He looks so young. Like Simon. The same kind of mouth, resolute but childlike. Frank has taken his shoes off and has no socks. His feet are so big. Halper tries to recall what Simon's feet were like but he can't remember them except when he was a baby. Yes, he remembers: the last year they went to Palm Beach for Christmas holidays, Simon could wear his beach shoes. Simon liked to wear his father's shoes. Halper touches the back of his hand to one foot and it feels cold. Frank stirs. He blinks. Halper finds a tablecloth that will do and covers the bare feet.

Halper says, "It's okay, Frank. It's only me. We can talk in the morning."

"My dad threw me out."

"That's good. I mean, that you didn't say 'like, you know, I mean, man, basically.' " (Claudius Ito has been kicking Frank in the shins and fining him a quarter every time he slips into that lingo.) "How long have you been sleeping here?"

"Two nights. I told my dad about Becky. He goes, 'If you can knock up a girl you can pay your own way big shot.' I can't, man. There's no good jobs out there. I mean, I'm just a kid. I got twelve hours a week pizza delivery is all. Do I quit school or what?"

"What do you want to do, Frank?"

"Me? I wanta go to school, man. I mean, I don't like it that much over there, but I like it here and I mean I'm not so dumb here."

"You're not dumb any place. You're smart. You just have a language problem but we'll work that out. What concessions would you consider if your dad lets you go back home? If I were your attorney negotiating on your behalf what kind of assurances could I give your dad?"

"Hey man, that's cool. My attorney." Frank sits up grinning but he stops abruptly. "He'd say basically — cut my hair, work in his warehouse Saturdays, scrub my tattoo, stop seeing Becky, pass at school . . ."

"Suppose I cut a deal where he gets three out of five. Which three will you give him?"

"My tattoo won't come off easy and I mean, anyway, I like it. I'll pass at school and work in the warehouse."

"One more. Becky or hair. I don't imagine he'll want you in his warehouse store with that hairdo. It makes a statement but not the one you think it makes as far as he's concerned. He thinks it says you're a loser, that you have no taste, no common sense. But it's your right to wear your hair as you please. On the other hand, you said in my law class that you want to stick with Becky right through the pregnancy and the adoption. But of course it's up to you. I'm just your attorney."

"Get the scissors, man."

Between classes, Halper is in the front office on the phone to Alison's school. His students are going to a matinee of *Showboat* and he is asking to have his daughter excused so she can join them. He is told the school is not authorized to release Alison except with permission from her mother or her mother's lawyer. While he is objecting to no avail, he sees Claudius Ito being marched into the vice-principal's office by a teacher clutching the back of his collar. Claudius is kicking and screaming, "Leave me alone!"

Halper knocks lightly on Duchok's door. There is no response. He can hear voices including Claudius's shouting but he can't make out words. He knocks again. No reply. He opens the door. Claudius is stamping his feet and swearing and kicking at Matsushita, the science teacher who brought him in. Halper knows Matsushita only as the union chairman planning the next strike.

Matsushita, still holding Claudius by the shirt collar, is doing a little dance to protect his shins. Duchok is standing behind his desk, his shoulders thrown back, his chest puffed up to full size. This is his official stance, one he strikes a dozen times every day as aberrant students parade before him one at a time.

The moment Claudius sees Halper he breaks loose and runs to him. Duchok is flabbergasted. Matsushita is open-mouthed. Claudius throws his arms around Halper's waist, buries his face in Halper's tie and cries.

Halper looks at Duchok and says, "Can I help?"

Duchok finds his voice and says, "Can't you see we're in the middle of something? This is none of your business."

Halper says to everybody, "What happened?"

"He picked on me," Claudius says. "He always picks on me."

"I see the judge," Halper says. "And I see the prosecuting attorney. But who's defending the accused? Nobody should have to be tried in a court like this without benefit of counsel."

Duchok's chest heaves and emits primal grunts. Cords and veins stand out on his thick neck like vines on a jungle tree trunk. He growls, "Get out!"

"Will you defend me, sir?" Claudius says.

"I'd be glad to Claudius, if that's your wish."

"Yes sir."

"Mr. Duchok, I request an adjournment so I can confer with my client. And I have a class now. Let us know the time our case comes up. Thank you." He backs out with Claudius by the hand and closes the door.

That day at noon, Halper combs Claudius's file at school and phones his mother, his psychologist and his former principal. He phones the school board office to ask if there is a file on Matsushita that is available to one of his science students in the same way the student's file is available to the teacher. The answer from the superintendent of personnel is no. That evening Halper interviews Claudius and has him write a statement. He also interviews several other students who have the same science teacher.

When the court call comes, Claudius is not included. Halper objects to Fenton but is overruled. Court is held in Fenton's office. Also present are Duchok, Matsushita, and the superintendent of personnel. Matsushita, behind big black-framed glasses, has the stoniest face of all.

Fenton calls upon the superintendent who makes a rambling, conciliatory speech that regrets these unusual happenings and trusts there has been some misunderstanding and things can get back to normal for the good of all concerned.

Fenton purses his lips and knits his eyebrows and says they can't have teachers intervening in front office discipline matters. Professional standards. Public expectations. The idea of students defended by counsel is ridiculous.

Duchok says he can handle Ito, that Midhill has an excellent record on discipline, that Ito needs to apologize and serve his detentions. They can't have students challenging teachers' and administrators' decisions.

"Why not?" Halper says. "It's the democratic way. Why should kids be the only ones subject to arbitrary arrest and detention?"

"The law gives us the right to act in place of kind and judicious parents," Duchok says confidently, pleased that he has recalled something appropriate.

Halper says, "There's nothing kind and certainly nothing judicious about the same arbitrary authority acting as lawmaker, police, prosecution, judge and jailer. That's Stalin's concept of justice. And there's nothing in school law or even school rules that justifies forbidding a student who has finished his assignment — including extra questions — from quietly reading a novel. My client says his book, *Something Wicked This Way Comes*, by Ray Bradbury, was yanked from his hand and thrown in the waste basket by Mr. Matsushita. When my client immediately retrieved the book — for which he had paid $5.89 of his $10 allowance — Mr. Matsushita again seized it. A tugging match ensued during which the cover and several pages were torn from my client's property. Exhibit A."

Halper takes what remains of the book and the torn pages from his brief case and whacks them down one at a time on Fenton's desk. Every eye is riveted to the nails Halper is driving.

"Further," Halper continues, "my client's psychologist trained him years ago to do exactly what he was doing — read to relax when he feels upset, bored, restless or rejected, and his elementary school principal confirms that it never caused any problem there. All of that is in my client's school file for any teacher to read. But according to guidance department records Mr. Matsushita has not read any grade nine files. My client is given extra questions with every science assignment and does them; though he regrets that more of the same is the best this school has to offer quick learners, he has never, not once, done anything but turn to literature for solace. Having made those points, my client has no objection to exchanging apologies with Mr. Matsushita and closing the case provided Mr. Matsushita pays compensation of $5.89 plus bus fare to get my client to and from the bookstore."

Matsushita lets out a hiss of air and simultaneously slaps his hand down on the table beside him and looks at Fenton. "What's going on here? Compensation? Apologize? Me?"

With the superintendent present, Fenton is studiously controlled, patriarchal. He shoots his cuffs in a businesslike way revealing his big glass cufflinks. He draws his chair closer to his desk and clears his throat in preparation for a senior-statesman pronouncement. His mouth opens.

But before Fenton can speak, Halper says, "If and only if there is no apology and compensation from Mr. Matsushita, my client will take his case to the school board and submit detailed evidence that on four occasions he has found Mr. Matsushita in error or confused on matters of modern science and my client has corrected Mr. Matsushita by reporting recent discoveries and theories in class. In every such case, Mr. Matsushita has failed to receive the correction graciously. Once he referred to my client as 'the pee-wee professor,' another time as 'the talking baseball cap.' Further, my client will show that Mr. Matsushita asked my client if he always wears a baseball cap to hide his hair — a racist statement referring to the fact that my client has brown hair so is obviously of mixed race. Several students heard Mr. Matsushita utter one word, a strange word, when he threw my client's book in the wastebasket. My client knows the word: *ainoko*, a derogatory term for someone of mixed race."

Matsushita is on his feet lunging toward Halper but Duchok intervenes.

They are eating Saturday lunch beside the railing at Mr. Greenjeans on the top level of the Eaton Centre. Alison is alternately picking at french fries and the Christmas gifts they have bought to send Jillian. Halper feels bombarded with noise: shoppers, loud music, and a fractious family at the next table arguing about food, money and gifts. The father declares last Sunday's Santa Claus parade not worth the long wait in the cold and this year's Santa at the Centre not worth lining up for; and besides, with all the perverts around these days, he doesn't want his kids sitting on strange men's knees. The two youngest children clutch the railing and look through at the spires of Santa's castle and wail about their lost opportunity. Alison seems not to notice.

She says, "You mean it's just one room? Not even a bedroom? You sleep in the living room?"

"That's all I need, sweetheart. But if you come to live with me all the time or part time I'll get a two-bedroom. We could fix it up together. Would you like that?"

Halper leans over to kiss her on the temple and feels himself float there on waves of tenderness. She is so pretty, so in need of him, and he in need of her.

"When would I stay there? Mummy and I are going to Bermuda for three weeks at Christmas. After that I'll be at school, then at camp next summer. Even if I go to your place some weekend, I won't know anybody around there. Anyway, Mummy says it's all strip malls and gas stations and she says you have a girlfriend, that Keiko Ito."

"A friend. Not a girlfriend." He wants to say, 'not a lover,' but the father-daughter boundary drawn by years of sanitized family prattle makes the acknowledgement of his own sexuality feel like taking his pants down in public. "She's never even been to my place. I've been to hers for dinner and business meetings. She'd invite you too. I want you to meet her. She has a son about your age, just turned thirteen."

"I'm fourteen, Daddy! Almost fifteen for heaven sake! Anyway, what could I do with him? He's Chinese or something, like her."

"Japanese. And you could do whatever you'd do with any boy that age."

"Which is nothing."

She is so like her mother. Halper feels her drifting away downstream, ever smaller, becoming a speck, leaving him alone on some unknown shore that dissolves beneath his feet.

"Is that all you want for lunch, french fries?"

"I'm on a diet. Why can't you just come and see me sometimes at school? Sports or choir concerts or something. Other girls have divorced fathers who do that. You could drive me to dressage competitions. Mummy gets tired of pulling my horse around behind her car." Alison is looking at the fry she is breaking in half. "Jillian might like this sweater and blouse but she said I should get you to send her money for Christmas."

Halper is looking through the bars of the railing at the family group from the next table descending the long narrow escalator, backs to each other, still audibly acrimonious.

The school office is decorated with restless clouds of silver cardboard suspended on white threads from a bright fluorescent heaven. They say, JOY TO THE WORLD on one side and SEASON'S GREETINGS on the other. The phone message in his pigeonhole from Keiko Ito says URGENT, so Halper calls her immediately from the front desk. She says, "The police have questioned Claudius, David. He's locked himself in his room. Very angry and upset. Inconsolable —"

Before she can finish, Fenton is standing right beside Halper tapping him on the shoulder with one hand and jabbing the other toward his office door and saying, "Now."

Halper says, "The principal is here and waiting. Can I phone you back?"

The second his office door is closed, Fenton says, "You were seen by two teachers kissing a male student in your car in the school parking lot."

"So what? There are kisses and there are kisses. Have you kissed Lincoln?"

"It's my duty to inform you that you're being investigated for child abuse. Two witnesses, girls from this school, have sworn statements that they saw you in a public washroom bending over a young boy with his pants down. A third witness, an adult, saw you hugging the same boy in the same washroom. The boy's name is known but can't be revealed of course."

Halper feels punched. Fenton looks at him expectantly. Halper tries to reply. But what? That it's all a mistake? That he was only looking at pubic hair? That he is being framed? His mouth is dry. It is desert hot in Fenton's office. He feels faint. He reaches for a chair shimmering in the heat and obscured by blowing, blinding sand that shifts dunes from under his feet.

When the air clears, he is sitting looking up at Fenton who stands confidently on top of a dune serenely surveying his desert.

Fenton waves papers, "And further, a respected witness, a retired judge, states that he found you and a boy asleep at dawn in that hang-out of yours where the two of you spent the night alone together. The boy confirms that; and he also says that during the night he woke up to find you feeling his feet."

TELL ME WHO YOU ARE. Halper grips the arms of his chair.

Fenton continues, "You're being transferred immediately to work at the board office. But take my advice, Halper. Look for another job. Even if no charges are laid, you're finished as a teacher. Your probationary contract won't be renewed here and nobody else will have you after this. You haven't got the right stuff to be a teacher anyway."

CHAPTER SIX

Gordon, Lincoln, Panther and Claudius are in Lincoln's car headed toward the Greenhouse.

Gordon says, "I've asked every teacher worth talking to. Most of them say we make matters worse by drawing attention to the lies. Leave it to the union, they say. Mr. Haynes says the union has a lawyer who does little else but handle false sex reports about teachers."

"How can we make it worse?" Lincoln says. "He's ruined anyway. And gone from Midhill. Besides, these particular lies were by members of the union so what good is their lawyer to us? I say we go for big media attention and fight the phonies publicly."

Panther says, "I believe in civil disobedience, the kind Jesus practised, and Ghandi. I think we should blockade the school, sit down in the halls, attract the media that way."

As he brakes for a red light Lincoln says, "We could take hostages. I just got my grandmother's gun back from the police after a whole year. Maybe the timing is fate. Fenton, Duchok and Matsushita bound and gagged in the window of the Greenhouse. That would attract national TV."

"But Maude wouldn't let us do it," Gordon says.

Claudius says, "We could blow up the school. That would attract international TV. CNN. I could do it."

Claudius is in the back seat with Gordon. Lincoln and Panther turn around and look at Claudius.

"Well I could," Claudius says. "The whole school or just Duchok's and Fenton's offices and Matsushita's science lab."

Gordon smiles and pulls Claudius's baseball cap down over his eyes and says, "How?"

"Lots of ways. Dust or vapour are easy in an enclosed space like an office or lab. That's why flour mills and mines blow up accidentally. To make it happen on purpose you detonate a small charge under a bag of flour or a can of gasoline. That's enough to blow dust or vapour and ignite the particles so they cause a secondary explosion, a big one, and a fire. For a nice added touch we could carefully place a cylinder or two of compressed oxygen or acetylene from the tech wing so the secondary explosion sets them off like rockets."

"And how do you detonate all this," Gordon wants to know.

"Lots of ways. I've used flash bulbs, alarm clocks, watch delay . . . That just takes a watch with hands and a battery. I once blew up my wristwatch that way so now my mother only gives me digital watches."

"Yes but what makes it blow?"

"Lots of things. Picric acid is easy. Just takes aspirin, alcohol, sulfuric acid and potassium nitrate — that's saltpeter. I used to make it at home. Twenty crushed aspirin in a third of a cup of sulfuric acid in a canning jar. Heat the jar in a double boiler and stir in —."

"Okay," Gordon says. "So the little nipper knows how to blow up the school."

"I think that would have appealed to my brother Arnie," Panther says thoughtfully. "But I doubt if Jesus would go for it."

"I like the symbolism of a school going up, any school, especially that one," says Lincoln as he parks at the strip mall facing Midhill.

Gordon says, "I'm not too crazy about fires if there's a chance of someone being burnt. I think Panther's right. We should start with a demonstration, a sit-in. Panther, you could get all the do-gooders and the student council, and the hockey team. I figure half the school would follow your lead. Between the two of us we can get most of the girls. I can get the swim team, all orientals except the ass kissers, most other minorities, and all the misfits."

Claudius says, "How would it be if we just blow Matsushita's car when he isn't in it? I can make a mini bomb in a little pill bottle with a screw top. Potassium chlorate, sugar, sulfuric acid, high octane gas, boiling water, one empty gelatin capsule and Elmer's Glue-All. Takes a day to make because the sugar and potassium chlorate and boiling water mixture has to dry out before it goes in the capsule. Then the capsule goes in the little pill bottle which is partly filled with the acid and gas mixture. Slip it in a car's gas tank and two hours later, kaboom. Scrap metal in small pieces."

Claudius is so bright-eyed and eager reeling off explosive

recipes that Gordon begins to laugh, then Lincoln, then Panther, then Claudius. All four are rolling about the car.

Gordon hugs Claudius and says, "If we ever write that spring revue, the little nipper does a cooking demonstration."

Before dawn cars are parked as barriers and marchers in the streets circle the school disrupting traffic on all four sides. Every motorist has to stop and is handed a flyer. Drivers phone radio stations to report the bottleneck and the cause. An inner ring of vehicles and marchers circles the frozen school lawn and parking lot. The lead vehicle is Dr. Ashman's white Rolls Royce driven by Gordon. Lincoln in his black Mercedes is next, then Keiko Ito in her red Supra. Panther's silver Jeep, top down, is parked by the flagpole as headquarters with phones and public address system.

As the sun rises, a traffic helicopter estimates there are fifty cars and five hundred people in the inner circle. Both entrances to the parking lot and all doors to the school are blocked by packs of kids in colourful sweaters and jackets. Dozens near the front entrance wear green baseball caps.

For the first time since its inception, the Greenhouse is empty at eight a.m. except for Maude Fenwick who stands in the window using the old brass telescope she brought to work because she knew she would need it.

The police, a TV news team and James Fenton arrive at about the same time and are allowed on foot as far as the flagpole.

Fenton shouts to Panther, "You've got one minute to disperse this crowd."

Panther says, "No sir, Mr. Fenton, you've got one minute to get up here on this microphone and tell the world you framed Mr. Halper."

While the TV camera rolls, Fenton climbs up on the Jeep, adjusts his navy blue overcoat, takes the mike and says, "Now listen to me everyone." The crowd roars but Fenton continues, "This is your principal speaking. Hear this. We believe in law and order." There are loud boos and catcalls. "Due process. Can you hear me?" Fenton is shouting. His face is red and his hot breath makes white bursts of fog in the cold air. "That's what's happening, due process. I'm not at liberty to comment on a matter that's under police investigation. But you can count on the system."

The crowd howls disdain but Fenton continues, heard by no one. Gordon pulls the white Rolls up beside the Jeep. Lincoln parks his black Mercedes on the other side. Both climb up on their hoods and Panther tosses them microphones.

Lincoln is about ten feet from Fenton and they glare at each other as Fenton finishes his unheard sentence and lowers his microphone. Lincoln holds up one hand till the crowd noise subsides and then says, "This man Fenton is married to my mother, and I lived in his house for over a year, so I know him, and I don't believe him. He's corrupt because the system is corrupt. All he knows is hypocrisy. How about a little democracy instead? We should decide who teaches us and we want Mr. Halper. Halper. Halper. Halper."

Over the chant and the cheers Fenton shouts, "I expect all of you in there on time. Classes begin as usual at nine."

Gordon says, "No they don't. There are no teachers in the school and we won't let any in unless Mr. Halper gets his teaching job back and goes in first."

Teachers arrive on foot, having parked blocks away. A few talk with students. Most tramp about finding each other, checking rear doors for entry possibilities. Duchok rams his way through a dozen students guarding a steel service door only to find it bolted inside. He ends up with Fenton, surrounded by four police cruisers circled like covered wagons, blocking all six lanes of Midhill Avenue. Bands of uncommitted students gather like displaced persons and sit on their bags in the strip mall parking lot.

Gordon, Panther, Lincoln, Bully and several other senior students make speeches. Becky stands up in the Jeep and says her father is sending free drinks and donuts for all people blocking doorways, and that anyone can use the washrooms across the street. Frank Stringer plays his personal library of music, announcing and accompanying every number with his own gyrations. There is dancing in the streets, on the steps, in the parking lot.

At 9:05 the director of education arrives with David Halper and there is a conference within the circle of police cruisers. After ten minutes Halper walks alone toward the Jeep. The music stops and Gordon starts a chant that swells, "Halper, Halper, Halper."

His own name being chorused is so far from his vision of himself and of schooling that Halper feels unreal. The body mounting the Jeep to speak is his but he is somewhere behind it, struggling to catch up, slowed by strange feelings and unfamiliar options. His body rises above the crowd on pillars of sound, the same roar that has elevated heroes through the ages. But he feels no exhilaration, just discomfort. The tumult subsides slowly according to some unconscious script. Silence. Halper reclaims himself.

"Thank you, all of you. I'm grateful. But the law says a teacher works for the school board not for any particular school, and the board can deploy a teacher at will in any school or the board office. So Mr. Fenton has no power to reinstate me at Midhill. But I'm told the chair of the board says she will convene a meeting of the board for that purpose. It's cold out here and getting colder. Some of you have light clothes. Some are sitting on cold cement. Your parents are calling the board office worried about you. And I'm worried about all that. You've made your point and I'm grateful. Believe me, your support is my comfort in this ordeal. Right now the director of education is here and wants to go inside with me to meet student leaders. Please come inside with us and return to your classes."

Halper jumps down from the Jeep and reaches up to shake hands with Panther. He does the same with Lincoln on the hood of his car, Gordon on the hood of the Rolls, and Claudius on the hood of his mother's Supra. He glances at Keiko Ito behind the wheel. She blows him a kiss and delivers it by extending her arm to the windshield and leaving her hand there palm up. Claudius grins. Halper reaches out for the gift, says thanks, and then turns toward the school.

Claudius jumps on Halper's back and rides with him. Panther, Gordon and Lincoln follow. Others fall in line. Their chant swells, "Halper, Halper, Halper, Halper."

As the pied piper marches toward the front door, the blockade melts and two rows of Greens whip off their green caps and hold them high on both sides to form a triumphal arch up the steps. When all the students have entered and the honour guard dispersed, James Fenton approaches the empty steps escorted by four policemen and the director of education.

The union boss is Clara Wilbar — Clydeside Clara — who has rushed in from head office in response to the first radio newscasts and a phone call from Matsushita. She is installed behind Fenton's desk and is briefed one at a time by Matsushita, then Duchok, then Fenton, all of whom wait their turn next door in Duchok's office. Mrs. Wilbar likes to hear the same story over and over again from different points of view so she can pick up on useful discrepancies.

Clydeside Clara has done with Fenton's chair what she does

with every chair she assumes: she has turned it into her power pad. She never moves from it. Coffee comes to it as surely as rocket fuel to Cape Canaveral. She is surrounded by her life-support system. Her handbag of natural cowhide yields up Kleenex, saccharin for coffee, Tic Tacs to suck and a notebook on which she scribbles occasionally. Her matching briefcase is open-mouthed and jammed in its shadowy depths with sneakers and smock for the picket line, a metal makeup compact, extra-hold hair spray, handbooks, bandaids and electronic aids — a tape recorder, a pager, a telephone . . .

Clara's impressive bulk, swathed in champagne silk and fine worsted wool, is planted firmly but slightly forward so that the threat of launch is ever present. Everyone understands the advantage of treading lightly because if launch occurs anyone may be incinerated in the burn.

Between interviews Clara checks the mirrored lid of her brass compact and pats her coiffure, a cap of curls cut to be as suitable for picket lines as for TV interviews.

Meanwhile, Halper is with Monica Stacey, the director of education, a calm tall woman who smiles often and listens politely. For all her easy manners, Halper thinks there is about her a sucked-in look as though always restraining flatulence. Her relentless niceness, unbreachable remoteness and professional evasiveness remind Halper of the efficient but unknowable doctor who supervised his recovery at age seventeen from the car accident on Dawes Road. Once again he is in trouble for driving too fast and again his recovery depends on an automaton.

Halper and Monica Stacey sit with Panther, Lincoln, Gordon and four other student leaders in the little infirmary which is the nurse's office. Panther has presented Stacey with written statements by every student associated with the abuse reports. Gordon is playing a statement recorded by Frank Stringer when

Fenton's secretary comes to ask if Halper can be excused to see Mrs. Wilbar.

Clydeside Clara says, "Have a seat David. Have a Tic Tac."

Twenty minutes into the interview Halper feels her bulk expanding with the gas of her own importance, filling the office, pressing the air out of it. Her voice, with its inflated residue of Scottish accent, rises and hammers him like the racket of rivet guns her union steward father and grandfather used to build warships in Scotland. Halper forces himself to think like a lawyer representing himself.

"You know and I know that these rumours are groundless, that they're malicious, that they'll be dismissed as frivolous within days. You know Fenton, Duchok and Matsushita purposely made something out of nothing. If you've got any guts, if the union has any, you'll take them on publicly, denounce them."

"To what end? We can't attack long-standing members for being on guard against possible abuse of students. That's their duty. Everything in the reports against you is literally true, however representative or unrepresentative of your intent. Your rebuttal is attached to every copy of their reports. And even if we did question their procedures — which appear to be within guidelines by the way — how would that benefit you? All new teachers are on one-year probationary contracts and my guess is the board won't renew yours. Why should they?

"Sex charges aside, your record is poor. You don't get along with other teachers or janitors, you constantly ignore the advice of your department head, vice-principal and principal. All documented. Parents complain that your students have excessive homework preparing lessons which they try to teach each other while you sit among the students in noisy classrooms. You made lesson plans at the principal's insistence after he visited your class and found you had none, but then you failed to follow them. You contravene school regulations, you counsel insurrection. You lack good judgement. All documented. Have a Tic Tac."

"Outside, this morning, the director said the board chair would convene the board to deal with my return to the classroom."

"That was necessary to restore law and order. You're a lawyer. You should recognize negotiating tactics. Oh, they'll deal with your return to the classroom alright. The board will hold a public meeting which will be jammed with parents disinterested in your motives. You hug students. You kiss boys. You bend over half-naked boys in washrooms. You touch. That's sex, they believe. Where there's smoke there's fire, they believe. The world is full of believers. To make matters worse you make dates and have private meetings with individual students at all hours, day and night, even weekends."

"All the students I teach will speak for me at a board meeting. More. Half the school was out marching this morning."

"Don't count on them. As soon as suspicious parents get into the act watch your student support drop off. The ones just out marching for a good time have short attention spans. A few of your supporters will show up at a board meeting. So what? Most students are too young to vote in school board elections. The board will let everyone have a say and when everybody feels purged by participation in the process they will quietly decide to keep you sorting papers at the board office till your contract expires in June. In the unlikely event of a prolonged fuss by your supporters the board will cite your dismal teaching record."

"Thanks for all the union support."

"We support you completely, on the sex matter. Our lawyer will see that the police investigation is meticulous and prompt. The moment you're cleared and no charges are laid we'll issue a statement, a press release too if you like. Our further support in that regard will depend upon your adherence to our advice that teachers refrain from touching or hugging students or allowing students to touch or hug them, and refrain from meeting with students privately."

"And the other charges? Poor teaching?"

"Mr. Fenton's documentation is by the book. There's nothing we can do about that."

"I can and do teach circles around Fenton or anyone else in this place. I can and do stand and deliver data when that's appropriate, which is about twenty percent of the time in the subjects I teach, but I'm damned if I'll disrupt the more important eighty percent of the time when students are self-propelled just to go into a fake performance because administrative morons like Fenton drop in and can't understand anything but teacher talk. And I'm damned if I'll stop one-to-one tutoring, or extended school hours. As for the little hugs of human interaction, I refuse to let you or anyone else paint them as salacious. Kids need to be touched so they don't grow up feeling like untouchables, stunted in their ability to relate."

Clydeside Clara is draining her coffee.

Halper continues, "You take my fees so I insist you stand up for my right to teach well — which includes my obligation to be available emotionally — and my right and obligation to challenge a model of schooling that's moribund, brain dead, on life support. You should be helping me pull the plug. The teachers union should be in the forefront, developing a new model of schooling. Instead you keep applying cosmetics to the old model without changing it. You should read a book called *Future Schools*. Or just come across the street to the Greenhouse and see a new model being born."

Clara is gathering her belongings, stuffing saccharin into her purse, turning off her tape recorder. "Interesting," she says. "But books always end up on the shelf, don't they. And a glimpse of your brainchild wouldn't tell me much. Send me an account in writing if you like. We always have committees looking at various aspects of education, writing reports, that sort of thing. I'll put whatever you write before an appropriate committee. If they see anything worth reporting, they can put it before the annual meeting next summer even though you'll probably have moved on to your next career by then. Have a Tic Tac?"

The black Mercedes, the white Rolls and the silver Jeep are on television every night. Lincoln is in charge of picketing the school board office and Panther the school. Gordon leads a convoy of banner-carrying cars that cruises from school to school and downtown. He cultivates the media people who follow him and is often on the phone to network news producers. All three boys make street-corner and school-yard speeches that draw curious crowds, sometimes big and noisy, usually small and attentive, always supportive or neutral, never hostile. All three are interviewed on television every night. All three miss all their classes and are declared illegally absent.

All three are suspended from school.

On television Fenton refers to them in a carefully prepared sound bite as 'three blackheads that had to be squeezed out because they were blocking the pores of the school.' All three boys have shocks of jet black hair so television reporters immediately dub them 'The Blackheads.' Fenton takes credit for the name.

The Blackheads like their name and make the most of it. So does Keiko Ito. First Claudius, then Frank Stringer, then all the Greens, turn up at Midhill with their hair coloured black. A few Midhill students who are not Greens go Blackhead. A few more.

A hundred. Two hundred. The fad spreads to other schools. At Keiko's suggestion, the Blackheads take to wearing all-black clothes. So do many other students. A week before Christmas break, while the world is turning red and green, schools are turning black.

A feature of the costume is a black kerchief worn pirate style. The prototype is designed by Gordon Wing and Keiko Ito and stitched by Keiko on the black silk square she keeps in her bag for unexpected showers. With a quick yank it can be pulled down over the face. There are two eye holes cut. It becomes a mask. No style-conscious student would be seen without one. To be 'in' is to be a Blackhead. Fenton regrets taking credit for the name.

Director of education Monica Stacey and her counterparts in other school boards decide to ignore the fashion statement on the ground that it will disappear over the Christmas break along with the entire Halper incident.

The school board meeting is two days before the end of term and at the peak of party season. Still, the visitors gallery is full by 7 p.m. and several people stand against the wall. A television crew has placed bright lights and two cameras. David Halper is on the agenda. Halper has not been asked by the board to be present but he sits in the visitors gallery flanked by Maude Fenwick and Keiko Ito. Fenton sits at the board table flanked by the director and the superintendent of personnel.

Restless students dressed in black and adults who look colourful by contrast sit silently through five routine agenda items.

The board chair says, "Item six. I am pleased to announce that a thorough police investigation has resulted in no charges being laid. That matter is entirely resolved. For reasons unrelated to the allegations, Mr. Halper will continue to work in the board office. It is not customary for any school board to discuss details of personnel placement in public meetings; however in this unusual case I am authorized by the board to make the following statement: Mr. Halper will not be placed in a school because our usual careful evaluation of new teachers reveals deficiencies in Mr. Halper's teaching performance which the board feels are detrimental to our students. We consider the matter closed."

Gordon Wing yells, "We consider the matter wide open and our evaluation of Mr. Halper's performance reveals that he's beneficial to students. We want Halper. We want Halper."

The chant is taken up and feet stomp. Black masks are lowered. Police move in, two from each side. The chair shouts, "This meeting is adjourned."

Gordon leaps onto a table and the chant stops. He lifts his mask and yells, "Then I convene a citizens meeting and demand the right to use this space which we the taxpayers own." Everyone recognizes Gordon from television. There is near silence. Most adults remain seated. The policemen look to the board chair. She confers in whispers with the director of education. Gordon continues, "We're ready to fight for our rights. Four cops and a hundred Blackheads. You figure it out."

The chair says, "This board will not be intimidated and will not tolerate threats or violence. However we are always open to suggestions, and always welcome community participation in school governance. We have no objection to this gathering being a forum for genuine public participation. Ideas from our parents are always welcome and of course our students are the voice of tomorrow, the very thing this board exists to promote —."

"Then I suggest you cut the crap, ma'am, and get on with it. We all know you're stalling while that guy going out the door phones for more cops. Who wants to speak? Hands up. I call on Keiko Ito, chair of the board of the Greenhouse, which is right across the street from Midhill but is a far better school than Midhill or any school run by this or any other school board. Ms. Keiko Ito."

Keiko stands and says, "Underneath one of those black masks is my only child, age thirteen. And a little child shall lead. It's come to this. Why is it our kids can see the road ahead and you elected politicians and hired administrators can only see the road behind? I for one like being shown a road map. I propose that this school board fund the Greenhouse as an alternative and auxiliary school with David Halper as principal. Alternative — for students so in need of getting up to speed in reading, writing and other skills that they should spend nearly all their time on skill building. Auxiliary — for students who are already self propelled and need more freedom, responsibility and challenge than Midhill alone can provide. Do I have a seconder?"

Maude Fenwick pops up and steps into the aisle. "Seconded," she says. "David Halper is a terrific teacher and he'll make a super principal. I've been around long enough to know the right stuff when I see it. I'm Maude Fenwick, director of the Greenhouse, and I can give you a first-hand summary of a hundred years of schooling. I remember my great aunt and my aunt who were teachers, and sixty years ago this fall they saw me off to normal school to begin my teaching career which continues to this day at the Greenhouse."

Maude sweeps open her black coat and drops it on the floor. Some people gasp. Some titter. Maude is encased in a nineteenth-century corset. She shuffles stiffly to the front. "This was one of the two straitjackets my great aunt taught in. Note the whalebone stays. Stays. The word says it all. Note the laced-in waist. I can barely breathe, let alone move. My great aunt's other straitjacket was the authoritarian model of schooling."

Maude reaches around behind and with a little help from

Gordon Wing, sheds her corset to reveal a smaller one, festooned with garters and decorated with lace. "A generation later my aunt wore this racy number to work. Note that hooks have replaced laces and metal has replaced whalebone. But a corset is still a corset. An authoritarian school with a few field trips thrown in is still a corset. The orthodoxy of stay, remains."

Gordon helps with the hooks and Maude sheds again to reveal another relic. "This little beauty is called a corselette but did the change of name change anything significant? More rubber. Less metal. Same orthodoxy. My mother gave me this one for work and a fancier one for courting, circa 1940, about the time most school systems got rid of state entrance exams for kids going from public to high school. More elastic. Same orthodoxy."

Maude sheds again. "Behold the girdle and bra my mother gave me in 1961 by which time I was forty-six and she had given up any hope of anybody courting me and was concentrating on getting me promoted to principal. The orthodoxy of stay expressed in two pieces. A perfect match for the two pieces, elementary and secondary, into which schooling has always been arbitrarily ripped. I've got three university degrees and a doctorate pending and sixty years of experience but I'm certified as an elementary teacher so officialdom says I'm not qualified to teach reading and writing to Midhill students even though I do it every day and Midhill teachers don't."

It takes some undoing by Gordon and wriggling by Maude to dump the bra and girdle. Every eye is on Maude. There is virtual silence. "And finally, ladies and gentlemen, the five pounds lighter girdle by Playtex, and the lift and separate bra my mother gave me just before she died. This is state of the art stay, but it's still stay. Lift and separate is rather like the rhetoric of streaming which is separate and lift. A good idea, but it doesn't work because administrative rigor mortis is characteristic of our authoritarian schooling, so academic streams freeze solid and become another example of stay."

Maude slides off the last items and stands there in her red running shorts and singlet slapping the Playtex repeatedly on a table top. "Interesting that all of these stay instruments were called foundation garments. Foundation. That's what everything else is built on. The foundation that women's lives was built on was stay. Interesting too that most of the time in the hundred years we've had universal schooling, teaching has been one of the few careers open to women. Women trapped in the orthodoxy of stay for clothing also trapped in the orthodoxy of stay for work. That's what's wrong with schools, the orthodoxy of stay. Hold, restrict, restrain, inhibit, tie down, dogmatize, lock in teachers and especially children.

"We got rid of girdles for women. But schools are still in authoritarian girdles and lots of regressive people want to bring back whalebones. Why don't we get rid of stay for kids, get rid of the universal authoritarian model of schooling? Ladies and gentlemen, David Halper is a born innovator, an inspired teacher, and my choice to lead us from the age of stay to the age of empowerment and self-propulsion for children. I call on David Halper."

The Blackheads clap, whistle and stomp.

Halper says, "I'm sure of three things. One: children have the right and obligation to learn a treasury of skills that start with reading, writing, speaking and listening and range through problem solving, discussing, computing, conflict resolution, parenting, and so on. That means we the teachers must know how to teach and test all skills and must go into diagnostic and remedial action every time frequent testing shows a student is not up to age/grade expectancy. Two: children have the right and obligation to be empowered and self-propelled, so we the teachers are obliged to make sure they have the requisite self-esteem and then we must teach them how to take charge of their own schools and lives. That means we have to teach them step by step how to do and how to take over many of the tasks teachers, coaches and administrators presently keep on doing.

"The third thing I'm sure of is that the present model of schooling can't accommodate either of the above because it's based on lockstep grades, not mastery of skills, and it's based on children being directed, not self-directed, on children being disempowered, not empowered, on children being reactive not proactive. A model of schooling and a model of childhood that are intrinsically authoritarian will never metamorphose in a cocoon of cosmetics and bandaids into new models of schooling and childhood that empower children.

"In my classrooms at Midhill and much more so at the Greenhouse I'm confronting the moribund models of childhood and schooling head-on. I'm trying to develop new models geared to the reality of childhood, not to the official model of childhood which is sentimental. That's what this brouhaha is all about. The old guard is running scared, protecting the only thing they understand — the official model of schooling which matches the sentimental model of childhood but not the reality of it.

"The official model of schooling, like the official model of childhood, is a virus that slipped into the human psyche a few centuries ago on an overdose of piety. Since then it has resisted every attempt to detoxify it; and it has successfully mutated while remaining essentially the same, as virulent as ever, as authoritarian, as disempowering of children. Potentially good teachers and administrators are as much victims of the present obsolete model of schooling as children are. That's my assessment. What's yours Mr. Fenton?"

Fenton is caught off guard. He expected to sit through the

meeting slipping occasional file items to the director or perhaps supplying the exact date on which Mr. Halper did or failed to do something. Fenton looks at the director and then at the chair of the board. Both nod. He stands and shoots his cuffs. He is wearing his nighttime navy blue suit and a white shirt which highlights the glitter of his ring and cufflinks.

"My assessment is that any teacher with three months experience is a rookie. He should sit on the bench and learn from experienced players. My twenty-three years experience tells me that all this talk about changing schools is just a smoke screen for bad teaching. Kids are still kids, always will be. School is still school, always will be. Good teachers are the ones who prepare good lessons and then teach them, always will be."

Fenton pauses to consider what he should say next. There is a ripple of applause from adults. It grows. Two or three people say, "Hear, hear." Fenton feels pleased with himself, bows his head slightly in acknowledgement of the applause, adjusts his tie, and decides to rest on his laurels.

Lincoln jumps up, lifts his mask, and is recognized because of his television appearances. "He's right about one thing. School is still school. That's exactly the problem. But kids have changed and he doesn't accept it. His kind of school doesn't accept it. A year and a half ago Mr. Fenton married my mother. In all that time he hasn't got through his head that I'm not a child of his sentimental model of childhood, which is Beaver Cleaver and Andy Hardy.

"I belong to the reality of childhood. I have my own money, car, computer and condoms. I have my own needs, hopes and ideas. He can't even acknowledge any of those, much less understand them. My ideas threaten his contentment and contentment is what Fenton and his kind are after. His own daughter moved out last year to live with her boyfriend. Years before that she started living a double life and stopped paying the slightest attention to her father, and he can't acknowledge any of that either. Is that the kind of man who can run a school for my generation?

"Along comes Mr. Halper and suddenly I feel like a real person talking with a real person who respects what I've got to say even if he doesn't agree with me and lets me know, which is often. Suddenly I'm working my ass off and I've got all kinds of responsibilities and I'm held accountable and I love it. I turned my journal account of moving to Toronto into a short story for Mr. Halper because he read us his own story about himself, warts and all. Now, somehow, he's got me writing three more things based on my journal, two stories and a prose poem travelogue with my own violin accompaniment. He's got me debating abortion in his law class, which spins into debating women's rights in his English class, which spins into debating children's rights at student council meetings. He's got me researching the computer situation at Midhill and writing a report for the school newspaper which Mr. Fenton censors because censorship is the automatic reaction of authoritarians to ideas that challenge theirs.

"Mr. Halper's got me doing what he calls 'a little project' comparing the *Globe and Mail* with the *New York Times* because he thinks that might be a good way to help an American kid like me become a Canadian. It started one day when he sat down for lunch beside me in the cafeteria and I was looking at something about NAFTA on the front page of the *Times*. So he pulls the *Globe* out of his bag and reads me what it says. Not the same. Some little project! Guess what? I find myself researching resources, culture, politics, government, religion, political correctness, gun control, neo-conservatism and about twenty other categories in both papers, and rewriting my report about a dozen times because his standards are so high I don't want to make a fool of myself.

"He's got me teaching him and a lot of kids how to use

computers. He's got me tutoring grade nines in reading, writing and math, and testing them, and then doing remedial teaching with individuals. He's got me working with three others to set up a flea-powered radio station and also to negotiate a Greenhouse television program on the local cable station. He's got me sitting on the board of the Greenhouse making decisions about budget and program. He's got me writing sketches for the Midhill spring revue which forces me to think through everything about school and teenhood that needs social commentary. He's got me — happy. And guess what? I'm in only one of his classes, English. Now that's a great teacher."

While all the black masks cheer, Lincoln lowers his mask and Panther raises his. Everyone recognizes him but he introduces himself, "I'm Bill Parr, Black Panther Parr as they like to say on television. I'm president of the student council, captain of the Midhillers hockey team, and president of the student Christian club. I work weekends on the wards at the hospital. I get at least a ninety-five percent average. But I'm suspended from school because I stand up for student rights and for Mr. Halper.

"Every one of us here could give a list like Lincoln just did of all the great things Mr. Halper's got us involved in. But there's another dimension. Because he spends time with us we get these conversations going and they just pick up again and again serial fashion whenever time allows, especially when we have lunch at Midhill or supper at the mall. Real conversations. None of that ignorance/innocence of childhood nonsense. We talk about everything — rights, responsibilities, sex, suicide, death, war, divorce, love, nutrition, rock music, sports, politics, clothes, drugs, teachers, school — everything, so I'll just tell you about the last supper Gordon, Lincoln and I had with Mr. Halper, which was at Kowalski's tonight before coming here:

"Gordon says, 'Christmas music is Chinese water torture

Western style. Simple syrup is dripping through the ceiling onto my pancakes from those bloody rooftop speakers.' Well, that makes me a little indignant because I like Christmas music and I just happen to be a Christian who intends to become a minister. Gordon just happens to be what he likes to call a post-Christian non-theistic rational humanist. Lincoln is halfway in-between and says he's looking for direction.

"So I say, 'Believers like me find the repetition, simplicity and sweetness of that music comforting.' Gordon says, 'Great. But do it privately because the rest of us find your syrup sticky and you've got no right to drown us in it.' The two of us exchange a few jibes about beliefs but it goes no place till Mr. Halper asks me, 'Are your Christian beliefs symbolically true or literally true, Panther?' I answer, 'Symbolically true, because the gospels were written seventy years or more after Jesus died so they were written in the spirit of storytelling, not journalism, and symbolism is the stuff of storytelling. The storytellers were believers like me who made up about 80 percent of what Jesus is supposed to have said to illustrate their own visions, and they probably got the other 20 percent close enough to be called paraphrased quotes. Same with all books of the Old Testament. They were written around 700 B.C. That's about five hundred years after the events they supposedly describe, so they have to be understood as folk tales.'

"So Gordon says, 'I figure Jesus was a travelling sage who went around challenging assumptions. That's my kind of guy. His followers were mostly outcasts — prostitutes, criminals, hippies, the unemployed, and guys like me.' Mr. Halper says to Gordon, 'If you had been a disciple, what would the gospel according to St. Gordon say?' Gordon finishes his mouthful of pancake and answers, 'That God is a process, not a being, not a thing. That God is the constant effort of people to uncover the ultimate mystery. Which means that worshipping God is working hard at questioning assumptions, which is what I do.'

"You need to know that Mr. Halper taught us that immediately shooting down an idea in any discussion is a cheap shot. Instead you should take an idea and run with it and see if it goes to a higher plateau or falls into a crevasse. So Lincoln squishes syrup on his last pancake and says, 'So — if God is the collective potential of people then I guess the search for God is the ever-increasing use of brain power.' Gordon says, 'Right. And the revelation of God is the unfolding of human achievement.' I add, 'So I guess prayer is the promise of individuals to apply their brains to bettering the world.'

"Mr. Halper says, 'Not a bad thesis, Gordon, that the collective untapped cortex of humanity is the raw material of refined thinking that will access the ultimate mystery. So what's the role of churches? What's the role of schools?' By then it's time to leave for this meeting and we have to divvy up the check, but you can bet the topic will surface again and continue from where we left off. Mr. Halper always leaves us with questions to work on.

"That's especially true at the Greenhouse. Maude Fenwick is our reading expert, Lincoln is our computer expert and Gordon our computer games expert. I happened to be there when Mr. Halper asked them a bunch of leading questions and now the three of them are creating computer games that teach reading and writing better than it's ever been done before anywhere. I predict their products will set the world standard. That's what happens when kids are empowered and mentored by good teachers. They take off."

Panther is interrupted by a composed, tweedy man in the front row who raises one hand and says politely, "Pardon me, Panther." He remains seated with his duffel coat folded neatly on his lap, a briefcase and deerstalker hat on top. "They take off, you say. Isn't it also true that when empowered by Mr. Halper they take off their pants for men voyeurs in public washrooms? Isn't it true that girls in his clubhouse get pregnant? Isn't it true that boys get kissed by men?" He stands up holding his coat, hat and briefcase in front of him and continues, "My name is Reverend Ben Gambell and I'm president of the Christian Rebirth Society." He looks at Halper and his voice rises, "Isn't it also true that you have study groups on how to do sex? Isn't it true that your textbook on sex is illustrated and pornographic? Sex seems to be a visual and performance art in your fun house, Mr. Halper. Meanwhile, across the street at Midhill you teach them how to have abortions."

Several adults applaud and say, "Hear, hear" while black-masked students stand to boo and jeer. During those first few seconds of noisy reaction, Claudius Ito slips from his place, streaks like a little black goblin in front of Reverend Gambell's confident face, and punches him in the eye.

Gambell drops his possessions, clutches his eye and sinks to his knees. Members of the board jump to their feet so fast that some chairs are overturned. Claudius melts back into the black block which closes ranks, locks arms and sways chanting Halper, Halper, Halper.

Gambell and most of his party are crawling around looking for his contact lens when all four entrances to the chamber burst open and riot police with shields rush in. The chair of the board shouts, "This meeting is adjourned."

Moments before a quarter to nine on the last day of school, black waves churn as usual up and down Midhill corridors between lockers and classrooms. Many people in and around the school check their watches and picture what Gordon Wing had promised the night before, 'The captain is sitting behind his desk as usual preparing to make his appearance on the bridge as the great ship Midhill sails intrepidly out of the black night of mutiny and inches into the safe harbour of Christmas vacation.' In his office Fenton blows on his mammoth ring, buffs it with tissue, pats his brow with the same tissue, shoots his cuffs.

A dozen black-masked figures veer suddenly, almost unnoticed in the morning surge. They pour into Fenton's office at the very moment his monumental cufflinks blaze forth. Simultaneously, Duchok in his office and Matsushita in his lab are confronted with black masks.

In each location black figures proffer a red-wrapped gift and sing in unison, "We wish you a Merry Christmas, We wish you a Merry Christmas, We wish you a Merry Christmas and a Happy New Year." The song is repeated while Fenton, Duchok and Matsushita beam. One black figure in each location opens the peace offering, while another rolls the desk chair and its obliging occupant around in front, and another holds a camera ready to shoot. From tissue paper, a velvet cushion is produced and placed in each chair. Each king sits triumphantly on his newly cushioned throne. The song swells. Cameras flash.

Doors slam. Gags whip across mouths. Locks click. Ropes descend. Knots are tied. "We wish you a Merry Christmas . . ."

In the Greenhouse window, Keiko Ito and Maude Fenwick check their watches and focus their telescopes on Midhill. They see a van move from the school driveway to a new position near the flagpole. It disgorges a television crew.

Black heads poke over the roof parapet and out of every window of Midhill and unfurl long black banners. While cameras roll, the huge corpse is dressed in a tattered shroud. At ten minutes to nine the body bursts releasing black gas which propels Fenton, Duchok and Matsushita onto the front steps tied to their chairs and wearing dunce hats. They roll to the very edge where the black clouds that surround them dissolve and drift toward the flagpole. Black-covered students drain from every orifice and flow to the pole. They lower the flag, hoist a black banner to half mast and stand silently with heads bowed.

When Fenton is untied and is being interviewed, he picks up his gift cushion to show the camera how he was abducted. The underside says DUNCE. Mr. Fenton can't see the cushion's message but television can. Cameras fastens on it and catch Fenton's every word as he holds the cushion to his chest. Close-ups of Fenton's fist show white knuckles and a gigantic ring with claws grasping as always but holding nothing. Duchok, newly released and rubbing his wrists, whispers in Fenton's ear and takes the cushion away. Fenton announces that classes are dismissed.

The term is over.

By the time police cars arrive with sirens wailing, the student exodus is well under way. Duchok confers with the officers and the police cars depart quietly.

On the floor of his office Fenton sees the glass bauble from his ring. He waits till the school has emptied, then he goes to the art room and glues it back in place with Elmer's Glue-All.

Mourners around the flagpole slowly drift away in every direction.

Internationally, newscasts show Fenton, the principal, as dunce in front of what everyone in the world recognizes as a typical high school draped in black, flying a black flag at half mast.

The next night, while Greenhouse board members watch a replay, Keiko Ito asks, "How many viewers elsewhere in the city, in the world, recognize the black figures dispersing as refugees with no place to go?"

At Keiko Ito's front door on Christmas eve Halper says, "This is for Claudius. Just a book."

"He's got something for you too, David. He made something. I think he took it with him to Lincoln's birthday party. Come in. It's freezing. Where's your coat?"

"In the car I guess. I don't know."

"I've got neighbours here for Christmas drinks. Maude's coming later. I've been calling you."

"I had my Christmas drinks early."

"Maude said you called from Vancouver."

"First I had some drinks. Then I flew to Vancouver. Then I called the Greenhouse. Jillian's gone from Vancouver. Gone for good. Simon's gone. Liz is gone. Alison's gone. My job is gone. I should be gone. But, I wanted to say thanks for everything. Really, thanks."

"Gone where? Bermuda?"

"No. I don't know where. Just gone. Wish Claudius Merry Christmas for me."

"Wait, David. We got a reply from the Ball Foundation in Chicago. Carl Ball, the president, has read *Future Schools* and likes what we said about the Greenhouse as a prototype. They've got some project with the University of Illinois called The School Design Collaborative. Three really new-type elementary schools actually operating. Maude says we could set up an elementary level Greenhouse in a wink."

"But foundations don't move in a wink. Anyway, I think that project redesigns existing schools in public school districts. Not independent upstarts."

"But they replied. And Gordon and I have talked to five software companies. Gordon actually spoke with Bill Gates at Microsoft via e-mail. Two other guys are also interested in our reading game. One is already talking development money. Gordon has written all that up on a Christmas card he made for you, so pretend I didn't tell you. And we've had a Greenhouse board meeting about hiring you. Frank's father and Mr. Kowalski are calling up all the parents to say each of them will match dollar for dollar every donation a parent makes. And the judge thinks you might get legal aid funding for representing kids in rights cases. Test cases like Claudius against Matsushita. Or foundation money to pay you as an ombudsman for kids in schools. Or both. Even without television I think we can raise half a salary at least."

"Television?"

"A cause célèbre television campaign for donations if you're willing. I've had two offers from local TV shows and one from CBC national news. And I've contacted four more locals and three network shows including Petrie in Prime. All interested. And I've had a nibble from Larry King Live. We have to talk. What are you doing for Christmas?"

"I don't know. Nothing."

"Stay here. Please."

"I don't want to intrude."

"You won't. Lots of room. Maude's staying for three days. Gordon and Lincoln are coming for brunch and dinner tomorrow. Panther for brunch. Tons of food. Stay."

"Are you sure?"

"I'm sure. And it would make a perfect Christmas for one small boy."

"I'd like that. Thanks."

"He'll be ecstatic. I'll call the Greenhouse."

"He's not there. I just looked for him there."

"With Gordon then likely."

"Gordon's at the Greenhouse. Panther too. A dozen kids and Maude, just sitting, trying to be cheerful for Lincoln's birthday. They said Claudius hasn't been there."

"It's after nine. I'll get on the phone. Come in."

"First I'll check whatever's open at the mall."

Midhill Avenue is almost empty of traffic. Bleak. Bare trees and dead grasses. Halper thinks how much more exactly it reflects his heart than the verdant mildness he wandered through in Vancouver. A thin layer of crusty snow is dusted with powder that swirls like apparitions onto black pavement and then dissipates. Some drive-ins have closed early for Christmas Eve. The rest have one or two cars. Blackness surrounding darkened factories looks to Halper as deep as his loneliness. Here and there decorated trees light up black voids the way thoughts of Keiko and Claudius light one corner of his night.

To the left, ahead of his car, he can see flashing green bulbs on the tree in front of the Greenhouse. Off and on. Off and on. Each time he wonders if they might stay off. The loudspeakers playing Christmas music on the roof of Kowalski's donut shop are outlined with strings of tiny flashing lights. Fake stars, fake twinkle. Halper is glad he can't hear the fake sentiment they disperse. At least his night is silent.

To the right, the school looms basalt black, like a precambrian shield. Dormant. Immovable. Eternal. The weight of it presses down upon him. *'If you don't suck Mother School's tit, she'll roll over and crush you.'*

A volcano erupts. Orange light rips the dark sky apart. The basalt shield splits wide open. Blast thunder rocks the night. The car shudders, veers. Halper clutches the wheel.

The Greenhouse shakes. Dishes fall. Kids stunned by the flash freeze in place.

Gordon Wing shouts, "Claudius!"

While the others are paralyzed, Gordon streaks across the empty street and through the front yard of the school.

Halper sees Gordon's dash and wheels his car into the school drive, onto the lawn and up to the flagpole. The centre of the school, where the old wing meets the new, is a fire storm.

Gordon turns and yells to Halper, "Claudius!" He disappears through what remains of the doors near the front office and heads for the science labs in the new wing. Halper follows.

Lincoln and Panther reach the flagpole in time to see Halper vanish into smoke. They follow.

In the Greenhouse, Maude Fenwick stands at the door blocking the exit of any more Greens. The second explosion feels like an earthquake. The black of night opens like a drape on a blinding white universe.

Maude is thrown backward against Frank Stringer. Greens who grab onto something and remain standing watch the new-wing roof burst open. Fiery rockets arc through the sky. Flames erupt from shattered windows and throw wild orange shadows on black smoke that belches above the labs. The school is engulfed.

From the roof of Kowalski's a choir sings 'Alleluia! Alleluia! Alleluia!'

Maude Fenwick, assisted by police officers, makes the first calls while the flames rage. Keiko Ito drives at once to the Greenhouse. Mr. and Mrs. Fenton are touring in Florida and can't be reached immediately. Dr. and Mrs. Bond are in Switzerland but will return on the first flight. Mr. and Mrs. Parr are at home in Renfrew and will await a further call. Mr. Wing is not at home and not at work. The police will try to find him in Chinatown. Mrs. Wing is out of town with a friend, her daughter is not sure where. No number or address for Liz Halper is readily available so Bermuda police will try to find her.

The crowd at Kowalski's donut shop is thinning but Maude and Keiko remain seated, staring out from the booth they have occupied all night, one of the few with a window intact. They are an island invisibly cordoned by respect for grief and surrounded by puddles and slush, piles of coats that smell of smoke and wetness, television cameras, sound equipment, reporters, firemen, policemen, coffee cups, cigarette butts, plastic film flapping over broken windows.

Becky Kowalski keeps plying Maude and Keiko with coffee which they hardly touch. Frank Stringer keeps reporters at bay. From time to time Maude nods to Frank and a policeman or fireman is admitted to the booth to ask a question or report that a body has been found. Maude does all the talking while she squeezes Keiko's arm or holds her hand. Once in a while Maude slips away to confer with officials and Becky sits with Keiko.

Keiko has been almost silent all night, sedated by shock. From time to time she tugs at her black silk kerchief. All night she has wrapped it around one finger after the other, pulled on it, rewound it, twisted it, tugged some more, stuck her fingers through the eye holes she cut and stitched.

Only one searchlight remains. First daylight reveals the burnt-out shell of the new wing and the pile of debris that was Midhill's old wing. Keiko murmurs, "Hiroshima."

Maude Fenwick is still wearing the huge hat covered with red silk flowers which she wore for Lincoln's party. In the light of dawn filtering through fine ash on Kowalski's window the red silk fairly glows. Maude puts the hat on Keiko and says, "The rising sun."

"I've never cared much for traditional symbols," Keiko says. She lifts the hat and looks at it. "Anyway, this one is too big for me."

Becky says, "Claudius left this at the Greenhouse." The band of the green baseball cap she hands Keiko says Claudius J. Ito, cap #1.

"This is more my size."

The fire captain clutches his hat to his breast and says to Maude, "Ma'am. We've found the fifth. The little one. I'm sorry. You're sure there's no more?"

"Five. Thank you. Thank your men for us. Merry Christmas." To Keiko she says, "We can go now. Come on, I'll drive."

Keiko stands up saying, "I'll be alright." She slips her arms into the coat that has been over her shoulders all night. "But you take my car. That's David's car over there by the flagpole. I'll drive it. I want to."

There are still a few officials on the fringes and some firemen probing debris, but the spectators have gone home to open Christmas gifts. Keiko Ito, a small figure in high-heeled party shoes and a green baseball cap, makes her way alone, across the dirty skin of packed snow in front of Midhill. Her heels punch holes like machine-gun bullets. She stands by the sooty flagpole and looks at the blackened front steps and the smoking debris beyond them. She opens the car door, moves Halper's trench coat aside and climbs in.

This is where she sat in her own car to blow Halper a kiss at the demonstration. She blows a kiss. Halper reaches out for it. Claudius grins. Halper turns away and Claudius leaps on his back. Green caps form an arch and they march triumphantly up the school steps and into a plume of smoke.

In front of the donut shop Becky and Frank stand with Maude beside the red Supra. Becky weeps quietly with both arms wrapped over her belly while Maude hugs her and murmurs about not catching cold, about the baby. Frank holds up his Greenhouse key and says, "I mean, do I open up the Greenhouse tomorrow or what?"

Across the street Keiko starts Halper's car and drives a few feet. She stops. Backs up. Steps out.

Frank repeats, "I mean like, is it open from now on or closed?"

Keiko ties green cap #1 to Halper's black coat with her own kerchief and hoists them up the flagpole. Maude wonders if she will leave them at half mast. No. All the way to the top. They fly smartly in the Christmas breeze.

Maude waves her red-flowered hat and honks the car horn. "Open," she says.

Keiko honks back.

They both drive off horns blaring.